HOUSE
OF
CLUBS

HOUSE OF CLUBS

House of Jewels, Volume IV

Amber Jakeman

Lorikeet Press, 2021

This is a work of fiction. Similarities to real people, places, or events
are entirely coincidental.

HOUSE OF CLUBS
First edition. 11 November, 2021.

Copyright © Amber Jakeman.

ISBN: 978-0-6489202-9-8

Written by Amber Jakeman.

Also by Amber Jakeman
House of Jewels series
House of Diamonds
House of Hearts
House of Spades
House of Clubs

www.amberjakeman.com
www.lorikeetpress.com

To those who let us into their hearts and
to those who remind us
to listen to our own,
lest nobody heed our dreams.

Chapter 1

The decades-old memories of Cynthia Huntley's Parisian honeymoon with Jimmy were still too perfect for her to crack open—so she flew into France through Nice.

Adrenaline surged as she made out the curve of the Mediterranean coastline with its celebrated fringe of beaches and marinas. Yes! As the wheels emerged with a soft thump in preparation for landing, ever greater detail came into view—soft hills encrusted with stone buildings, a sleek railway line, yachts, apartments, red roofs, and a large plaza encircling a statue and fountain.

She unzipped her make-up bag, frowned at her messy hair and red eyes, then gave herself a wink. It wasn't as if she was meeting anyone. She'd have preferred to look her best as she stepped foot in France for the first time in thirty years, but even the flight crew were tousled, and they were experts at travel.

She brushed her hair, refastened her sleek bun, and gave a polite smile to her taciturn neighbor. She was desperate to tell someone her childhood dream of living in France was finally coming true. No response. Never mind.

Inside the terminal, she waited for her one small suitcase, enchanted by the French advertisements and snippets of overheard conversation, fear and joy at the boldness of her adventure washing her hot and cold.

Was it really only a month ago, her daughter, Nicole, had challenged her to escape her pleasantly boring rut?

On impulse, she pulled out her phone, took a selfie and sent it to Nicole, then frowned at the background. Grey concrete. The picture could have been taken anywhere. "I'm here!" she texted. "Nice, France."

Her phone rang. It was Kath, her oldest school friend, actually born in France, now happily Australian.

"Cynthia! You missed the reunion!"

"I'm in France. I've just arrived in Nice."

"No!"

"Yes! Nicole challenged me, and I listened, so I thought; why not?"

"Well, I never thought you'd actually do it," said Kath. "Good for you. Hope it's everything you dreamed it would be. How is it? Nathan Carmichael was asking after you, by the way."

"Oh?"

"He goes from fame to fame. He's won some international architectural competition and now he's on some judging panel in Europe. Should I tell him to drop in on you?"

"Kath! What's Greta going to think about that?"

"They're divorced."

"No! After all these years. That's such a shame."

"Well, Nathan was in fine form. Why is it that some older men become more distinguished as they age?"

"Nate was always ..."

"Wasn't he! And he was wearing these amazing round glasses. Super arty. Google him, Cynthia."

The two women laughed. Nathan was voted most eligible the year they graduated, but Danish exchange student Greta had swooped in and claimed him before any of them had had the chance to date him, and she'd clung on tight, clearly with Nathan's approval, of course, at least until lately...

Cynthia was sad for them, then, for a brief moment, the concept of dating the debonair Nathan hovered in her imagination, but she laughed it away.

"There's absolutely no point, Kath. I've told you. Jimmy was the great love of my life. No one could ever compare."

"But that doesn't mean you can never fall in love again."

They'd had this conversation before. After Jimmy's death, Kath was one of the first friends to try to set her up with someone new. No matter how many times Cynthia tried to explain, Kath didn't get it. The only solution was to change the subject.

"Anyway, could you thank the organising committee for me, please?" Cynthia said. "I sent my apologies via Camilla, but maybe she forgot to pass them on. I actually booked a session with Rennie to glean all he knows about buying property in France, before I left. That husband of hers is a genius. And he insisted he wouldn't charge me. I have beautiful friends. I'm sorry I didn't tell you sooner, Kath, but I didn't want you to talk me out of it. I'm doing this French adventure boots and all. I'm finally ready to look forwards, not backwards. If I hadn't left quickly, the impulse may have passed. Not sure if you understand."

"I'm trying. You're not usually so impulsive, but I know how obsessed you've always been about France."

They shared another laugh. Way back in high school, the instant Cynthia had discovered Kath the new girl was French, she'd barely left her alone. Kath, for her part, carefully absorbed Cynthia's Australian

8

accent and mannerisms, eager to lose her "Frenchness" and fit in as quickly as possible.

"As for France, well, you won't be surprised. It's exactly how you predicted, Kath. The baggage carousel is exactly like any other, as was the airplane, but at least most of the people around me are speaking French. I love it."

"Well, you're a surprise, Cynthia Huntley. How long are you away?"

"One-way ticket! I decided to get on with it; seize my childhood dream of living here instead of simply collecting French antiques forever. Nicole told me I was becoming a French antique. That got me going."

"Well, yes, but…"

"I haven't been this excited in thirty years, Kath. I'm glad she dared me. James is running Huntleys now, as you know, along with Jim and Nicole, and Will, in theory at least. They haven't needed me for years. The country house will be fine. It's so new there shouldn't be any leaks or problems. I put sheets over all the furniture; and packed just a few things. And now that you and Bob are downsizing, you can come and visit me any time. It's spring over here. Divine. I've asked James to give the car a run now and then for me. Oh look, here's my bag now. *Au revoir*, Kath!"

"Keep in touch, Cynth! Be careful."

Cynthia smiled as she claimed her bag. Dear Kath. Her high school friend always downplayed her French roots, while Cynthia never stopped craving a French lifestyle. And now she was here!

Outside the terminal, Cynthia inhaled deeply, excitement bubbling. The spring air was cooler than the autumn bite she'd left behind in Australia's Southern Highlands, but the smell of the sea held a promise of the bonus summer to come.

She blessed her wheelie bag as she stepped off the kerb—and almost into the path of a small truck. The driver beeped and gave her a two handed rebuke. Oops. Yes, she was used to being alone, and she could speak and understand some French, but Kath was right. She should take care.

The young woman at the hotel reception insisted on speaking English to her, despite Cynthia's attempts in French. Never mind. The shower, clean sheets and sheer horizontality of the bed were luxury. She melted into oblivion.

Next day she wandered through Nice, stretching her legs, wondering at the history of the old town by the water, with its intriguing jumble of narrow lanes, pale yellow and cream low rise apartments and street-level shops. She practically clapped in delight at the breathtaking beauty of the flower market on the Cours Saleya, bursting with the color and fragrances of early spring blooms.

A walking tour deepened her understanding of the prehistory as well as all the layers of Greek, Roman, Italian and French influence. She learned more about the town's popularity with the wealthy wintering British and Russians, this playground of the rich.

Being a tourist was exhilarating, but she was on a more permanent quest. She arranged to inspect a few apartments with their art nouveau architectural embellishments like so much piped icing, and their tiny balconies, but wasn't convinced she'd be happy in such a busy centre for holiday makers.

Next day she explored more widely in the region, her house-seeking mission giving her sightseeing additional intensity. An eight-hour round trip by train to Avignon and back again left her wonderstruck by the beauty of the pale stone houses on lumpy little deep green hills, their green pine trees so tall and narrow they could have been painted by Van Gogh. Between them, the glimpses of the strips of beach and Mediterranean, blue as an aquamarine, were tantalising, but Cynthia had lived most of her life by the coast in Sydney, and this adventure was all about having a change.

She hired a car for a week, and turned her attention to the north, an enchanting world of hills and slopes pulsating with purple lavender plantations, with ancient stone villages in the valleys.

Three inspections later—an old farm converted into a holiday home that felt too isolated for her single status, an apartment in an old mansion where the glances of suspicious neighbors already gave her the spooks, and a too-large abandoned biscuit factory turned art gallery—she was beginning to lose hope.

On her way back to Nice, she found her future. It was a charming town, nestled in hills to the north west. She'd felt a kind of recognition in her bones as she drove into the village, with its central fountain and a small square surrounded by ancient stone buildings. She parked and walked, treading carefully with her sandals on the ancient cobbles, and snapping photos with her phone. She loved the faded pastel window shutters and wooden doors with their brass knobs and knockers of every shape and style, pigeons the same soft grays as the old stone walls, the steeple of the church, the patchwork of red roofs.

As she inspected the fountain in the little town centre, she jumped. A kitten was sniffing her ankle! A group of them romped together in the sun and she stopped and admired their golden eyes, perfect whiskers and pink paw pads. Full of life they pounced on each other, chewed and lapped at her gifts and sniffed her fingers before she wandered on.

Then, the moment she saw the old corner store with its "*à vendre*" sign, she could barely look away. Every detail enticed her. The property was empty. Large windows on two sides, facing south to lap up winter sun, met at the pale blue wooden doors, classic French shabby chic.

She stepped closer and ran her hands over the old wood. Clover leaves were carved into the surface near the lock, encrusted with countless layers of paint. She traced them with one finger, and pinched the dust that came off with her thumb.

Even the *for sale* sign was dusty and a little faded. Had it been for sale long? She peered inside. Sunlight streamed in, onto black and white floor tiles; the same as she'd chosen for her Southern Highlands home, back in Australia, but originals!

She stepped back and examined the building from the other side of the street. Her heart raced. With two upper floors, she could live here and there'd be plenty of space for visitors. She had no firm plans for the place. She only knew she wanted it; that this was where her future would unfold.

She arranged to meet the agent two days later. A jumble of cautions flew to her mind—and then out again, chased by the certainty she only lived once. Cynthia laughed as adrenaline surged through her veins.

She barely slept ahead of the inspection. Feverishly, she researched how to buy French properties, checked comparative pricings, tried to understand the local property laws and teed up a building report. She phoned Camilla's husband again. With his part share in a French chateau, a law degree and a number of clients with properties in Europe and the US, his advice was invaluable, but her heart fell when he told her she'd probably have to wait three months for all the legal checks to be completed.

"But it's empty! I need to live somewhere. Do you think the *notaire* would rent it to me while we wait to finalise it all?"

"Maybe. It can't hurt to ask."

Cynthia had promised to send the family regular photographs, but thought twice about snapping herself with the serious real estate agent, *l'agent immobilier*. Maybe not.

This agent actually appeared to be immobile. He sat at his desk, his elbows planted on the arms of his chair, fingers tented above his considerable girth. This man enjoyed his meals. She glanced at her watch. Perhaps it had been unwise to insist on a two o'clock meeting. Maybe his brain was on a siesta. The clock ticked slowly. Three months could pass before he said anything.

"*Votre mari?*" said the agent, looking at her wedding finger where Jimmy's engagement and wedding rings still glinted, the marquises bright as tears. This old-fashioned assumption that only a man could buy a property! Sexist.

"*Je suis seule,*" said Cynthia, alone, always alone; alone for more than a decade. "*Je voudrais le faire; je peux le faire, il faut le faire.*" She must do this. She faced the agent with a polite, determined smile. On her second visit, the unmistakable aroma of ripe cheese filled his office. She tracked it down to a basket covered with a blue and white cloth, asked about it and was treated to a rapturous lecture about his *fromage du jour,* his beloved cheese of the day.

Three cheeses and three days later all was explained, all signed—rental for three months then ownership, subject to standard legal checks—and the keys handed over.

Best of all, the key for the shop door was the same clover shape as the carving in the doors, the shape of clubs in a pack of cards. The metal key was old and heavy and real.

Considerably the wiser on cheeses, Cynthia inhaled deeply—a *chèvre,* or goats' cheese rolled in charcoal, as it turned out—then sighed with satisfaction and relief.

Even now the agent barely met her eye, but she was so thrilled, she invited him to lunch with her in celebration.

"*Je ne peux pas*," was all he said, his polite "no" as ponderous as ever. A pang of doubt intruded, threatening to burst her elation, so she pressed the point.

"*Mais pourquoi pas*? Why ever not?"

He shrugged, then moved his hand slowly back and forth in the air between them, as if to indicate an impossible distance. "*Ma femme*." Oh. Of course. His wife.

So now, as the taxi puttered away in the blue dawn, she stood outside her new home with her roller bag in the morning mist, turning the clover-headed key over and over in one hand. Her heart jumped with excitement. So much to do! First, she'd remove the "for sale" sign.

She pulled on the sign. It bent, but stayed anchored in two corners. Sounds and smells of her new town awakening swirled as she tugged again—the aroma of freshly baked bread, a baby's muffled cry from an upper floor somewhere up the street, and distant traffic.

As the sign refused to budge, a tiny note of fear stabbed at her chest. What had she done? Blown most of her retirement savings on a pile of old stone where she knew nobody? No furniture, no friends, not even a screwdriver or pair of pliers to remove the sign—what kind of a fool was Cynthia Huntley?

Then again, wasn't this the adventure she'd craved?

An old-fashioned motorbike rounded the corner, idled past, then looped back towards her on the narrow street. The rider, tallish and nimble, dismounted. A robber? A spy? She was alone. If she screamed, would anyone hear?

He was lanky in his black leather jacket and helmet, with striking eyes—hazel with a touch of gold, curious, full of light—and there was an odd scar, low on his left cheek. She caught her breath as they stared at each other. He ran his eyes up and down her figure, then met her own gaze with a question she didn't understand, as he reached into his pannier.

A gun? Fear lodged in her throat and she took another step back, eyes on the stranger.

He withdrew a pair of pliers, stepped forwards, and in less than half a minute, twisted the fastenings and removed her sign. He rested it against the wall, then remounted and revved his engine. It was an old-fashioned motorbike in excellent condition. She breathed again.

"*Merci*," said Cynthia and she leaned forwards, relief and shame making her gush her thanks. "So chivalrous! *Un café?*"

The rider gave her a lopsided grin, shook his head, pulled down his visor, waved and took off again down the street, a puff of oily blue smoke in his wake.

Heart soaring, she laughed and waved back. On impulse, she blew the generous stranger a kiss. Did he notice it in his rear view mirror? His random act of kindness had propelled her adventure to new heights. All doubts evaporated.

She turned back to her blue doors and traced a finger around one of the clover carvings again. What was the meaning of the shamrock, the symbol of clubs, or the French "trèfle"? The three leaves stood for faith, hope and love. Of course she'd bought the place. Bargain! She plunged the key into the lock, twisted it and her door swung open.

Chapter 2

With its two walls of windows, the empty front room was full of light. More than three hundred years old, the agent said. A dozen generations of families had lived within these ancient walls. Businesses had set up here and thrived, and failed and thrived again.

Perhaps she'd establish another, but Cynthia had only recently escaped the responsibilities of Huntleys House of Jewels back in Australia, gradually handing over complete management to her children James, Nicole and Will since Jimmy's death. While her aging father-in-law, Jim, continued to make most of the special rings, James, in his early 30s, was well and truly up to the task of handling strategic and day-to-day decisions. Nicole tackled the marketing, and Will, her restless one, 29, was travelling, hopefully finding new international suppliers and markets.

Cynthia knew she'd chosen her new French home hastily, certain only that it had plenty of space for friends and family to visit and that its location in the centre of the village and its orientation—soaking up the southern sun—were timeless assets. For a moment, she stood in the empty front room and dreamed. If James ever found someone less selfish than Helene there might even be grandchildren to visit her here one day. There were so many wonderful and worthy young women in the world. Surely James would find a special one soon, or one would find him, and ...

The front room was strangely empty. Wires dangled from the centre of the ceiling, calling out for a fitting. Cynthia frowned. What this room needed was an elegant chandelier. She closed her eyes and imagined it. Yes. The right chandelier would transform it, would draw the light in from those generous windows and dress the old room magnificently, like the crown on the head of an aging monarch.

She closed the door behind her and explored the corridor behind the sunny front room, and the rest of the ground floor. A small kitchen overlooked another square. Upstairs were more rooms. She counselled herself not to panic at the obviously ancient status of the electrics and plumbing, mere flesh wounds in a building with such noble bones.

Previous owners had stripped and whitewashed the rooms, maybe to showcase it for rent or sale. Well. She knew how to furnish a place. She'd just spent the past few years building her Southern Highlands home and filling it with French antiques. This time there'd be no need for interior decorators and antique furniture dealers. Here in Provence, she couldn't be closer to the source of her favorite style.

Cynthia hired a car to visit the antiquities market in L'Isle-sur-la-Sorgue, several hours away. Famous throughout the world, it lured dealers and tourists alike. Much of the furniture she'd bought in Australia may well have passed through this market, she mused, as she parked and strode towards the stalls.

There were so many treasures, at prices a fraction of what she'd paid in Australia, she hardly knew where to begin. Two dozen antique crystal champagne glasses caught her eye but she forced herself to hurry past. No need to blow the budget straight away. Surely some basics would be more sensible, before the best finds were snapped up and gone.

Linen, silver spoons and candlesticks, brass door knobs and door knockers, old windows of every size, wrought iron bed heads, wardrobes and Louis XV chairs—she wanted them all. She should have hired a pantechnicon!

At an instant, a myriad of sparkles dazzled her, bright as sunlight on Sydney Harbour when a westerly rippled the water.

It was an enormous chandelier, its hundreds of lustres shooting light towards her as she approached. It lurched to one side as it rested on a table, calling out to her to rescue it and hang it anew. Cynthia circled it, practically clapping her hands with glee. She knew she should be buying furniture first, but this piece would be ideal for the shop room facing the street corner. What a treasure! This beauty was made by artisans, not in a factory production line. She knew she had to have it. *Now*.

"*Celui ci, s'il vous plaît*," she gestured to the seller. He stood to one side, chatting with several other men. As more tourists arrived, her need to secure this treasure was urgent. More loudly, she waved and pointed. "This one, please."

The seller glanced at her; their conversation halted.

"*La petite Anglaise*," said one, amused. Foxy little English woman, huh? No. She wasn't a fox. She wasn't even English, and this definitely wasn't about flirting. She was a customer, actually.

As the men laughed together, she turned her face from them to roll her eyes. Though her French swear word vocabulary was somewhat limited, it was the way they spoke and snickered and gestured and muttered sexually suggestive things that implied she was rich and privileged. Their assumptions were offensive.

Was she really a spoiled white English woman? She was Australian, for starters. And if she had an allowance, she'd earned every cent of it and had every right to spend it how she wished.

"*Australienne!*" she corrected them. It slipped out before she thought twice. What did their prejudices matter?

"*Bah, non!*" They laughed. Their patter was rapid, and despite her proficiency in French, she could only catch a word here or there.

18

"Poor husband," indeed, she managed to translate. Jimmy had died at 42, a decade earlier.

She turned and faced them again, arms crossed. She fixed the seller with the steely glare that every jewelry supplier who'd visited her empire back in Sydney knew meant business. What right had they to judge her decisions, these casual slouchers of men, whose wives were doubtless cooking up their casseroles, cleaning their homes, and raising their children unaided as they stood in the spring sunshine and made jokes about their international customers.

"She wants it," they'd repeated in French and guffawed. Were men the same the world over, with their sexual innuendos? These men reminded her of the builders and mechanics of her teenage years, back in Australia. She couldn't walk past without them whistling or nudging each other or commenting on her anatomy.

Surely the stallholder wanted a sale.

"*Est-ce qu'il y a une probleme?*" she asked in her best French. Now it was their turn to look uncomfortable. So, she'd understood their banter. Let them fester there as she stared back.

"*Mais, c'est déjà vendu,*" said the seller with a Gallic shrug. Already sold! No! He gestured at one of his companions, bantering with the best of them, the tall one, the only one without a beret.

She stepped towards them, opening her purse with purpose and drawing out some euros. Surely everyone understood money.

"*Voici l'argent,*" she said, offering the money in cash. She could already see that glittering chandelier in her front room, lit with the light of her two walls of windows. Their insults only made her more determined. This was the tenacity that had kept Huntleys House of Diamonds afloat even in those difficult years in the wake of the Global Financial Crisis as Jimmy lay ill, and especially in the worst months after Jimmy's death, and subsequent years. Despite her slight frame, Cynthia was no pushover; no quitter.

Cynthia wanted that chandelier so much, she actually batted her eyelashes at them. If they'd noticed her gender, she might as well use it to her advantage.

"Please?"

But as she found the purchaser's eyes, recognition dawned. That scar on his cheek. Even if there was a French type, long limbed and rangy, moody, they couldn't all have identical scars. This was the exact same man who'd helped her remove her sign. Would he remember her?

"*Vous*," he said, formally. Her heart jolted. His hands were out, conciliatory and his English excellent, though heavily accented. "I am so sorry; but, I need it; to match the other—for my client, you understand."

"Oh," said Cynthia, crestfallen. So. Some kind of tradesman or builder; he didn't even want it for himself. What a waste.

"But then," she said, and she pointed to two other chandeliers, under the stall table, which matched each other. "What if I buy these two for you, and you could let me have this one after all, and your client could even have a spare."

She repeated it carefully in French and smiled triumphantly, crossing her own arms and drawing herself to her full height to match his determined stance.

The banter around them stopped. She broke the silence by pulling out more notes. His companions cheered.

"*Je suis désolée,*" said the tall one, his large hands open, his regret obvious. "I am desolate to disappoint you" went the rough translation. It was the most polite form of "sorry" but it was still a "no."

Shame washed over her as she replaced the notes in her purse. Clearly money couldn't sway everyone. How crass of her. She shrank a little. She'd hated the big spenders at Huntleys who'd never take "no" for an answer, like the man who'd bullied Jimmy's mother into selling her anniversary ring all those years ago, that ring that led to all the trouble.

Cynthia cast another long look at the chandelier, heaved a sigh and gently touched the large multifaceted crystal at its base, a farewell gesture. It shot out a dazzle of sparks as it swung. Such a beauty.

"*Moi, je suis désolée,*" she repeated quietly. She was the one feeling desolate. Such a loss. Another one. Jimmy's death continued to haunt her, that ache at the centre of her being, never fully extinguished. She almost sobbed, but pushed her shoulders back, turned and wandered on, chastising herself. It was only an object, after all; not a loved one. And she'd survived the loss of Jimmy.

The morning was young.

She rapidly purchased a slim and elegant folding drop-leg table and four almost-matching spindle-back chairs—one a little rocky—so she'd at least have somewhere to eat her meal this evening, then halted in front of a stall full of marble and ornate wooden mantelpieces. She'd need five of those but there was no way she could lift even one of them.

A tape measure would have been handy. Still, there was no shortage of space in her largely empty house, so much so that she hesitated. Maybe it was some kind of regional scam, and she'd end up buying back the very fireplaces the last owner had stripped from her property.

Unlikely. And yet, here she was, with every other enthusiastic foreigner and a few locals, her cash helping drive the local economy, in a never-ending restoration racket for foolish Francophiles like herself. No matter. In for a penny, in for a pound.

For a moment, the enormity of her task overwhelmed her. What was she doing here, spending a fortune? She took a deep breath. Everything was fine. She was simply creating her new future. At this age, after a lifetime of service to her family and the business, she was entitled to a fresh start. The Huntleys expense allowance was generous, thanks to the sale of Eleanor's childhood home. She closed her eyes in deep gratitude to Jimmy's late mother. So many of her friends struggled with their mothers in law, but Eleanor had been a dream—generous and loving to the end. Eleanor would have wanted her to enjoy this adventure to the full. Eleanor would have approved of that chandelier; would have seen it as a perfect investment in her new property, a signature piece as perfect as the right diamond for an engagement ring.

Decorating her new property cleverly and furnishing it with style would add value. It was an investment. With the right look, if she ran out of money, she could Airbnb some of the rooms—even fund her retirement. That was a plan. She'd dropped in on the tourist office the previous day, where Nanette, a non-stop knitter, had welcomed her and explained that even though the village was relatively quiet, it thrived in summer, when visitors from all over the world flocked to admire the lavender and drink the wine.

Spend money to make money, Cynthia said, patting her purse. Did the French have a saying for that, too? *Dépenser de l'argent pour gagner de l'argent*. Except of course at the chandelier stall. Indignation surged, along with frustration.

She cast a glance back at the stall. That tall man was hauling it away, its facets flashing in protest. Pity. She'd truly loved it. It would have been so right for her front room.

For a moment she thought of Kath. The two often discussed Cynthia's abiding fascination with all things French.

"There's nothing actually all that special about France," Kath insisted. Cynthia countered that Kath would have no idea, since her family had moved to Australia when she was only nine.

"Sure, the language is special, but the things people discuss are really no different to what everyone discusses anywhere—what they're eating for lunch, who's getting divorced and why, and what they plan to do on the weekend…"

They could argue all lunchtime when they were at school together.

"Name one Australian philosopher," said Cynthia. Kath stayed silent.

"Or clothes designer."

Of course there were famous Australians, and many more now, but back then … Kath remained silent.

"I rest my case."

There were famous Australians in every field of endeavour, Cynthia was to discover, if not exactly like Rousseau and Chanel.

"What about Jacques Cousteau," Cynthia said.

"What about him?"

"He's hot."

"Well, he illustrates my point," said Kath. "Cousteau dives all over the world, not just in the waters around France."

Maybe Cousteau had been a silly example after all. Kath's theory was that life in France was exactly like life everywhere else, with the same hopes, triumphs and disappointments, so why make a change?

"You talk about it as if it's some kind of promised land, Cynthia, as if nothing bad can ever happen there."

"Well it didn't work out too well for Marie Antoinette, I know that."

"That's exactly my point."

So if she were to tell Kath the way she felt about missing out on the perfect chandelier, Kath would laugh at her, and Cynthia already knew better than to compare a retail disappointment with the French revolution.

But it would have been perfect for her front room. Truly.

Kath would call her shallow, but ask anyone who'd just bought their first car, or first pair of high heel shoes. Ask any of Huntleys customers who purchased jewelry, with that special light in their eyes that told her they were honoring themselves or another with a beautiful gift, validating their own desires and fulfilling them. Things mattered. And once you'd bought them, they were yours. As long as you looked after your own precious items, and they weren't stolen or wrecked—you could rely on them to be there when you wanted to use them or admire them.

The whole of western society relied on materialism, and, better still, the ownership of beautiful things was harmless, wasn't it? The retail industry craved customers, as did every market since the beginning of time, including this one. Back in Australia, at Huntleys House of Diamonds, Cynthia had devoted most of her life to trade.

Best of all, things didn't leave you, unlike people. Each of her babies had grown and changed and moved on, and even with the best medical care, her beloved Jimmy had sickened and died, leaving her bereft. She'd never make that mistake again—investing time and emotional energy in a partner. It had taken every fibre of her being to reinvent herself in those terrible months after he'd died, to focus on Huntleys, to fulfil Jimmy's duties to the business and try to be her children's father as well as their mother.

No. Cynthia knew the value of a good thing. Shopping wasn't called retail therapy for nothing. She hadn't simply wanted that chandelier. On some level, she'd needed it, and to know she'd missed out on it truly hurt. The loss of it resounded in her gut like grief.

24

Chapter 3

The chandelier seller and his friends patted Émile on the back. They congratulated him and laughed, but Émile's eyes traced the small woman's figure as she wandered on between the stalls, the set of her head so sad it turned the sunny morning to a minor key, as a cloud blocked the sun. Why had he been so quick to reject her offer? It was creative; workable; reasonable.

But he was a renovator now, not a charity for rich tourists. She'd get over it, and fixate on the next French antique she had to have. But his disappointment on her behalf lingered.

"Second thoughts for the little Australienne, eh, Émile?" his friends ribbed him. He punched the seller on the arm and they talked about the football, but it bored him and his mind wandered back to the incident.

Something about the woman was familiar. That was it!

It had been a couple of weeks since Émile had visited his old plumber friend, Jacques, in the village. In the thin blue light of dawn, on his way back to the villa he was renovating, he'd motored past the woman as she wrestled with the sign on that corner shop that finally sold.

Unlikely to be the estate agent, and very alone in her chic coat, she'd clearly needed a hand.

"You're too soft, Émile," said the voice in his head. He marvelled that his wife's opinions still held such sway, considering he'd left her as far behind as possible.

That morning in the village, he'd carefully executed a u-turn, stomped the kickstand down and left the engine idling as he'd pushed up his visor and reached for his pliers within the motorbike's black pannier.

Not wanting to frighten her, he'd approached slowly, to give her a hand and be on his way.

He'd smiled when her momentary alarm turned to gratitude, the fierce determination replaced with a delighted smile. With her animated face and intelligent eyes was she Parisian, or English? What would she do with the shop, and why wasn't her husband here helping her? There was something soft about her; a vulnerability; and the way she'd accepted his help had made his heart swell.

He'd been tempted to agree to the coffee she'd offered him in thanks, but was already running late. Other builders were waiting for him. Perhaps another time. If she'd purchased the place, she was likely to be there for a while.

Her smile and wave as he'd headed out again warmed him. She'd even blown him a kiss. A smile like hers could thaw any regrets. As he'd kicked up a gear, he'd laughed at himself and shaken his head. The last time he'd fallen for a woman he'd had to endure twenty-five years of unhappiness. He'd only just escaped.

But now—what he wanted more than anything was to see the Australian woman smile again. If his friends hadn't been watching, he might have considered her suggestion more carefully.

"Okay. *On y va*; let's go," he told his friends, as he hoisted the chandelier into his van, its facets shooting out light as if it were alive. It was certainly a beauty.

He wended his way slowly back and forth along the road next to the markets, straining to catch another glimpse of her, to at least discuss the matter—to no avail.

. . .

Alone in the front room of the old shop, Cynthia stared up again at the empty socket where that chandelier belonged. Curse those men at the markets with their easy banter! It was alright for them. They'd grown up in France, where one chandelier was much like another and the passage of time gave every item a patina of age, a depth and beauty Australians could never hope to truly replicate. She knew.

Planning her exit from the family business, she'd surrounded herself with French decorator magazines and architectural journals. French doors were the first item on the architect's brief for her rural retreat, and when Nicole showed her all the extraordinary decorating photos on Pinterest, she'd created a mood board so entrancing she'd been filled with an urgency to begin the project.

But first she'd had to sell the big harborfront home Jimmy's mother, Eleanor, had inherited from her own parents. Old Jim rattled in it after Eleanor died, not long after they'd all lost Jimmy, the couple's cherished only son and her husband.

Cynthia and Eleanor had liked each other from the moment they'd met, and if working in the family's jewelry business had had its challenges, there'd been plenty of good times, too.

Jimmy's death would have had far worse repercussions had the family not owned that beautiful home. Even her ability to stand here in her own property in France and grumble about a fancy chandelier was due in no small part to Eleanor's family's prudent property decisions generations earlier.

After Eleanor died, Jim insisted he rattled in it, and being there made him sad. He spent so many nights working and sleeping in his studio at the top of the store they modified the top floor to create a small apartment for him, while she stayed in the old house as her children finished school and stretched their wings.

Once they were out and about with friends every evening instead of sitting down to her home-cooked meals, Cynthia was overcome with loneliness. Jim was right. The harborfront lawn and views of the city and harbor were special, but the house was too full of loss. She kept expecting Jimmy to run up the stairs or walk in the front door, or hear Eleanor calling out to her from the kitchen, but there were no smells of cooking when she returned from a long day selling jewelry and wrangling with suppliers. No chatter. Will was often overseas, James would be out with Helene or friends, and Nicole was in a shared apartment with friends.

After a week of rain one winter, Cynthia forced herself to face the truth. Jimmy and Eleanor would never return. She lifted her chin and came up with a plan, since no one else was going to solve the problem for her.

Eleanor called everyone to a Sunday lunch and announced her idea. If they sold the place, James, Will and Nicole would each receive a substantial windfall with which to buy their own apartments. The business, often strapped for cash, would be able to fund repairs, fire safety upgrades and a fresh shipment of gems and gold. After a lifetime spent keeping the business afloat, she would take her share of the money, retire and build a dream home in the Southern Highlands.

To her delight, everyone agreed. With proceeds from the sale, young James, Nicole and Will each bought a new apartment near Huntleys with their share of the money, but Cynthia's dream was the rural retreat. She bought acreage near the Southern Highlands a couple of hours south of Sydney, and sketched out her ideas to an architect. From paper, it became bricks and tiles and windows with shutters and French doors leading to a courtyard, orchard, tennis court and roomy "stables" for cars.

But once completed, she suspected her attempt to chase her girlhood dream of living in France by building a French-style country retreat in Australia was a mistake.

She'd filled it with French antiques in a frenzy, taking up decorator recommendations and visiting one antique dealer after another, hoarding treasures. Kath asked her once why she wanted "all that old stuff."

"It's classic, it's classy, and it's truly beautiful," Cynthia answered. "You only have to look at the styling to appreciate the craftsmanship. Look at these curves and the glow of the wood. And every piece is unique and handmade. Don't you agree? If every piece could talk, imagine the stories. Some came through the revolution. These treasures have survived the test of time, the wear and tear and changing fashions—and they still look great."

Kath wasn't convinced. She lived her life in motion, playing netball, then tennis and later, golf, outdoors. "You can't even put a glass of water on top without worrying it will leave a mark."

"But the marks are part of the history," said Cynthia. "Look at this one, the one that started it all."

Cynthia took her friend to the small chest on a side table in the hall and smoothed her hand over the top of it. "This was my first piece."

She told her friend how, after Jimmy died, and they were all grieving, tiptoeing around the old house, Eleanor called her to her dressing room and pointed to the box, a simple rectangle with an angled opening, and insisted she take it. She'd explained how it was her grandmother's, long before the department store which became Huntleys was built.

At first Cynthia assumed the heavy box was for jewelry, but when she opened it fully, it became a sloped surface. There were small compartments at the top, one with an inkwell, and another with old nibs—a writing chest.

"There's more in this than meets the eye," said Eleanor, standing behind her, one hand on her shoulder.

29

In the days and weeks after Jimmy's death, through the days of planning, the funeral and wake, and the legal matters and finance meetings and nights and nights of silence, the strange old box was a curiosity and a comfort. The fact Eleanor entrusted her with it, and others in the family, now long gone, treasured it, really mattered to Cynthia.

It opened her eyes to the beauty of antique furniture. Blended with her love of France, it was only to be expected that she'd furnish her new home with French antiques, and she'd loved the process.

She'd enjoyed herself for a while, inviting all her Sydney friends to visit her gracious new Southern Highlands home. She'd hosted a tennis party, a garden party, and a number of dinner parties with French food, her friends and their husbands staying the night, with croissants for breakfast. She'd even started a local book club, and they'd aimed to read books by French authors, but as soon as her visitors vanished, her fine imported antique French furniture stared at her, unmoving, and a loneliness descended she could never quite quell.

Despite her careful research and the years of planning and procuring French finishes and furniture, her Australian home smelled new, because it *was* new. In autumn, when the sun dropped a few degrees and the wisteria leaves yellowed and tumbled, and the birdbath was full of moss, the place took on the atmosphere she'd craved, of a French country home, but mostly it remained large and new and empty.

Nicole sensed the emptiness at the centre of her life, and challenged her. Nicole, her second child, wasn't known for her tact.

She'd visited for her birthday and they'd enjoyed canard à l'orange on Cynthia's Limoges china. They'd washed and dried the precious dishes carefully by hand—a task Nicole resented but tolerated for her mother's sake—and were warming their toes by the fire, sipping on Cointreau, when Nicole asked the question.

"So what will you do now, Mum?"

"What do you mean, Nic?"

"This place is perfect," Nicole said. "There isn't another thing you need. You made your dream come true, so what's your new one?"

"Well, this is your birthday, darling. Let's talk about your own dreams," said Cynthia.

"I'd like my Mum to be happy," said Nicole.

"I am happy."

"Alright then. I'd like my Mum to be joyful—full of joy. Everything's tasteful here, and you're as beautifully groomed as ever, but I worry that you're bored. I can't remember the last time you laughed."

Cynthia chuckled then, but Nicole was right. Her life was as forced as her laugh. She was merely going through the motions.

All that night she lay awake, reviewing Jimmy's early death, and her subsequent struggles and achievements. Once she'd handed over the running of the business to the children, she'd enjoyed building the new house; but now it was finished, it was true. She'd fallen into a pattern; too predictable and not satisfying enough.

When friends returned her hospitality, they always tried to set her up with the single men in their lives, still uncomfortable that her situation no longer mirrored their own. Their well-meaning efforts embarrassed her. No one could replace Jimmy, the love of her life.

Cynthia had truly loved the exhilaration of attending furniture auctions and stocking her house with French treasures, but Nicole had a point. Was this really how she was meant to spend the rest of her life?

"If you love French style so much, why don't you just go and live in France?" Nicole asked her as the fire burnt low.

For so long, going to France had been impossible—her girlhood dream of speaking French and living in France only expressed in her purchases, movie choices and recipe books.

Now, with her children running the business, nothing stood in her way. If she travelled to France for a month or a year or longer, nobody would miss her. She worried about Will, her youngest, always so wild and free, but he'd been given the same opportunities as James and Nicole, and if he chose to throw them away, well, he was an adult. There wasn't much she could do about it.

Next morning as the soft dawn sunshine lit up the far side of her small slice of Kangaroo Valley, turning the tops of the trees gold and creeping down to illuminate every leaf, an excitement grew in her she hadn't felt since she was a teenager; since before Jimmy's proposal—the realisation that her life was in her own hands—that she was finally free to act on her deep interest in France, to go there and live, for as long as she wished.

With one conversation, Nicole had given her permission to buy that one-way ticket to France. The idea set her whole body aglow, bright as the valley's sunshine.

"You must have slept well, Mum," said Nicole.

"I didn't sleep a wink."

"Are you okay?"

"Never better. You were right to call me out, darling. I'm going to France. As soon as it's sensible. Give me a month. I'll need to see Scottie senior and arrange my finances. And I'll throw some sheets over the furniture and lock up carefully. You're welcome to use the place as a weekender. Use the tennis court and keep an eye on it; take home some flowers from the garden. Enjoy it. I know you and James will look after it. Who knows; maybe some day soon James will find someone special to spend the weekend with here."

"James is still hankering after Helene—but Mum, you're not serious. Did you really say you're turning your back on the place, turning your back on us?"

"Oh Nicole, my dear, I'll be on the other end of my phone, as usual." She took her daughter's hands and smiled into her eyes. How strange it was that a child could parent you—boss you around and tell you to grow up; then be best friends; and then revert to dependency—all in one conversation.

"Now give me a hug, Nic," she said, and folded her grown daughter in a warm embrace before searching her eyes again. "You were right to tell me to get my act together. You and James are mature and independent. It's time I behaved the same way. There's nothing to stop me. I won't leave for a month or two. Let's have lunch at the club together in the city a couple of times before I leave, and I'll let you know how my plans are going. Monday week? Will you be free? I'll need to be in Sydney to see the lawyer and sort out my finances with Scottie senior."

Her daughter's admiration—or was it alarm—shone back at her. She astonished herself as well as Nicole. After putting off her dream for three decades, she was actually going to live in France.

Chapter 4

1979

Cynthia's father couldn't understand her fascination with French, though her mother told her that so many other people felt the same way, there was even a word for it—a Francophile was a person who enjoyed French culture and language.

"French!" her father said when she announced her plans to study it in high school, and then he'd shrugged. Little Cynthia had been no trouble, so pretty with her blonde curls. Why this odd obsession?

"Why not? It's good to have an interest," her mother said. She'd been home when Cynthia returned in a dream from her first French lesson, describing the French teacher's perfume. The French classroom was a revelation, another world, every window plastered with French tourism posters to make the classroom dark enough to show movies. Cathedrals, stonework, canals, snow mountains, the Eiffel Tower…

"If all you ever do is watch movies, it sounds like the teacher's lurk," said her father, who'd thought History might have been a more useful subject, or Commerce.

They'd learned everything in French—about Napoleon and his mistresses at least.

"How useful is that?" her father muttered when Cynthia won the French prize at Speech Night year after year. Her mother patted her arm, to reassure her his opinion wasn't the only one.

The only Commerce subject that would have interested teenage Cynthia was how to afford a plane ticket to France.

She scanned the newspapers and magazines for any news about France, including the ads for French cosmetics and fashion. The language was a magnet to her young and eager eyes and ears.

The following year, the possibility of a school excursion to New Caledonia was a bright beacon which helped her through the drudgery of the rest of her schooling. There was no money for the plane fare, so Cynthia worked and saved. A job at the local library helping to shelve books did the trick.

Noumea was full of everything French—businesses in a tropical setting so colorful, the mountains so pointy—that Cynthia became more certain than ever that France held the key to her future life.

Even the poster on the bus—*Il est interdit de fumer*—was special. She had no interest in smoking, but the construction of the sentence was fascinating. It is forbidden to smoke. There it was, a living language— no mere exercise on a chalkboard. She was all eyes and ears.

Addicted to anything French, she was in heaven. The trip to the fun park that very night was electrifying, even though it rained. She and another little group of friends fell in with some local boys their own age, who were happy to practise their English, and next day, Samedi, a Saturday, they accompanied them to the zoo.

When they paired up as couples, the French teacher gave a Gallic shrug, so from then on, whenever her new French friend Eric wasn't in school, he took her places on his moped, past palm trees and beaches and trees in flower in the balmy air. He arranged a trip for her to a lighthouse, where a guitar player sang French love songs, the notes resounding, enchanting.

"*Où se trouve le bureau de poste, s'il vous plaît?*" She relived the triumph of the first question she'd asked a real French person, and the fact she'd been understood, and able to understand the French answer in return.

Cynthia wasn't in love with Eric. She was in love with his culture. They went to the aquarium, the town, the gardens, a local dance where it wasn't just Eric who tried to dance too close, and she discovered what it was to be alluring—the power headier than the aroma of French food.

She returned home determined to go to France proper, and as soon as possible.

"I told you we shouldn't have let her go to Nouméa," she overheard her father say to her mother when she'd gone to bed. Her mind was wide awake with the excitement of her travels, the discovery she'd been able to decode so much, and even be understood.

Ah, the post office, the pen friendship with Eric, her French pal.

"No, he's not a boyfriend," she insisted, though she loved to receive his cards, with their tropical vistas and French stamps, and she loved to write his address and the little tag in the top left hand corner of the envelope "*par avion*" when she replied.

She was, truly, madly in love with all things French, and always would be. The plan to go to France never left her mind, and the moment she left school she tried to secure a job with a French shipping company, so she could travel to France by boat.

"It doesn't work that way," her father said. "You'd be better off going to university and studying French and becoming a French teacher."

He might have been right, but she couldn't bear the thought of delaying her life in France for another three years. The job with the French shipping company never materialized, but she did manage to get work at Christmas time at a large department store, helping sell French perfume to dazed men seeking gifts for their wives and girlfriends.

But it was only a holiday job, and she knew they only hired young people whose labor was cheap. Next year she'd be too old, even with her experience.

She comforted herself by translating the French text at all the makeup counters, those magic words, those vague promises:

rajeunissant

soin de la peau

crème nourrissante

When makeup samples were handed out, she pounced on Lancôme, Givenchy, Dior. Any of it, all of it. She pored over French magazines, snapped up French brands in second hand clothing shops. She borrowed anything French she could find at the local library, scanning the jobs columns daily.

"Dad thinks you should take any job, darling," her mother said as the New Year rolled around and she hung about the house. "You have retail experience now."

So she did.

A friend of her mother's had heard that Huntleys House of Jewels in Bondi Junction was seeking a sales assistant. Cynthia dressed carefully in her most chic outfit—a white school shirt she'd altered by removing the collar and cuffs, topped with a cropped pale gray jacket and cream trousers. She twisted her hair in a chignon. Her mother appeared and held out her hand, her best pearl earrings shone in the palm.

"Really?"

"I'd love you to have these, Cynthia. To sell beautiful jewelry, you'll need to look the part, as if you value it yourself."

"Well, I do! These are beautiful! *You're* beautiful, mum!" Cynthia kissed her mother's soft cheek in thanks.

Now she was set, but for the shoes.

"Borrow mine?"

"Thanks, Mum, but they're too big. I need stilettos."

"You'll need to be comfortable if you're on your feet all day, dear."

"I need to get the job, first! I'll find something on the way. Wish me luck!"

"Show me your hands, dear. They'll be studying your hands and especially your nails. It's a fine shop, Cynthia. It has the best reputation. Everyone who's anyone buys their engagement rings at Huntleys, and they'd be lucky to have you."

"And you think I'll be able to use my French?"

"I can almost guarantee no other applicant will be able to speak French. Don't forget to mention it, Cynthia!"

Her mother painted her nails with clear lacquer, then shared her hand cream with her, first putting it on her own hands, then smoothing it over her own. It was a strangely intimate gesture, transmitting her mother's love and good luck vibes to her, skin to skin.

Only later, when her mother died and Cynthia had her own children, would Cynthia reflect that her mother nursed her from when she was newborn for so many months and years when she'd been oblivious to her care; that the love and care continued virtually—that her mother would have gone to Huntleys herself to convince them to hire her.

Cynthia held her head high as she opened the door, with the insouciance of the French models she'd studied in their fashion magazines, as if she already owned Huntleys.

Cynthia considered simply pretending to be French, but maybe that would be going a bit far.

Jim and Eleanor Huntley took her up to the VIP room to grill her, but she'd noticed their expressions in the mirrors in the elevator and knew they were keen. They wanted her to start straight away, so she did.

The only trouble was another young staff member, Jimmy. Self assured, he kept bossing her around.

"Not like that," he said, after she arranged the chains in the hanging cabinet as Eleanor requested. "You need to turn all the tags over so the customers have to ask you the price."

He might have been right, but it was easy to take offence. Jimmy wasn't much older than she was, and she knew she was good with customers. *She'd show him.*

She took to walking quickly ahead of him when they were both on the floor, flashing her brightest "can I help you" smile to catch a browser's interest.

When an older man stopped at the chains, she slipped beside him and peered down, too.

"Some lovely ones there, sir," she said.

"Hmm."

"Allow me to show you the quality." She unlocked the cabinet, pulled out the tray and laid it gently on the counter, selected a medium weight gold chain and held it out, as Jimmy's eyes bored into her back.

"If you hold out your hand like this, sir, … you can appreciate the weight of the gold."

"Yes," said the customer. "Indeed."

"Do you have an idea of how much you'd like to spend? Is this a gift?"

"For my granddaughter. She's turning 21."

"Oh, congratulations! That's very special," she said. "We have some beautiful pendants, too, right here, for a truly unique combination. When's her birthday? You're probably aware one of the January birthstones is garnet; and February, amethyst. March is aquamarine, my favourite. Of course, you can always select something in the colors she enjoys."

"She's about your age, actually. You choose something. You seem to know about these things."

"If your granddaughter's not happy, you can always bring it back with her and swap it for something similar. Huntleys is amazing that way. What's your granddaughter's coloring? Blonde, brunette? And how tall is she? In general, the taller someone is, the longer the chain, though of course it becomes a personal preference. We can always alter a longer chain, and perhaps make a bracelet from the extra section. Mr Huntley's a goldsmith."

Cynthia rang up the sale, carefully boxing a thick, long chain with a champagne topaz pendant — "they call it champagne, but really it's 'clear' so will go with everything. I'd love a gift like this. A future family heirloom!"

She wrapped the box in several thick layers of tissue paper, secured them with a gold HHJ sticker and slid the package into a shiny purple bag with the same HHJ gold letters and gold ribbon handles.

Her pleasure at handing it across to her customer was real, and magnified as he walked out the door.

Jimmy sidled up to her. Expecting congratulations, she turned to him and smiled.

"We don't do returns," he said, his face dark. "Why didn't you check with me about that?"

"That happy customer won't be back. He made the right choice. I know about these things, Jimmy. Didn't I just sell several thousand vials of Perfect perfume over Christmas? The whole city smells 'perfect' because of me."

"You're very confident."

"That customer needed 'confident.' I can also do 'meek.' Besides, who are you to tell me what to do?"

"I'm more experienced in selling jewelry, that's for sure."

"Alright. Let's find out who sells the most value this week then, Jimmy."

By the end of the week, Cynthia sales amounted to well over Jimmy's. She'd watched and kept count. In the tearoom, she confronted him.

"So. Who won, then?" She wanted to hear him say it.

"Pretty pleased with yourself, aren't you?" said Jimmy. "It's only because you flirt with the male customers."

"As if you don't do the same thing! I see you with those middle-aged women, flattering them about how young they are and their 'discerning taste'. I heard 'discerning' about twenty times in the last week. How about some new lines, Jimmy? Like 'it's very cultured' or 'understated elegance' or 'very flattering'."

"What are you? A thesaurus?"

"Jimmy! What's this bickering?" Eleanor entered and headed to the sink to wash her hands. "We prefer a happy team at Huntleys."

Cynthia flushed bright red and bit her tongue, suddenly ashamed. She'd barely been there a fortnight, and wanted to stay.

Jimmy cleared his throat but remained silent.

"It's these late Thursday nights," said Eleanor, more gently. "We're all tired on Friday mornings, but it just means we have to try harder to get along, and be more patient with each other, don't you agree?"

"Yes, of course, Mrs Huntley," said Cynthia, only too ready to tone down the rivalry if it meant keeping her job. Why didn't Jimmy say anything? She glanced up at him. He stared back, his expression unreadable. She stood straighter. Was there teacake on her cheek? She left her mug on the corner of the bench and rushed out to the ladies' room to check.

No sign of anything amiss in the mirror, she made a vow to herself to simply ignore Jimmy from now on. If it took two to fight, she would never take the other side.

When he turned up on her floor on Monday morning, she found an excuse to go upstairs.

Once, when he followed her upstairs, she grabbed a cloth and polished the mirrors in the lift. Another time, she took herself to the storeroom to replenish the box stock under the counters. And then wished she hadn't. She'd never forget Eleanor and Jim's exchange she overheard in the corridor outside.

"I don't like his attitude," said Jim.

"All young men need some freedom, Jim."

"He's forever off tinkering with his friend's car, or wandering along Bondi Beach sunning himself."

"Ron Scott's a lovely young man. What would you rather have them doing, Jim? Going off to war, just because you did?"

"My country needed me. This generation is lost. Not every young man has his advantages. He takes them for granted."

Were they talking about Jimmy? Did they always care so much about their staff? Jimmy might be about to lose his job.

Her curiosity and sympathy piqued, Cynthia paid more attention to Jimmy after that, to the shadow that passed over Jimmy's face every time Jim spoke to him, the way his shoulders stiffened, as if expecting a rebuke.

He wasn't an unpleasant young man, not like the ones who drank beer in the train and whistled or made lewd comments about her to each other as if she were deaf, or like the young men in Woy Woy who cared more about their surfboards than anything else.

In fact, she quite liked aspects of Jimmy.

As autumn descended, he took to leaving with her on Thursday nights after the shop shut, and walking with her to the bus stop in the deepening twilight. He'd stand with her until she was on safely, and give her a wave as the bus pulled out.

Part of her wanted to argue she was perfectly capable of walking herself to the bus, but part of her enjoyed his quiet company. It was old fashioned, gentlemanly, and very unusual.

One day she caught him staring at her as she polished the tops of the cabinets in a few quiet moments and stared back. The light in his blue eyes wasn't quite aquamarine, but something finer—a sensitivity, an intelligence, an unasked question.

A customer entered and the moment was broken, but she found herself staring back at him more often, at a nick in his chin—how awkward to have to shave every morning! She liked the deep honey color of his hair, and it was always clean, not as long and messy as most men's hair in those days.

Most of all, she liked the way he stood straight, with confidence. Some young men grew hair to their shoulders, and slouched. They'd never be offered a job in a jewelers as classy as Huntleys.

One afternoon, Jim Huntley the elder summoned Jimmy upstairs to his workroom at the very top of the building. She'd never been in, but it had a mythic quality among the staff, as if a dragon lived there, breathing fire.

"You should see the blowtorch," Lorna told her. "I was up there once. There were jewels all over the bench, like dragon's tears, and the flame was something awful. I don't know how Mr Huntley can stand it up there in summer."

Jimmy was so quiet on his descent, she went up to him and touched his arm. His answering glare threw her — so much pent-up emotion in those blue eyes. Strange she'd never noticed his eyelashes before. She'd never stood so close.

Had he just lost his job?

"Want to talk about 'upstairs'?" she said. "After work?"

He looked her up and down, as if to test her attempt at friendship. Had she been so awful to him at the start?

"I was going for a run on the beach," he said. "But I can change my plans."

"The beach is good," she said. "I'd love to come with you. I haven't been to Bondi for ages."

Chapter 5

1984

It was a chilly afternoon, already turning dark, a strong southerly scattering the breakers. Cynthia shivered with cold. Or excitement.

The beach was bleak and beautiful with its backdrop of deep grey clouds, the sea dark and shiny and alive. Jimmy took off his shoes and socks and rolled up his trouser legs, so Cynthia kicked off her stilettos and held them in one hand, suddenly full of energy. She hitched up her tight skirt.

Jimmy was surprised.

"I thought you were too stitched up," he said.

"I love beaches," she said. "But I can hardly wear a bikini to work selling jewelry, can I? Do you come here every afternoon?"

"Only when I need to let off steam."

They set off, dodging abandoned sandcastles and the footprints of thousands of strangers, down towards the water's edge, where wave after wave smoothed the sand like a polishing cloth and the last of the daylight cast a silvery sheen across their path.

They ran the full length, Jimmy adjusting his stride so Cynthia could keep up. Half way back, Jimmy slowed to a walk. He was smiling, his shoulders relaxed, a different person.

"How long have you been at Huntleys?" she asked, then winced. Should she have mentioned work?

He stopped and turned to face her. He brought his hands to her shoulders, then dropped them, as if she might sting.

"You don't know?"

"Sorry?"

"I've been there forever. I can never leave."

"Your job?"

"My life. I'm Jimmy Huntley, Cynthia. Jim and Eleanor are my parents." Jimmy's laugh was huge, with a trace of bitterness. Did he regret his opportunities?

"Well, I'm an idiot," and she laughed with him. "You could still leave, though, if it's not working out; if it's not what you want to do."

"It's not perfect, no. Dad doesn't accept I'm not a total clone, even though I'm his only child. But I can't ever take over his goldsmithing. He got me an apprenticeship and I totally failed at it. That wasn't fun. This afternoon he tried to talk me into giving it another go but it doesn't interest me, staring at a bench and a flame all day. I won't do that, and he won't accept it."

He stared out at the horizon and kicked at a wave that came close.

"But there are other things I love about the business; the selling, for example," he said. "That's why I was cross at you, Cynthia. You're so good at it, and I'd always been the best. Jim said I was using my sales skills as an excuse not to knuckle down and do the hard yards. Hiring you was strategic. He wanted to prove to me that salespeople can be hired and fired, that I was expendable in that role, that I should be helping him produce more stock. But there's so much competition these days, and my going into manufacturing won't make the slightest bit of difference."

"Why not? I don't disagree, by the way. I want to learn more about the business."

"Mass producers will always undercut us. Huntleys having two goldsmiths won't solve the problem. So much jewelry is imported these days, we can never compete. We need to import, too, while keeping up the exclusive high-end designs. I need a business degree, not a blowtorch, but he won't agree."

"But you can enrol yourself, can't you? You can spend your own money on whatever you like, including education."

"You're right, Cynthia." He turned to her, and offered both his hands to her, and as another wave washed in around their ankles, she reached across and took them. They were warm in her own, warm as the sensation in her stomach, something new, something exciting as she stared at the light in Jimmy's blue eyes.

"I can and I will," Jimmy said, staring back. "Why didn't I think of that? It's that simple. If it takes Jim a while to get used to the idea, so be it."

He dropped one of her hands but he held on to the other and swung her arm as they walked back together.

"Eleanor's always very reasonable," she said.

"But they're from a different era. Are your parents like that?"

They talked for hours, the barrier between them dissolving as they sat on the concrete steps and stared out to sea. Jimmy's arm crept around Cynthia's shoulders and she leaned into his warmth, and told him of her dream to live in France.

"No one can stop me," she said. "Once I have the money."

Jimmy pulled her closer. His kiss was a surprise, a nice one, warm; delicious. Just right.

He broke away.

"Fish and chips? Hot pie? I'm starving. Are your toes like icicles?"

They were a bit numb. She dusted the sand off her feet and pushed her stilettos back on.

"I need to get home."

He helped her up and held her hand all the way to the bus stop, kissing her again as it arrived. This kiss was awkward, more public. Their noses bumped, but it didn't matter. Not at all.

This time when he waved, she waved back with a new kind of smile.

A few days later, Cynthia was taking a late lunch in the staff kitchen when another overheard conversation sent a chill down her spine.

"That girl has to go," said Jim. "She's a complete distraction. Jimmy's making mistakes."

"Nonsense," said Eleanor. "Isn't that what my father said about you? Have some patience."

"This situation is completely different."

"Is it?"

There was silence then. Cynthia nearly choked on her sandwich. What were they talking about?

"Well, if that's the case, she's far too wily," said Jim.

"She's a young woman with dreams," said Eleanor. "What's wrong with that?"

But if Jim was having second thoughts about her value, Eleanor had taken a particular liking to Cynthia, who'd been given responsibility for the lower value items, including silver charms and lockets. The older woman patiently showed her how to count the change into someone's hand, totting up coin by coin from the price of the item in small money to the note she'd been given.

One afternoon, three weeks into the job, Eleanor called her aside.

"Come up to the office with me, please, Cynthia," she said. They took the lift, Cynthia's heart beating double time. She hadn't stolen anything; hadn't stretched her lunch breaks. Had Jim put his foot down? Would she be served her notice?

Eleanor sat at the old wooden desk and gestured to Cynthia to sit opposite. Eleanor leaned forward and extended her hands, palms open.

"Show me your hands, please, Cynthia."

Mouth dry, Cynthia held out her own, her palms clammy with fear. What was going on?

"It's alright," Eleanor said. "You've been doing very well. You have lovely hands. You keep your nails so neat and clean, and your skin is creamy and flawless."

"Sorry, Mrs Huntley. What's this about?"

"Oh, my dear," Eleanor laughed. "I can tell you now. I didn't want to say anything in front of the others, because there's jealousy. I've seen it before. Huntleys needs a hand model, and you'd be just right. We're going to put out a catalogue. Would you like to model some of Jim's rings? The photographer is coming next Tuesday."

"Oh, I'd love that, Mrs Huntley. Is there something I should wear on that day?"

"Beige or white would be suitable, and maybe something black to swap into; clothes that are simple and don't distract."

Cynthia's heart pumped all day. It wasn't as if anyone was likely to recognise her from her hands, but she felt an instant affinity with the French models she'd studied in fashion magazines all her life. She'd add this experience to her resume at the very least.

When the photographer arrived with her heavy bags of lenses and lights, Cynthia watched Eleanor greet her and usher her into the lift. Her heart pounded. This was a different sort of day. Huntleys this week. Tiffany's next.

"Meet us in the VIP room at eleven o'clock, please, Cynthia," she said.

The VIP room was smaller than she'd imagined, but it retained the grace and style of a respected establishment, if a little outdated.

The two large windows on two sides were flanked by velvet curtains, and there was gilded fretwork and a large chandelier reflected in the other two walls, hung with two enormous, gold framed mirrors.

The photographer sat on the ornate deep blue velvet couch. A deep purple velvet cloth was draped over the circular marble table and a shiny brass music stand. On each side were lights on stands.

"Beautiful natural light in here," said the photographer with a smile as she studied the set up. "But it never hurts to get some extra sparkle. So, you're our model?"

Cynthia swallowed and nodded. How hard could it be?

Jim entered with a ring case, his face stony, unconvinced. Eleanor was close behind.

"You can leave us to it, Jim," said Eleanor, but he stayed to observe, frowning slightly.

When Cynthia had first met Jim, she'd found him kind, like Eleanor, but now it was easy to imagine the pressure Jimmy was under; the unspoken criticism.

He might not be aware she'd overheard him say she was a distraction to Jimmy, but she knew he couldn't fault her sales. They were excellent, and so was her service. She was always prompt, taking the earlier train each day to ensure she was still on time, despite frequent rail delays.

And if there was a new vibe between her and Jimmy, an invisible thread that turned her head towards him as he entered her floor—a snatched kiss on the staircase when no one was watching, or an eagerness to delay as he walked her to the bus stop, to find out all about his course options and progress and to share something new about France—she never let it interrupt her attention to customers' needs.

Cynthia held her chin high as the photographer switched on the extra lights. If Jim had doubts about her, all she could do was remain polite.

"Right," said the photographer. "If you sit here on the edge of the chair and place your left hand here, I'll do a light check."

She turned to the camera on its tripod, twisted the lens a few times and announced "let's go."

Jim opened the case and handed a ring with a green stone to Eleanor, who pushed it onto Cynthia's ring finger, removing any fingerprints with a soft cloth.

Light shot out of the luscious emerald at all angles. Cynthia was mesmerized, dazzled. She'd admired some of Jim's rings in the past, but not this one. It transformed her hand as ornaments transform a bare Christmas tree.

A ruby ring followed, and a rosette of emeralds, the centrepiece the deepest blue imaginable.

"That's good," said the photographer. "Turn your hand a little more. Excellent. Your skin tone is perfect. Lovely work. Try a few different hand positions, please. Yes, that's good."

Under the spell of the photographer's patter, Cynthia began to act, pretending she was Marie Antoinette, placing her fingers beneath her chin.

"Yes. Lean in. You're happy to include your neck and chin?"

"Do I need some makeup?"

"No, no, that's great. Stunning, actually. Ever modelled before?"

She shook her head.

"How about the diamonds, Jim?" said Eleanor. "Did you ever do anything with that pear and the Asscher?"

Jim stood and locked the door. He placed the case on the edge of the table. He lifted out the top tray of rings, exposing a lower layer, and pulled out a simple gold ring with an enormous square cut diamond, each corner faceted. The gold band tapered away from the striking centre stone, flanked by three tiny squares on each side.

"That's an absolute beauty, my Jim," Eleanor said.

"I was going to keep it a secret. It's for you, for our anniversary."

"Oh, Jim. It's so beautiful. You are the most incredible jeweler; you have prodigious talent. It's more than a skill, what you can do. It's an art."

"Don't let's start this again, Eleanor. Anyone can set stones. It's the beauty of the jewels that's on show."

"No, Jim. You're wrong. It's the setting that makes a stone so beautiful. Put out some diamonds. They're nothing if they're not set right."

"Oh! What are these ones?" said Cynthia as Jim emptied a small bag onto the velvet cloth. Slivers of ice sparkled up from the lush material, but Eleanor was right. There was something lonely about them without a setting. They could have been shards of glass—a bit ordinary.

"Marquises," said Jim as if it was all that needed to be said.

Cynthia's hand was right there. The photographer was busy winding up the film cartridge, tipping it out into her palm, then inserting a new one and winding it on. As they waited, Cynthia pinched the slim diamonds and lined them up, centre to centre, the largest in the middle.

Jim's eyes pierced hers. Did he imagine she'd steal them? She snatched her hand away, fingers spread, to show there was nothing in her palm.

"Cynthia," he said, and he drew in a breath. Was she in trouble? "I've had those diamonds for nearly a decade, and never thought to arrange them like that. That will work. So, you're not just a salesgirl, then?"

Eleanor shot her a special smile, then nodded at Jim.

Cynthia's hand felt ordinary when the shoot was over; naked. At the time, each ring felt heavy, but now they'd left a shadow of their presence on her fingers. She opened and closed her hands as if to rid herself of the sensation.

"Thank you very much, Cynthia," said Eleanor. "I believe you have a real flair for our business."

Cynthia flushed with pleasure, even though Jim declined to comment. He was busy replacing the rings in the tray and locking it carefully, as the photographer collapsed the tripod and put the camera back in its case.

"Thank you very much for the opportunity, Mr and Mrs Huntley," said Cynthia. "I'll pop back down and find out if Jimmy and Lorna need a hand."

Jim nodded. He didn't smile, but at least he didn't frown. Perhaps he was mellowing. Had she passed some invisible test?

The catalogue was a wild success. Customers entered pointing at the pictures of her fingers with all the different rings.

"I'm afraid that one has sold, madam, but our goldsmith is here," she'd say. "Would you like to speak with him and discuss your sizing? And you might like an extra diamond or two on each side, or a garland across the stone."

Huntleys installed an intercom system to save staff time racing up and down the stairs to summon Jim.

Cynthia was given a small raise in the coming months. Jim wanted to recognise her expertise with customers; her ability to translate their wishes into custom designs, a skill he finally conceded neither Jimmy nor Eleanor could match.

"You have an eye for these things," he said. "You could get an apprenticeship."

"Thank you, Mr Huntley," she said. His praise was rare. In the corner, Jimmy raised his eyebrows, making her smile.

She loved working at Huntleys, but an old ambition nagged at her. She wanted to travel, to go to France and use her French. She'd been saving for her ticket for ages.

Friday was pay day at Huntleys. Cynthia received hers in a small brown envelope and peeped inside. They were all in there, in a stack of orange and blue notes, more than two hundred dollars for her efforts. This pay was significant. This was the one that brought her up to the mark. Now she could buy her one-way ticket to France. She would do it.

"We need to celebrate," she said, catching Jimmy's hands when she passed him in the corridor.

"Why's that?" He pulled her in close.

"I've got enough money! My dream's about to come true." Did a shadow flick across his face? He should be pleased for her. They'd agreed on reaching for their dreams. He'd enrolled in an after-hours business course. He was yet to break it to Jim, but she knew he loved it, devouring the concepts.

He'd been telling her about supply and demand; how it made sense to him; that Jim's rings would always be good business, and would eventually become collectors' items, far more valuable than the sum of their parts, because he was an artisan, and each ring was unique.

"Friday night. Let's go out, then! A mate told me about a French restaurant, near Town Hall," he said. "Come and try out your French, and we'll toast your success."

She looked at him and smiled.

"Is this a date?" she said.

"Maybe. If you want it to be."

"So, it's not just because it's French, and you're always hungry, and you need me to translate the menu? And because I need to celebrate."

"Well, it's all of those things, Cynthia, but I'd also love you to come out. With me. On a date. My shout."

"Tonight?"

"Why not?"

She freshened up in the ladies' room near the VIP room, giving herself a spray of her precious Perfect perfume and brushing her hair into a neat chignon. Starry eyes stared back at her in the mirror as she pinched her cheeks for more color.

Jimmy was waiting for her in the foyer. He'd swapped his pin-striped double breasted suit for jeans and a denim jacket.

"Trendy," she said. "Did you dress up for me?"

She noticed a tiny cut near one of his sideburns. He'd shaved again, for her. He smelled good, like cologne. She ran the tips of her fingers down his smooth cheek and he snatched them and kissed the top of her hand.

"Smoothie."

"Gotta keep up with the French," he said.

They caught the bus to town together and walked to the restaurant, hand in hand, swinging their arms. It was good to be on a date with Jimmy— James Huntley the Second—better than good.

The restaurant featured proper tablecloths and candles, and a menu Jimmy found incomprehensible.

"So, your dream is coming true," he said, over a glass of Burgundy, rich red in the candlelight, as beautiful as one of his father's rubies.

Cynthia nodded.

"You'll have to come up with some new dreams," he said.

"Why?"

"It's good to have a dream."

"Well, this one hasn't totally come true yet, has it? I'm not actually in Paris yet."

"But you will be, soon. I suppose you'll resign. We'll miss you. I'll miss you."

He looked so sad across the table, Cynthia almost had second thoughts. Maybe she should stay and save a bit more money. How would Eleanor and Jim manage without her? The catalogue was a wild success. Business was as busy as ever, even though the rush of Christmas was months away. Was she a fool to throw away such a good job?

Was it the wine, or was Jimmy wistful?

"I'll miss you, too, Jimmy," she said. "But I've been planning this for so long, all through high school."

"You'll love it. But it will be very cold over there in December and January and February. Maybe you could keep saving, and go in a few months instead. How long do you plan to stay? You could take leave without pay."

"I only have enough for a one-way ticket. Do you want to come with me?"

"I can't. I've got exams coming up, and I need to graduate and stay here to run Huntleys."

"Your dream."

"And I'll need to help Mum and Dad through Christmas. It's like 'harvest time' in retail. We always need all hands on deck for a financially successful end to the year. And given that catalogue, we're on track to be busier than ever."

Jimmy held her hands across the table. In the soft light he was handsome, suddenly serious, older than his years.

"Dreams can change, Cynthia."

"Maybe."

"Will you marry me?"

She snatched her hands away and took a deep breath. Did she hear correctly?

Jimmy was a friend, a good one, but they'd only known each other a few months. Surely he wasn't serious. Was this to stop her going to France? For all his talk about dreams, marrying Jimmy would derail her plans.

She liked him; more than she'd ever liked any other man. But at eighteen, was she ready for marriage?

"That's a big question, Jimmy. Do you really want a wife? We're so young."

"I know I want you."

"For the rest of our lives, though? We're barely out of school. I was going to live in France. Next month."

"That's what worries me," he said. "You'll go over there, and meet all those Frenchmen, and never come back. I'll lose you."

"You want me to drop my plans and stay here for you?"

"I didn't say that. Look, I've got an idea. Don't give me an answer yet. Think about it. Can you give me a few weeks, Cynthia? Maybe we can have our cake and eat it too. I have a plan, but I have to check it with Eleanor and Jim. Besides, if you work with us for a bit longer, you'll be able to save enough for a return ticket, too."

She squeezed his hands and smiled at him across the candlelight, this earnest young man, so handsome.

Suddenly she burst out laughing.

"What?" said Jimmy.

"You proposed on our first date!"

Chapter 6

But now, far from Australia, in the French property she'd claimed as her own, Cynthia stared at her empty light socket. She was so cross with the tall Frenchman who'd snaffled that chandelier she actually stamped her foot. She knew it was churlish. She'd run a business for a decade, raised three children and built and furnished a house, dealing successfully with teachers and tradespeople and suppliers of all ages and genders. She wasn't accustomed to failing to secure a transaction. It riled her.

She stomped back through the corridor to the other end of the building where she'd parked. Her anger gave her energy, and she lugged the slim antique gateleg table out of the back of her car and through the back entry and hallway into the front room. She followed it with each of the chairs. At least this setting was something—not a proper dining table, but useful enough to serve a meal upon for now. She towelled them down gently with warm water, then headed out with a shopping basket to buy some bread and cheese and olives for dinner.

The local market would fill the square with life again tomorrow, as Nanette had promised. In the meantime, she used the hired car to fill her new home with some basic pots, pans, linen, cutlery, crockery, a blow-up mattress, pillow and linen, and then return it.

Chandelier or not, she was happy, wasn't she? If for a moment she wondered if she was repeating her most recent mistake by simply filling another empty house with French furniture, she pushed the thought aside. At least it was actually happening in France. She was living the dream.

No matter that the shopkeepers still refused to speak French with her, despite her own best efforts. She stocked up on a few groceries and turned for her new home.

As Cynthia rounded the corner, swinging her string bag with its heavy hunks of paper-wrapped cheese and a jar of jam, the bread stick tucked under her arm, there was someone at her door. Odd. He was peering in the windows.

She approached with caution.

"*Oui?*" she said. She really must have her eyes tested, throw vanity to the winds and purchase some glasses. She leaned closer. As he turned, with a shock of astonishment, she recognised the tall man again, the one from the market, the one who'd helped her with her sign, and then snaffled her chandelier.

"*Puis je vous aider?*" she said. It was polite, considering her fury about the chandelier.

"Perhaps I can help you," he said, throwing her words back at her.

"Yes," she said, her emotions see-sawing. "You already did. You kindly removed my sign for me, but then," she swallowed and took a breath, planting a smile on her face.

"Would you like a coffee after all?" she said. She wouldn't mention the chandelier. It was too childish. At least this Frenchman actually spoke French with her.

"*J'ai quelque chose pour vous,*" he said. He had something for her.

He led her around the block to the rear entrance of her home, to a big, deep blue van. He swung open the rear doors, and there, between racks of drawers, was the chandelier!

Cynthia's hands flew to her mouth and she threw her arms around him. He was solid and strong, and she sprang backwards, embarrassed.

"Oh, I'm so sorry," she said. "You haven't even named your terms. I apologize. I'm behaving like a spoiled child."

"No, no. It is I who apologize to you." His accent was deliciously French, his tone conciliatory. "With my friends, I was weak. Your solution was ... intelligent. I bought the other matching chandeliers. My client is happy. And this one? It is for you."

She could barely speak with delight.

"But why ... Oh."

"It is a gift; my gift to you."

"Oh no. I really can't accept."

"But you must accept."

"I'd love to, but at least let me pay you. I really did want this one so badly."

"No. Please. I will not hear of payment."

"No." She drew out her purse, and he placed his hand on hers.

"*Non.*" His touch was firm and cool. Pleasant. When he took it away, she felt the loss of it.

"But ..."

"Do not insult me."

"Pardon?"

"When you've lost everything, sometimes all you can give is kindness. Do not deny me this dignity."

That silenced her. She stood taller. She'd have to tell Kath she was wrong about the philosophers. Here was one, an everyday one, she seemed to have picked up at a market. Was France full of them? But what could this debonair yet practical Frenchman have possibly lost?

"And as you see, I can hang this for you. Show me the position."

Should she let this stranger into her house?

She didn't hesitate long.

He stood in the front room and stared at the socket.

"But this is perfect. I will hang it now."

"Oh, you're very kind, but I'd like to clean it first, and I don't have a ladder. But please, stay for lunch, and then perhaps you could come back another day."

As Émile left to bring in the chandelier, Cynthia rushed inside, tidied her few possessions, washed her hands, checked her careful French twist and lipstick in the mirror, and laid the lunch on the tiny table. All she had was a couple of mugs, a chopping board and a knife. She really must buy some more necessities. Fortunately the local market was only a day away.

"*Fou*," Cynthia said to herself. Mad. Foolish. Yet thrilling.

He returned with the chandelier. It lurched sideways in the sunshine near one window, shooting out rainbows, a glorious tumble of sparkle.

Emile pulled from inside his coat pocket a bottle of bubbly.

"Really?" she said.

"But of course."

"But why?"

"Émile," he said and leaned towards her. Oh. The cheek kiss routine—too familiar by far. She didn't want to offend, but they hadn't even met. Not really.

Cynthia leaned backwards and shot out her hand.

"Cynthia Huntley," she said. "Delighted to meet you, Émile. Welcome to my adventure."

"Enchanté," he said, popping the top off the bottle. "Cremant, local. Nice?"

"Very nice," she said. Enchanting, indeed! The tiny bubbles fizzed on the roof of her mouth.

"To your 'adventure,' Cynthia," he said, the soft "th" becoming a hard 't'. "Cyntia." She loved it. She laughed.

He really was quite handsome, with those eyes full of light, and the little scar. Her eyes were drawn to it, and to his lips. She blinked and smiled.

"To your generosity. Émile. You haven't told me why you changed your mind."

"It is very simple," he said. He poured more foaming liquid into their glasses, and she was relieved he wouldn't be going up a ladder after lunch after all. "I wanted to see you smile."

"That every stranger should be so lucky," she said. As she touched her glass to his, their eyes met and a jolt shot through her. Talk about testing the power circuits ... She dropped her gaze.

Their simple meal of bread and cheese was delicious, washed down with the bubbles.

"Tell me about your work," she said. "Do you chat up every stranger who moves to the south of France, and then do up their ancient houses for them?"

He shrugged. "One job, it leads to another, yes."

"Tell me about your client with the chandeliers, Émile."

"It's a villa outside Nice, a couple of hours away."

"You've driven all this way to give me your chandelier?"

"There is time today. The tilers; I cannot work when the tilers are there."

"You subcontract?"

"Sometimes, yes. It depends on the job."

"And do you often give single women fittings for their houses? That would be great for your business." She hadn't meant to imply he was so mercenary. Perhaps he truly did just have a kind heart.

"And where do you live?" she said, rapidly moving the conversation elsewhere.

"South," he said, with a new reticence. Had she offended him?

Cynthia smiled brightly. "*Sud.*" Maybe if she repeated his word in French, he'd be more specific, or open up a little about his past.

"*Sud.*" Then silence.

Did he flee something? Or was he seeking it? If so, how would he know when he'd found it?

His eyes met hers as she searched his face for clues. He'd piqued her curiosity, this kind and generous stranger, perhaps her first new friend. Was she right about what she glimpsed there in those dark eyes? A world of pain before steel gates swung shut.

But then he smiled, and the sun came out.

Chapter 7

É mile leaned back in his chair and enjoyed bread and cheese with this beautiful woman. Her questions were intelligent. He wanted to think before he spoke next.

If he asked her about her plans for this place, she might accuse him of fishing for work. Instead, he simply wanted to be with her, and not be nagged, and not be criticised, and not worry about the future or the past.

"You still haven't named your terms, Émile," she said. "I'd love you to hang the chandelier, once I've had a chance to clean it. Are you an electrician, or can you recommend someone who can help me? These switches are ancient. I didn't want to look too closely when I bought the place. I love it because it faces south and has enough room upstairs for me to live and the family to visit, or maybe I can rent out some rooms one day if I have to. I was probably a fool, but what's life for if you're not taking a few risks. Oh, and thank you again for my chandelier. It's perfect for this room, don't you agree?"

He smiled. He loved it that the drink loosened her tongue; the way she relaxed with him. Her voice was eager and pleasant, her French good, the accent different. Australian. Kangaroos. Koalas. Sydney Harbour Bridge. A very long way south.

"Tell me, Émile. Do the French have 'damsels in distress?'" she asked, leaning forwards to cut up a pear. She pushed half of it towards him with the knife and he took a piece, nodding his thanks.

"You've helped me twice now, Émile. You turned up at the right time on your motorbike on my first day here, and now you've spoiled me with this gift. I can't explain why I had to have that chandelier. You've totally indulged me. You're so kind."

He winced at her words. At least "so kind" was different to "too kind," Bertha's constant criticism. For too long, his wife had badgered him, that his kindness towards their son would mean he'd grow up weak; that his kindness to their hardware shop customers meant they'd always take advantage, expect discounts, and pay them late or not at all; that his kindness towards shoplifting school children to save them from a life of crime was sheer madness.

"We're not a charity, Émile! We'll go broke!" Her rebukes were embedded deep in his brain. Émile winced and offered Cynthia more champagne.

"À votre santé," he said. "Good health."

"I'll drink to that," she said, tilting her glass forwards for a small top up.

Here in the sunny room, with Bertha a long way north, he poured himself a little more champagne, and privately toasted himself on his escape.

...

Cynthia never drank alone, and the crisp bubbles were going right to her head, but what could it hurt? Her knight in shining armour was impeccably behaved. His hands were clean, his manners fine, and his conversation informative. How would she know if he had a criminal past? There was plenty he wasn't saying—yet she understood the need to enjoy the moment, without clouding it with regrets.

Why shouldn't two strangers enjoy a meal and a drink? Besides, she longed to ask his advice about what she should tackle first. Perhaps he could help her to quantify and prioritise the repairs her home would undoubtedly need. She'd invite him back and ask him to quote. No matter that he now had a distinct advantage over other builders. She admired entrepreneurship; the master stroke of a master builder, perhaps.

"I'd love to see some of the places you've done up, Émile," she said.

"You are checking my credentials," he said, his smile guarded.

He finished his drink, sat back and wiped his mouth with his handkerchief.

"Of course. Is that a problem?"

His face fell.

"You will excuse me," he said. "Thank you for this meal. I must go."

With a little bow, he unfolded his lanky frame from the chair, stood and took his leave, out her powder blue doors and around the corner.

Cynthia ran to the back of her house and peered out the little window in the vestibule. His expression remained muted, brooding, as he climbed into the cabin of the van, turned the key and backed out of the square.

She hadn't even asked for his card. Would she ever see him again? What had she said that so disturbed him? Did she cross some unwritten cultural boundary? Or a personal one? She hadn't meant to offend him.

She tried to read the sign on the side of his truck. "Eméliorations." *Ameliorations* by Émile. Repairs. Clever. But he was gone before she noted the phone number.

The front room was empty without him as she gathered up the remains of their meal and brought them back to the old kitchen. She'd need to buy some plates and cutlery at the very least, in case he popped by again, or some other stranger arrived with something she'd always wanted. Maybe it was a local custom.

Chapter 8

At night, the ancient house was too silent. The thick walls admonished her. If she opened the windows to the sounds of the village—a dog barking, a mother calling her children—the loneliness was worse.

She punched her pillow and turned over again at two in the morning. In the dark, the charm of the small town was invisible and her isolation, wild and pounding like her heart.

What madness had brought her here, to a town where nobody knew her; to this empty old building with so many unknown problems she could renovate for the rest of her life and still find things to fix?

The shopkeepers were just friendly enough. They bantered with her in the same way she'd welcomed her regulars at Huntleys, ready to praise and listen to whatever she said, for the sake of loyalty and ongoing sales. It was a thin veneer. They were curious about her, she knew. She overheard snippets of their gossip. They suspected she'd left her husband, or that he'd rejected her. Here, women her age were immersed in the care of their grandchildren. If she could have caught their eyes and had a decent conversation, they would know how much she longed to hold those warm and heavy bundles of babies with their dark eyes and rosebud lips, to rock them with lullabies and chant nursery rhymes.

They might have all had something in common if ever they'd conversed properly, but they always hurried away.

Like the men at the markets, the local women distrusted her. Despite her careful French, or because of it, she'd always be a foreigner. Though they'd stop and kiss and talk to each other in the cobbled streets, they slipped past her as water flows around stone.

A few were curious about her plans for her building. They'd stop and talk if she was coming in or out, but only to ask what she was doing. Were they friends of the other shopkeepers, sniffing out the threat of competition?

"Not sure yet," she'd say and smile twice as wide as necessary, despising herself, even though it was the truth.

So she turned to her old refuge, even as she knew she was doing it, of decorating herself and decorating her house.

When Jimmy was dying, Cynthia took greater care than ever with her appearance. With full makeup and every hair in place, strangers might never guess her own world was falling apart. If it took her an extra hour every morning to face the day, it was more than worth it. She wasn't sleeping anyway. Her makeup was her armor, as much for herself as for others.

At the time, Kath's reaction confirmed the strategy worked. They met in the city for lunch every few months.

"You look better than ever," Kath had said.

"The doctor says he has only weeks now."

Kath had clutched at her, as if she were the one to be losing her husband, her children's father and the mastermind of their business.

"It's okay, Kath. We'll be fine." If she kept her back straight and her expression pleasantly neutral, she'd manage.

The trick always was to have a task worth doing, and now, with her French property, there was no shortage of tasks, she'd remind herself every morning, when the soft light of dawn brought back a sense of perspective, hope and excitement.

As she did in Australia when she planned the whole Southern Highlands house, she drew up lists. If she could make her French place look like a home, maybe it would start to feel like one.

Her mood lifted immediately, and with the village market due to open the following day, she slept more deeply than she'd done since she arrived.

Calls and hammering woke her. Out the window, the square was transformed, with vans and stall holders setting up their tents and tables, stringing up second hand clothes and carpets, and joking with one another.

She pulled on her jeans and a shirt, slipped on some shoes and grabbed her purse.

Everywhere she looked were things she needed; even a shopping basket to begin the task.

The day passed in a frenzy as she flashed her card and dragged her purchases home. She bargained and she bantered, picking up new slang and the local accent. The merchants were happy and so was she.

Cynthia inadvertently bought five kilos of tomatoes after pointing to five different sorts. The merchant was so thrilled she didn't have the heart to explain her mistake, and she lived so close she just dumped the bags on her counter, then went back out to explore again.

As market day drew to an end, she was still shopping hard, picking up well-priced items as the stallholders began to pack up.

Old bevelled mirrors, side tables and chairs made of twisted metal wire, winged chairs that needed re-covering, a jug and nest of bowls, a set of saucepans and an omelette pan.

Last to leave was the plant seller. She hadn't planned on plants, having no garden and no gardener.

"It's not important," said the young seller. He was clever. "That is why I am here every week. Your plant dies, you buy another. You'd like one plant? Two plants? I give you eight. For your windows. For free."

He pointed at some wooden boxes.

Of course Cynthia agreed, suddenly so pleased with the plan she also bought five pots of herbs for her kitchen window. She'd save money. European parsley with every meal! No need for vitamins. She was thrilled.

By the time she'd dragged all her purchases inside and into vaguely the right rooms and rearranged them, she was tired.

An omelette with parsley was a fine meal, and that night she slept again, better than ever.

Reupholstering her armchairs was beyond her, so she draped beautiful fabric over them.

She piled the tomatoes high in a colorful Italian fruit bowl she'd found at the markets. The green, gold and red display reminded her of the abundance of Christmas in Australia's high summer. The aroma of ripe tomatoes was heady, and after a couple of days, she sacrificed some of her fresh basil and made tomato paste.

She took most of it across to Nanette. The heavy jars clunked against each other in her string bag as she walked, remembering her own days as a single parent. It wasn't easy to keep coming up with meal ideas while raising children and holding down a job.

When Cynthia reached the tourist information centre, Nanette's daughter, Inès, in her tweens, was doing homework at the far end of the counter, brushing her cheek with the end of one of her two long braids as she contemplated an English translation. When Cynthia explained a point, she rewarded her with a beautiful smile. Though Nanette was usually busy giving advice to visitors, Inès was one of the locals always happy to speak French with Cynthia.

While Cynthia's new place still needed replumbing and rewiring, it became more and more welcoming, and her days full of purpose.

If Cynthia was lonely, she refused to acknowledge it.

A phone call from Nicole reminded her that her family cared about her, even if they couldn't meet at her place for Sunday lunch every week, as the rest of the town seemed to do.

"How's la France?" Nicole said.

"Marvellous, darling. I'm so glad I came. How are you? How's everyone?"

"Do you really want to know?"

"Of course, Nic. Why wouldn't I?"

"When you handed over the business to James and me and Will, we got the impression you were totally over it, and we had to solve all the challenges ourselves, Mum. 'Been there. Done that' were your exact words, though you were polite about it. You smiled."

"It doesn't mean I'm not interested. What is it?" Cynthia sensed Nicole was troubled.

"I'm furious, actually," Nicole said. "This was supposed to be a brilliant evening. I'd planned to phone you for weeks to tell you how well everything went."

"What happened?"

"We had this publicity event. It was my idea, and it was so good. We'd all agreed it was going to give us the optimal boost ahead of

Christmas—really put Huntleys back in shoppers' minds, but you won't believe what happened."

Nicole's pain and frustration oozed through the phone like vitriol as she described how some newbie stallholder out the front of Huntleys stole their limelight.

Cynthia listened to every detail; how Nicole managed to secure a top movie star to appear with the diamond necklace that had been stolen in the plot of her latest movie, *Heist*, with Huntleys in the background. There was no doubt Nicole's plan was brilliant.

"And then this little upstart, this stallholder making junk jewels, elbowed right in on all the action. The movie star didn't help. She did her thing with our necklace, but she ended up giving this newbie all her genuine attention, and the rotten media gave her all the limelight. They came and drank all our champagne alright, but social media had already picked up on *her* business—Stellar—not Huntleys. I'm so furious, I could scream, Mummy."

What was she doing here, on the other side of the world, unable to comfort her daughter?

"Nicole, my dear. Those stalls were always going to be a problem. Jimmy and I tried to stop the council allowing them there in the mall, but they wouldn't listen. They insisted the stalls would bring life into the place once they'd closed off the street, after all the tram tracks were pulled up. The council meant well, and they do keep the place busy to an extent, though why they didn't simply keep the street open, I'll never understand. Our customers really missed being able to park out the front, that's for sure."

"Well, I'm going to lodge a complaint. It's totally unfair."

"You do that, darling. It might make you feel better, if nothing else. Now, when are you coming to visit me?" Maybe if she changed the subject, Nicole would calm down. Nicole tended to take things to heart.

Cynthia herself had had to learn that business wasn't everything. If you let the profits and losses dictate your moods, you'd go mad.

"What's there to see in France?"

"History. Food. Effortless style. It's beautiful here."

"Meh." Nicole belonged to the generation who found everything they wanted online. "Will's in Europe, Mum. I can't believe he hasn't been in touch yet."

"Well, you know Will. I suspect he'll contact me when he runs out of money."

"It's irresponsible. He is so indulged."

"It's true. Jim and I were both a bit soft on him, but Will was my baby, and you and James were always jealous."

"Well he's not a baby any more, even if he behaves like one. I don't suppose you've seen the latest headlines? Did you hear he was engaged to some high flyer in Italy?"

"No."

"Well, none of us did. But now that he's broken it off, it's the biggest gossip column news you ever saw. 'Huntley heartbreaker'. The usual. It's all over socials."

"Oh dear."

Nicole sighed.

"I suppose it's not all bad, Nic," said Cynthia. "It keeps Huntleys in the headlines one way or the other."

"If only column centimetres translated to sales."

"Not going so well?"

"That's James's department. He's got another meeting coming up."

"Oh, with that lovely Scottie? How's your love life by the way, Nicole, my dear? Seeing anyone nice?"

"Mum, you are transparent. You're bad. Why would you ask that at the very same moment you mention Scottie?"

"Well, he always was rather fond of you, Nic."

"How's your own love life, Mum?"

"I haven't thought about my love life since I married your father."

"Well maybe you should. Then you'd stop prying into mine." That was Nicole, blunt as ever.

"Maybe you children wouldn't like it if I fell in love again."

"Why should you become a nun just because Dad died? We're bigger than that. Surely you're lonely sometimes. I know you resisted all those set ups right after he died, and that was sensible. But Dad's been gone for so long now. It would be okay, you know. We'd still love you … Mum?"

Once again Nicole's directness took away Cynthia's breath. It was only because of Nicole she'd finally moved to France, and now her daughter was suggesting she date. In her fifties. Really?

"I'm thinking about your words."

"You really don't need to be alone, Mum."

"Well, Nic. I could say the same of you. Honestly, this is a new thought for me. When your father died, I focused on the business. There was more than enough for me to do. What with all the school fees, going belly up was never an option, that was for sure, and then when you and James and Will were ready to take it all on, I was so busy creating my Southern Highlands hideaway …"

"Yes, and then you decided you were bored…"

"Not exactly."

"But you're glad you're in France?"

"I am! I'm having a ball. I'll send you some more pictures. The place is really coming together."

"Good to hear, though I never doubted it. You have a real eye for how to arrange things."

"It's pretty easy when your taste is French provincial and you're living in Provence! Can't go wrong."

They laughed. Cynthia was glad Nicole was getting over the disastrous PR campaign.

"But I'm not only talking about the place, Mum. I'm talking about your heart. What about some sexy Frenchman."

"You're a great one to talk, Nicole, my dear! Tell you what. How about you open up your own heart. Find somebody nice, who treats you well. You're like all young women. You want someone perfect. And yes, you should have high standards. But it's not necessarily about their looks. It's about the way they treat you—whether they respect you; whether they actually care about you…"

"Yes, Mum."

"I mean it, darling. Let a new chapter of your life unfold. What if it's staring you in the face and you're just not open to it?"

"Alright. But, Mum. This is a deal. I'm willing to give it a go, if you're willing to give it a go."

"Your father Jimmy was my one true love, Nic."

"I know, but Dad especially wouldn't want you to be lonely."

"I'm fine, Nic. I've never been remotely interested in anyone else. I'm very happy in my own company. But thank you for the thought."

Chapter 9

Cynthia sent Nicole three more photos of the interior after their call, singing to herself. It was a shame the chandelier was still on the floor, though at least she'd had the chance to clean it thoroughly. She gave every facet of every lustre a careful wipe, wondering at the skill of those who'd made them, and imagining all the people who'd walked beneath it in times past.

Émile had not returned to hang it, let alone give her a quote on fixing the electrical circuits, but she could hardly complain, given that he'd gone so far out of his way to hand it over. She would have liked to see him again. He'd been excellent company over the simple meal they shared.

"Gorgeous!" Nicole messaged back. Thank goodness for technology. She could be on the other side of the world and still be in touch with her children.

She'd interrogated herself before about this, when she moved to the Southern Highlands, how she'd tried to be both mother and father to them as they finished school and started work. But she'd known that solving all their problems for them wasn't necessarily doing them any favors.

James was older when Jimmy died. He'd been at uni, already living his own life; and with his strong sense of responsibility, he'd almost taken the inevitable into his stride, accepting the role of chief proprietor. By the time she fully handed over the financial reins, he was more than ready to shoulder the load. He loved it. It was a shame about Helene, his long-term girlfriend. What a disappointment she'd turned out to be, hooking up with one of his old university mates, a stockbroker. James didn't deserve that, her fine son, who had left university to help her run

Huntleys. He'd needed someone more generous to stand by him, someone with a bit of grit, someone less greedy than that shallow, fickle Helene.

Will was more of a worry. For all the media made him out to be made of Teflon, surely all those "playboy" headlines couldn't be easy to live with. Being handsome wasn't everything. Laughing and having fun and sweeping up one new lover after another wasn't necessarily any more healthy than having none at all. And as for this new Italian incident…

Well, there wasn't much she could do about it. Will ran his own show. Always. She'd hear from him when he was desperate, and not before. She suspected she"d always been too soft on him, but he reminded her so much of Jimmy. She forgave him everything.

She sighed and stared at a cobweb in the corner. She needed a broom with a longer handle.

If Nicole's conversation found a chink in Cynthia's love-life armor, she didn't admit it to herself, though she did find herself thinking about Émile—his kindness in bringing her the treasured chandelier, and his chivalry in offering to hang it for her.

She was content to think of him and smile, to say to herself he was the kind of Frenchman who might appeal to her at some stage. Someone able to admit he'd made a mistake, someone generous, not to mention someone so handy at repairing things. Only as a friend of course. No one would replace Jimmy in her affections.

What had Émile called his business? *Emilioration.* How clever was that name! Even Nicole would approve, with her marketing mind.

Cynthia set out to buy milk and bread for the day and to feed her stale bread scraps to the kittens who lived at the well. Half wild, they tolerated her tickles under their chins, and contemplated her with those tawny eyes.

The window boxes of the village were full of flowers, in all their host of colors, the yellows, the reds, the oranges and purples all nestled together with the vivid greens of their leaves—the sheer proliferation of blooms was spectacular.

Standing at the well, she turned her feet and another vista opened up, another peek up another ancient street, with its cobblestones and crooked buildings and windows, their shutters opened wide, and more window boxes with tumbles of blossoms, and arches of roses carefully trained up the facades, bursting with pink or white blooms.

"Lovely," she said. "Too beautiful. Yes!" This was the promise delivered. Vibrant abundance. Beauty. Fragrant, delicate, temporary, wild with life in the abundance of spring and summer; here for her discovery, for her to appreciate.

"And I appreciate it," she said out loud.

About to go on her way, she noticed Émile at a corner table outside the wine bar. Surely not. At ten o'clock in the morning! He was with two friends, under a cloud of smoke in the morning sunshine. On the table were several carafes of red wine, most of them already empty.

She stared, then hoped she'd backed away quickly enough so that he didn't notice her. So. Émile was a lush, just some drunk Frenchman ready to meet anyone for an excuse to drink. There were men like that in Australia, and women, and, even though she knew she was being a prude, as a stranger in a strange land caution was only sensible.

She chastised herself. Imagine building Émile up in her mind to be so fabulous, when, after all, he'd been almost as obnoxious as his jeering friends back at the markets. Their lewd comments still made her smart.

So, all that "gentleman" business might have been an act. The jury was now out on Émile.

"Cyntia!" he called out now, with a "t" again, the way that made her heart jump. He stood, and then he staggered and his chair fell backwards. Drunk and disorderly in the middle of the morning!

She walked more rapidly away from them all, from him. Too bad if she was being rude. The last thing she needed was a dose of wine-fuelled nonsense, in French or otherwise.

The aroma from the boulangerie a few doors up was irresistible. She pushed open the door with its little bell, bought a croissant and long French loaf, stowed them in her string bag and headed off around the corner, breaking off a corner of croissant. How did the French make their treats so deliciously light and crunchy on the outside and perfectly gooey in the centre?

Behind her, a motorbike engine clattered into action. Was it Émile's? Surely he wouldn't attempt to drive with so much wine on board so early in the day. She took a side street, picked up her pace, slipped in her back door and locked it behind her, leaning against it to catch her breath. She placed her purchases on the kitchen bench.

"Cyntia!" He banged on the blue door at the front of the building. "Cyntia!"

It was too late to pretend she wasn't home. He knew she was there. Where else would she have gone?

"Cyntia?"

Awkward. Should she tell him to go away? No. He'd been decent to her. She hadn't been afraid when they'd lunched together, nor on her very first morning in this town when he'd helped her with the sign. He'd been friendlier than anyone, before or since. Apart from the shopkeepers who sold her their goods, no one here was particularly keen on the foreigners who forced up their house prices. But she wouldn't open the doors to her house to him and let him into her haven; not now; not while he was drunk.

Taking a deep breath, she grabbed her keys and went out her back door, locking it behind her.

He was still knocking on her front door when she approached him from around the corner.

"Émile?" she said. His eyes were red rimmed and he smelled of alcohol. What made him imagine he could come to her place like this in broad daylight, making such a ruckus? Did he presume he had a lifetime guarantee on her affections because of the chandelier? Worse, was he unhinged? She knew nothing about him. Only that he knew her address. She vowed to have her locks changed. Who knew how many people had keys to these ancient doors?

Émile flinched as if reading her thoughts.

"I apologise," he said, swaying, the emphasis on all the wrong syllables, very French. He held his hands out and down, as if to calm a frightened horse. "I will explain. I was with my old friend Jacques all night and will go back to him. His wife, she just died."

"Oh," said Cynthia, the ground knocked out from under her feet. How quick she'd been to judge!

She reached out to squeeze Émile's forearm. Now it made sense that Émile was unshaven. She knew that grim set of his mouth.

Now she was the sorry one. "What do you need?"

He returned to his bike and motioned her across, then, from the pannier, he brought out a black bundle of fur.

"It is injured," he said. "Just after I saw you ... You can help, perhaps? You like the kittens."

So, had he watched her feeding them at the well?

The kitten's fur, tail and legs stuck out at angles, claws spread. It bit and scratched at Émile's fingers, its golden eyes wide with fear. Instinctively, Cynthia reached for it and held it close to her chest, covering it with her jacket.

"But why me? Isn't there a vet here?" she said. "Where can we find the doctor?"

Émile shrugged. She peered inside her coat. The golden eyes were wide with alarm, but the struggling stopped. It was basking in her body heat. Cats were resilient. It might be alright if she fed it and kept it warm.

In the darkness, against her skin, the tiny cat began to purr. She'd looked after injured kittens in her childhood. They were tough creatures. They wanted to survive. All they needed was a dark warm space, a box, with something soft inside, and soft food, and to be left alone. Did the French also say a cat had nine lives?

"A tourist bus came too fast, and the driver was talking, not taking enough care. This one ...."

"No!"

"I am so glad. You will help, Cyntia?"

"Of course," she said.

"I ..." His words trailed away as he stared back the way he'd come. "I must return ... to Jacques."

"Yes," she said. "I'm sorry to hear about your friend's loss." The words never went far enough. She sought his eyes, saw the pain in them, and closed her own to remember Jimmy's death and prevent that ricocheting echo of losses. She reached out to squeeze Émile's arm again, and he brought his hand across to cover hers. That warmth. She breathed again.

"Au revoir," he said, the wonderful French expression that promised the goodbye was only temporary, that it would only last until the next time they saw each other. His hazel eyes. With that arresting glint of gold, they lingered on her own, and her heart lifted. Émile understood loss and could comfort his friend; and he trusted her with this wounded creature.

"À bientôt," she said. Until next time. Yes. She wanted a next time with this strange Émile, so practical, so sensitive and kind, even to an injured kitten. Intriguing.

Only after he'd gone did she remember she needed his contact details, for quotes on repairs, but he'd be back to check on the kitten, wouldn't he?

Chapter 10

Cynthia tiptoed in to inspect the kitten several times that morning. Bright eyes peered out from the darkness of the box, reassuring her it was still breathing; and toward the afternoon, she noted it had moved to the other side of its bed. When she dipped her finger in her sweet tea and held it out, she was rewarded with the rasp of a warm tongue. The kitten accepted more and more, so she left some in the saucer nearby.

She leaped when her phone rang. Would it be Émile?

"Mother!"

Will always addressed her so formally when he wanted something.

"Darling!"

"I'm in France. How about I drop in? Nic says you're in Provence somewhere."

"Oh Will, that's wonderful."

"So, what was wrong with Australia? What's all this upping sticks to the south of France on a whim. What kind of example does that set?"

"That's hardly fair, Will. I took a month to set my affairs in order."

She well remembered her meeting with Ron Scott and his wife, Dianne—pronounced Deeane. Ron and his son Scottie were their family's long-term financial advisors and business accountants. Ron insisted she come over for dinner, and she'd brought flowers for Dianne as always. How many dinners had they had in that room, the four of them, first as young business people and firm friends?

She and Dianne discovered they were expecting within a month or two of each other. They'd compared their waistlines, and then their chubby babies, and as the years rolled onwards they'd discussed schools, enrolled the two boys together, stood side by side at the edge of sports fields in all kinds of weather, celebrated speech days in unison, and laughed and shared so much.

Jimmy and Cynthia had broken the tragic news of Jimmy's diagnosis at one of their dinners, shattering forever the perfect symmetry of their friendship. Their get-togethers became less frequent, more strained and hushed. Even now, Jimmy's empty chair brought back the grief as if it were fresh.

Cynthia sighed and swallowed and forced a smile.

"I know I thought I wanted to move to the Southern Highlands," she began.

"It's beautiful what you've created there, Cynthia; a real achievement," said Dianne.

"And a good investment, too," said Scottie senior. "It will only increase in value, a property like that, with the improvements you've made to the land."

"Yes, but I've found I don't really want to live there."

"It's quite spacious. Is it lonely?" Dianne said, her tone gentle.

"It's not that exactly. It's just … You know I've always loved French decor and French movies. I don't know if I ever shared with you my childhood dream of living in France."

Dianne nodded. Ron's expression was less accepting, veering towards alarm. That would be right. Ron's life was planned and methodical. But here he was, with his own child bride Dianne right there beside him, and all going along swimmingly, while Cynthia still lurched from the loss of Jimmy. And if she wanted to move to France while she had enough time, money and energy, she'd do it, whatever Ron might advise.

"So I've booked a one way ticket," she said. "I leave for Nice in a month."

Ron stiffened but she ploughed on.

"And I'd love it if you could help me arrange my financial affairs, please, Ron. I know the investments should give me a steady income, and I have the expense allowance from Huntleys. I've redirected the mail to you, so the bills will be paid on time. I won't rent out the house. I'm really hoping James and Nic can have some use out of it as a weekender. You and Dianne should go, too, Ron. Have a hit of tennis and stay the night. Why not? I don't want to sell it, in case France doesn't work out."

"Of course," said Ron. "That would be an even more major decision."

Now, she strode through her new French property, banishing the memory, focusing on her wayward son, Will, and their phone call.

"So I've bought a fabulous place, darling. Can you come down? It's between Avignon and Nice. I have plenty of space."

"Brilliant. Text me the address. See you soon."

Typical Will. He'd hung up before giving her any idea of his timing, and then wouldn't answer when she rang back.

She sighed and smiled. Her youngest had always been self-centred, but he was also a joy, with his easy charm that reminded everyone that life was for the living. She hadn't seen him in months and longed to show off her purchase. He might even lend her a hand with furniture and repairs.

The kitten continued to make progress, venturing out of the box on spindly legs to lap at a saucer of water and bread several times a day. Cynthia replaced the newspaper on the floor of the box from time to time, and placed a sandbox nearby. Eventually it let her scratch it under the chin and run her hand down its back.

In her rambling property, the kitten was company and she loved to tempt it with morsels of her leftovers, mostly soft cheeses. It needed a name. Minette? Hadn't she read that name in an old French picture book?

Cynthia's Saturday began again with the thump of tent pegs being driven into the ground outside her door. Market Day! Markets had been held here on Saturday for at least 800 years, Nanette told her. One by one the vans appeared with their colorful tents and tables and goods— olives, fresh produce, including tomatoes that actually smelled like tomatoes. Handmade wooden kitchen utensils, second hand stores, cheeses, leather goods, linen clothes and pots of plants so colorful she almost needed sunglasses to gaze at them. No wonder this town was so popular in summer. Window boxes were kept well stocked with flowers of every variety. It was like walking around a Hallmark garden wall calendar.

For Cynthia, every market was a revelation. In Sydney, the treasures in her favorite stores were carefully clustered with other eye-catching desirables, the colors and shapes a magnet to women of means with plenty of time and money and the impulse to decorate. Here, every item had potential, and the jumble was the main attraction, the quest unending and the prices a steal. Cynthia was in heaven.

She bought jugs and other kitchen utensils, unmatched Limoges plates and cups, more crystal glasses than she knew what to do with, dining chairs, candlesticks, armchairs—every item charming—small tables and larger ones, serving plates and trays, lamps and cutlery, a sideboard to put them all in, an armoire for linen sheets with embroidered initials, remnants of a way of life that had passed.

She laughed at herself. Nicole might accuse her of hoarding, but there was plenty of room in her new house. Certainly, some of the items needed mending and reupholstering in matching fabric, but she had no other calls on her time.

She sent another photo to Nicole, Kath and Dianne, this time of a set of five copper frypans, a nest of ever smaller sizes, the smallest no bigger than a cup. They'd look superb on the long wall of her kitchen.

Her phone rang. Kath! She sounded tired. Downsizing did that to you. Cynthia remembered those months of cleaning out four generations of clutter from the Huntleys harborside mansion; how her hands and arm muscles ached from all the sorting, but her gut ached more—for all the memories of good times gone forever in the great rush of busy-ness that had been her life. She didn't envy Kath.

"That's so funny, Cynthia," Kath said. "I've only just got rid of three boxes of kitchen junk, and there you are over there buying more! You're not turning into a hoarder are you?"

"How are you, Kath? I remember cleaning out Eleanor and Jim's place for the big sale. It took weeks and weeks. I definitely didn't hoard any of that. I only kept Eleanor's old writing box and a huge wooden sideboard with mirrors for my Southern Highlands place. Originally it was from her parents, and it was the right size for that alcove at the end of the hall."

"I see. So you only hoard antiques. Not sure if that's technically hoarding, and no one doubts your taste, Cynthia. So I'm going to get through this? I have dreams of being crushed by old toys. Our weekly junk pile is the latest neighborhood treasure trove. At least the family room is done, and half the kitchen. Only eight more rooms to go. I'm ashamed to admit I found not one, not two, but three unused fondue sets at the back of our cupboards; one orange, one lime green and one purple."

"You won't need them all for your housewarming party?"

"No, I will not. We'll have it catered, or just invite our friends over one or two at a time. The new place is small."

"But it's beautiful."

"It is. And it's blissfully, neatly, wonderfully empty. I'd like to keep it that way. At this stage in my life, it's all about spending time with my husband, my friends, my children, my grandchildren, and travelling, not dusting nick nacks. I am done with it, Cynth."

"I do know what you mean, Kath. But …"

"You always loved to browse and collect. You are a hunter gatherer at heart, my friend."

"So good to talk to you, Kath. You'll be pleased to know I do also buy food at the markets. You wouldn't believe the variety of tomatoes on display, and the berries, and cheeses, and fifteen kinds of olives … I'm in heaven!"

As late spring became high summer, the town swelled with tourists, and Cynthia was glad to retreat into her hideaway, so close to the action, but hers and hers alone, a place to heal. In a way, she was like the kitten. Self sufficient. Or was she?

Had she imagined Émile's interest in her, that flicker of mutual curiosity? Maybe all Frenchmen made women feel desirable. Maybe Émile really was a model citizen, helping out everyone equally, then getting on with his life, without her. Maybe he had a string of single women waiting for his visits.

But she would have liked to show Émile Minette's progress. She was now twice as big, twice as bold and practically running the place, plonking herself in the sun in the front room, opening her golden eyes to acknowledge Cynthia's presence, and twirling around her ankles to indicate she needed more food.

To say Cynthia was lonely was wrong. She revelled in phone calls from her family, though the sibling rivalry wore thin. It was one of the reasons she'd tried to move on. Planning and setting up her Southern Highlands home engrossed her for a while, but family squabbles had a way of following her, even to her Provence hideaway.

"James is being a bore," said Will on another call out of the blue. "James says he wants to dock my expense allowance. He's so jealous. Probably wishes grandpa Jim told him to head out overseas instead of me, but who would he leave in charge? He's always said the business would collapse if I were in control. Even if that were true, now I'm out and about, he bangs on about me not doing enough for Huntleys; but you understand, don't you, Mum? Being seen at the right parties gets us publicity."

"Mmmmm. Maybe not exactly the right kind, darling," said Cynthia, who'd recently fielded a call from James, complaining about the media coverage Will received.

"More 'bad boy' headlines, Mum. We don't need them," said James. "Why can't Will stay out of trouble for once? Did you see it? 'Aussie playboy in trouble: Huntley ditches rich hitch.'"

"You're all grown ups now," said Cynthia, tickling Minette under the chin. The kitten had staged a full recovery and was paying back Cynthia's hospitality with purrs. "I can't always be the peacemaker. I'm living my own life now. It's up to the three of you to make it work."

"But listen to this one, Mum, under another 'Huntley heartbreaker' headline: 'The daughter of Italian opposition leader Rosa Bianchi ... is reportedly suing her former fiancé for breach of promise after he failed to show up at their wedding'. Tell me how that's good for our business."

Next time Will phoned, she asked him about the spate of wild parties and whirlwind affair with a marchioness, but he just said the media was being unkind again, blaming him for breaking off the engagement with the daughter of the high-profile Rosa.

"The whole thing was a beat up, as usual," Will said. "It was her mother's idea. We broke it off quite amicably, and the 'suing' thing is a complete lie. Even so, Mum. Maybe James is right for once. I wouldn't mind dropping out of the limelight for a while. Where exactly are you?"

Will wasn't known for following through with his plans, but she might as well furnish the extra bedrooms in case he arrived and needed a bed.

She returned to the distant antiques markets where she'd found the chandelier, certain there'd be bedheads there again. This time, she caught an early bus, hoping to clinch some deals before anyone beat her to it, and, if she was buying four or five of the things, surely delivery could be arranged.

Stall holders were still setting up when she arrived. On market days, her careful skirts and matching tops made way for jeans and a pale t-shirt with a cashmere cardigan draped casually over her shoulders. Jeans were ideal for fending off rust marks, rips and snags, though she'd never be dressed so casually back in Sydney or the highlands. Always careful with her appearance, she'd taken even more care when she'd married Jimmy. So many friends and acquaintances who'd admired her engagement ring ended up becoming Huntley customers, she always felt she was on display.

When Jimmy died, her efforts filled the gossip columns with photographs of handsome young James and Will, and Jimmy's slim widow in an acutely stylish black coat and sunglasses at his graveside. Only Nicole exposed her grief to the world, mascara smudged and hair lopsided as usual. Cynthia still cringed to remember the shoes Nicole wore to the funeral—a pair of old black runners.

"I don't give a stuff what I look like, Mum," Nicole said at her gentle suggestion she try some court shoes. "Dad's just died."

It was the last thing Cynthia wanted to admit to herself. Nicole's mini tantrum and a trip to the hairdressers were essential diversions.

Until now, Cynthia had avoided organising proper beds, but with a visit from Will more and more likely, she wanted her home to be as welcoming as possible. For that matter, she'd love Nicole and James to visit, too, with or without partners, and some of her old friends, but certainly not before the place was properly furnished.

As Cynthia wandered, it was impossible not to stroll past the chandelier stall. Would she find Émile there again, bantering with his friends? The stall holder was in earnest conversation with some shoppers. No Émile. Her heart clouded over for a moment, until she smiled at the memory of him turning up with the thing at her doorstep. Such a kind man.

Though she fossicked among the bric a brac and antique furniture, her eyes were drawn to the crowds. This time she admitted to herself she was scanning them again for the tall Frenchman. If Will ever did turn up, she'd love to introduce the two of them.

While Will would be her first guest, there was still the matter of her own bed to settle. Would she choose a single one at this stage of her life? Certainly not. There was space enough for a king-size one in the master bedroom, and no decorator magazine ever featured anything less, except as a daybed.

The problem was that many of the most stylish old French bed heads were narrower. It would be a shame to pass up an antique for a new bed she could have bought equally well in Australia.

At the very least, she should have a look at what was available. Perhaps something could be adapted to fit a modern mattress.

As Cynthia found the bed merchant, he was still unpacking his van. With so many bedrooms to furnish, her excitement bubbled as he pulled out one bedhead after another. He set up one or two that were complete frames with feet, but most were stacked, leaning against one another. There were more than a dozen.

"Celui-ci," she repeated. *"Est-ce qu'il y a l'autre côté?* 'The other side.' The end?"

"I like this one," she said, seizing on an ornate iron frame with three ceramic knobs in the centre. "Does it have a foot?"

She put her hands to work, turning them into a bedhead and feet. Was the stall holder teasing her? Surely everyone had the same question about his beds, be they Spanish, Italian, German or Australian. He shrugged, cigarette hanging out the side of his mouth. It was infuriating.

"Et celui-ci? Moi, je voudrais cinq lits aujourd'hui," she said. She held up her hand again. "Five beds today." The man was a merchant, wasn't he? Surely he recognized a keen customer.

She would have given up and taken her business elsewhere, but she'd visited several other markets in the previous month, and this man had the best collection by far.

Besides, she glimpsed one in his van she loved, of extruded metal thicker than her thumb, bent and twisted into a whimsical heart shape. It would match the other metal chair she'd snatched up the previous week, totally made of thick bent wire. All it needed was a circular cushion. The metal set would go so well in her room. She knew it.

Once again, she mimed, pointing out the bedheads she wanted and seeking the matching feet. Would he help her? A busload of Americans arrived and headed their way.

She pulled out her purse and flicked to the cash section, brandishing a couple of €100 notes and making to remove another, but he pottered about, as if there was all the time in the world.

She began to drag the bedhead she wanted out of the stack, and they fell with such a clang that the general market bustle stopped and everyone stared at her.

Now the man came to life, gesticulating at her and unleashing a torrent of French she'd never been taught at school, though it wasn't difficult to guess the meaning, given the tone.

As she stooped and inspected the tangle of wrought iron and brass bed heads, a tall shadow fell across her. "*Puis-je vous aider?*" It was Émile.

"Gaston," came his familiar voice, placating the man. Émile's tall frame dwarfed the merchant as he laid a hand across his shoulder.

"Émile?" Cynthia was so pleased to see Émile she practically hugged him. She held herself back by wiping her dusty fingers on her jeans, then regretted it.

"He doesn't understand me; *il ne me comprend pas*. I want to buy five bedheads, right now, but I need feet for them, too, of course and full frames."

"I'm sure that can be arranged," said Émile. Swift French followed, the man outraged and Émile conciliatory.

Once again she recognised "*petite anglaise*" as if it were an insult.

"*Mais non*," said Émile, with an emphatic "no" and he rushed on with slang or dialect too rapid for her to understand.

A couple more merchants turned up. Did Cynthia recognise the chandelier seller? Now they were all nodding and laughing at Émile and his "*petite australienne*."

He leaned towards her and put his arm around her, whispering into her ear.

"They think we're a couple," he said, his proximity sending shivers down her spine. "This could work for you."

At that moment, Émile was her hero. How she would have loved to push her fingers through the dark curls at the back of his neck and pull him closer, to give his friends an exhibition they'd remember, but that would be going too far.

She slipped her arm around his waist, the first time she'd held someone other than family so close for longer than she could remember. When she gingerly placed her other hand against his chest, he seized it with his large warm fingers as if they were old friends.

The security of his casual embrace was a balm. Her blood pressure shot up, then down. She wanted this more often, possibly more than the beds.

"*Et voilà,*" said Émile, calm and in command. "*Nous avons besoin de plus d'un lit. Cinq lits, s'il vous plaît, Gaston.*" We need more than one bed. We need five, please.

He dropped her hand to pull out his wallet. Cynthia pushed it away and extracted her own purse. She pointed at the beds she wanted. Émile and his noisy friends did the rest, selecting all the bits and pieces she would need. How extraordinarily useful that Émile had come to her rescue, however appalling it was to think that a single woman needed a man's assistance in contemporary France.

"*Émile, il y a un autre,*" she said. "There's another." Cynthia grabbed Émile's big hand, led him across to the merchant's van, and pointed out the heart-shaped bedhead inside. The merchant frowned, dubious.

Again, Émile went into bat for her. Cynthia could just make out the gist of his banter as the men began to applaud again, and blood rushed to her cheeks in a beaming blush. Was this really happening? Hopefully no media were about, or she might cop a dose of Will's treatment. She loved being anonymous here in Provence.

The transaction complete, and all her beds and frames neatly stacked together, Émile rested both hands on the tops of her arms and offered to fetch his van to transport them for her.

"*Un moment, ma chérie*," he said. Surely the "darling" was a bit much, but if the charade was necessary, so be it. As long as she secured the beds, she'd be happy. She wasn't sure how to thank Émile, but doubtless there'd be an opportunity.

Their chatter was light as he drove her back to her village, the beds and frames all safely tied inside his van.

It was late afternoon when they arrived. Émile scooped up Minette in one hand and exclaimed over her size and shiny fur before offering to set up the beds.

"Only if you agree to stay for dinner," said Cynthia. "You're so kind. I can't imagine how I would have managed without you. Not everyone is as kind as you. I worry that the people in this town resent me."

"They believe foreigners like you push up prices."

"Isn't that good?"

"Not everyone says so. I say everyone is entitled to a fresh start."

"Thank you. I agree. And I really am grateful to you."

"Of course you would have managed," said Émile. "It was I who took advantage of you." His eyes sought hers as he stroked Minette. Frenchmen were good at eye contact, and Nicole was right. This was romantic. What would happen if she simply stared back, longer than necessary. Was it a game, a dare?

She laughed and shook her head and asked what food Émile might like, listing the ingredients in her small refrigerator.

"Good company," he said.

"Smoothie."

"No, not a smoothie, thank you."

"Oh, I didn't mean the yoghurt and fruit drink," said Cynthia, laughing. "'Smoothie' means ... oh, never mind."

Émile placed the kitten carefully on its four paws and headed out to his van to bring in a tool chest and various drills and screws, while Cynthia washed and chopped some vegetables and worried that her cooking skills might be sub par. Did all Frenchmen cook well? Émile was good at everything. Still, he'd already put her at ease by suggesting her company was the main attraction. Was he lonely sometimes, too? He must have a home somewhere, and surely he wasn't all work and no play.

She hummed as she worked in the kitchen, grateful for various clunking noises upstairs as Émile wrestled the parts of the bedhead into shape.

His van signage included "locksmith." She'd have to ask him about that, and about the power circuits. Maybe he'd finally hang her chandelier and give her that estimate on rewiring and plumbing.

She'd open some wine. Though she rarely drank by herself, she'd bought a few bottles for when her children visited, or in case of an occasion like this.

On impulse, she reached into her top cupboard where she'd stashed some candles in case of another blackout. Why settle for a 1950s light bulb when better options were available? She hadn't cooked for a stranger like this for longer than she could remember.

She picked some pansies from one of the window boxes and settled them in an old glass inkwell she'd picked up at one of the markets. Why not dine in some style?

The vegetables were steaming and the aroma of the mushroom and beef casserole was making her own mouth water an hour and a half later when Émile came downstairs.

Busy at the stove, her back to the doorway, Cynthia felt him hesitate. She liked that he was careful in her space.

"Can I help you?" he offered Cynthia with a smile.

"Have you really finished with all those beds? Do you think … I'd love you to put the chandelier up, please, now I've cleaned it. Maybe you can't fix all the wiring in the house and replace the plumbing before dinner is ready, but I'd love to see how the chandelier looks in the right place."

"Of course!"

"And then we can eat beneath it. Thank you. Usually I eat here in the kitchen, and there's not a lot of room for a visitor. You'd have to stand! We'll sit under the chandelier, just the two of us. Let's celebrate our friendship."

Chapter 11

"A celebration, yes," said Émile. He was in no position to object to her term for their relationship. If "friendship" was a little on the cool side from his point of view, it was a good start. A much better position than when he'd felt the full force of her disdain, when they'd fought about the chandelier.

Cynthia turned off the stove and showed him her rooms full of furniture. He set up the gateleg table under the chandelier, then returned to retrieve two whimsical wire chairs, just as Cynthia extracted an ornate candelabra in need of a polish.

"Allow me," he said, whisking it away to his truck.

By the time he'd returned, the rest of the table was set and they both sat down to eat, with a toast of red wine in old crystal goblets. The candlelight shot their shadows around the bare room. It glittered in the chandelier above and glowed in the polished silver.

Émile looked into her eyes as they clinked their glasses "to life". His friend's wife had just died, but here they both were—alive, and Cynthia's meal was warm and delicious after a busy day. He appreciated every mouthful.

She asked him about his life. He kept details brief, explaining he'd owned a hardware shop but converted his business to a mobile service and headed south, dreaming of sunshine.

Outfitting the truck was his best decision so far, allowing him to make a living wherever he stopped. Odd jobs came to his door, large and small, and many leading to much longer stretches of work.

"Tell me," Cynthia said.

He shrugged, finished some bread, and began.

"Families inherit estates—farms, chateaux, wineries—or they sell them to wealthy foreigners. Some are very big. All are very old. You have seen. Everything is very old."

"I love old things. Australians can't get enough of these things. Rustic or refined, we love them all."

"'Rustic' is one step away from 'broken.' Gates, doors, windows, stairs, furniture, taps. Maybe in one family there is someone who can fix things, but in others, the children have moved to the cities. They are urban. They buy 'new'. They do not have these skills. The people who stay behind, they get old. They cannot see so well. They value old things. They don't want to buy 'new'. We should all fix more things. It gives people jobs; does not waste resources. My 1933 Lionne, my old motorcycle, for example. That was my grandfather's. For me, this is very satisfying; to keep it running."

Émile gladly accepted a second helping and kept talking. Cynthia was a good listener. He topped up her wine.

"I shouldn't," she said. "I hardly ever drink these days. You French people drink all the time."

"Rarely before lunch."

"How's your friend?"

"Thank you. It will take a while. They were married for forty years."

Cynthia nodded as if she understood. There was sadness in those eyes, but he didn't want to draw her out on something that made her unhappy. Instead, he continued his story.

"I never realized how fixing one window can lead to fixing windows throughout an entire chateau."

"Really?"

"That job took more than three months. The other workers—the plumbers and carpenters and electricians and stonemasons. They'd move on to other jobs and ask me to come and work with them. I accepted every job that took me further south. One job, it leads to another and then I am the one to find the work for my friends."

"You're a rolling stone," she said.

"The rock band?"

"You gather no moss. It's an English saying. You move along, you collect no baggage."

"'Baggage?'"

"No … family." What was she asking him, this beautiful woman from Australia, with her blonde hair up in a chignon shining in the candlelight, her posture so elegant, and her food so delectable. He wasn't ready to share his full story. Not exactly.

"If you are asking whether I am invited to dine with beautiful women very often, the answer is '*non*' and I appreciate your invitation, very much, and I thank you."

She smiled.

"Some fruit? If I'd known I was going to ask you to stay I'd have baked a dessert."

"A little fruit. Thank you." Did she mean "to stay" for dinner, or for the night, or perhaps for ever? He'd drunk too much of her good wine. He must be on his way. If he didn't overstay his welcome, perhaps there'd be another invitation.

"Will you show me my bed?" said Cynthia as they gathered the plates and brought them into the kitchen together. And then she blushed.

Was she offering him more than dinner? Of course he'd love nothing more. As she placed the dishes in the sink he came and stood behind her. Their eyes met in the reflection in the window, and he bent his head to kiss her neck, just behind her ear.

She smelled of clean things, of coconut and the hyacinths he'd loved as a child in his grandmother's garden.

Time slowed. It was impossible to stop his mind wandering; not to wonder what it would be like to make love to this Cynthia, to be her lover.

Yes, he would kiss her, if she wanted this.

The ringing of her phone broke the moment and she moved away to answer it.

"Nathan?" she said. Her face lit up but not for Émile. She glanced at him as if she was already on to her next adventure and he should be gone by now.

Of course she'd be married, a woman like Cynthia. What was he even doing here so late at night? Some rich husband was doubtless paying for her lifestyle, wherever he may be.

If he wasn't a rolling stone before, he must become one now. He gathered his leather coat and gloves, put his hand on his heart to mime his gratitude, and went to slip out her back door, but she put her hand on his arm.

"Yes, of course you'll have to come and see me," she said into the phone. "I'll let you know."

"Nathan Carmichael," she said as she hung up. "An old school friend. Well, he's a famous architect now, and he's here, in the south of France. He's going to visit!"

"But of course," said Émile. Of course she'd have friends, this beautiful woman. Was Nathan single? Had he come to France to pursue her?

"Could you recommend somewhere I could take him, please, Émile? Maybe a local restaurant?"

Émile took another sip of wine, considering. If he suggested "*le dépôt d'ordure*," the garbage dump, she might take it the wrong way. The thought was unkind of him, childish. Who was to say this Nathan was a rival for her affections?

"Jacques talks of the wine co-op. There's a chef there on Saturdays. But you have to book. It is very popular." He described the bank of bowsers along one wall, and how anyone could turn up with an empty jug or case of empty bottles and fill them, as if pouring petrol into a car from a gas station, paying by the litre. When the chef was there, the wine could be sampled at simple tables, with a set menu of local produce, harvested and foraged.

"Oh, how wonderful! Great idea. Thank you! Nathan is very well travelled. He likes interesting places. That sounds perfect."

Émile was glad to see her enthusiasm, then chastised himself. Why hadn't he thought to take Cynthia there himself? Now it would be too late.

He gestured at the dishes in the sink.

"I'll clean up," said Cynthia, excusing him. "There isn't much to do. It's the least I can do after all you've done for me. You're a fine friend,

106

Émile. I'd still be there at the markets, arguing with that merchant, and even if I'd managed to buy the beds without your intervention, they'd remain a pile of old metal, awaiting attention. Please come and see me again, won't you?"

He stood straighter as he nodded. At least she appreciated his work.

"In an old house, there is much to fix."

"And you can fix it, Mr Fix-It! Mr *Emeliorate* it. Mr Émile! Oh, I'll grab my purse. How much do I owe you?"

"*Non*. This is my gift to you. For my dinner. For your company."

How beautiful she was, this Australian woman, with her not quite English accent, her hair glowing silver and gold, her soft cheeks echoing the curves of her shoulders and hips. Elegant, alluring. Bright eyes.

Her smile as she played with the words of his name and business caught his own lips, coaxed them up at the corners, but he forced himself to look away. Not everything could be fixed. The little things, perhaps— pipes and wires and bits of furniture—but not the things that mattered.

He must go, gather up his tools and be gone, back down south where the work awaited him.

In the dark street outside, a hooded figure with a backpack loomed up and peered in through the window. It was a young man, athletic. Émile stepped between the glass and Cynthia.

Every protective instinct within him kicked into gear. She was vulnerable here, alone, this beautiful woman, unfamiliar with France despite her language skills. Yes, she could be strong and fierce, but physically, she was slight. He lowered his shoulders, clenched his fists and glared at the stranger, willing him to disappear, to wander on, away from them, up the street, and make trouble elsewhere.

107

Bewilderingly, Cynthia slipped in front of him.

"Oh stop it, Émile," she said.

When she turned the key and flung open the door, the stranger lurched forwards and grabbed her.

Just as Émile was about to wrench the man away from her, Cynthia stepped back, holding the man at arm's length, smiling and admiring him.

"Will, dear! What a wonderful surprise! Why didn't you tell me you'd be here this evening? Oh. Meet Émile, my French friend. He's been helping me!"

Will? Her son? Adrenaline still pumping, Émile forced himself to unclench his jaw, to breathe and relax, though there was nothing friendly in the way the young man regarded him. No. This Will was possessive, resentful of his own presence.

"So wonderful to see you, Will," said Cynthia, all delight. "You look a bit hungry and tired, darling. I'll get you some food. Have my chair; I'll be right back."

Eyes still locked on Émile's, the man slipped the hood of his jacket down and took it off. Good looking as a movie star, he was fair, like Cynthia, with striking blue eyes and that casual insolence that only the very confident can get away with. He sized up Émile with a half smile.

"Chill, grandpa," the interloper said. "Make love not war."

As spoken by a child untouched by real war, whose own country had barely suffered the horrors of his own, still scarred to its very foundations, the farmers still digging up bullets, the cracks in the bombed buildings still there for those who cared to look, the losses enshrined in families' memories.

Impertinence dripped off him. No child liked a father replacement, but Will's hostility was palpable and an insult to all of them.

Émile shook his head. Australians had fought side by side with his countrymen. Why fight now with this young Aussie?

Will opened his hands, as if to protest innocence, then turned his scrutiny to the old room, dismissing Émile, frowning. When he noticed the chandelier, he gave a nod of approval. Did he know Émile's role in securing the treasure for her? Will hadn't finished goading him.

"So, you're Mother's new lover, are you?" Though he spoke in English, every Frenchman knew the term "lover."

Cynthia entered with a steaming plate of casserole and green beans in one hand, and an empty glass and cutlery in the other.

"Émile, would you mind?"

Émile gathered up the empty plates to make space, loped back into the hallway and returned with a spare chair and another bottle of wine. As he returned, he overheard her telling the bed story.

"So it's Émile you have to thank for your bed tonight, Will."

"For the beds," said Will. "How very kind." His eyes were dubious as they sized up Émile again, as they both took their seats, their movements stilted—a sitting down standoff.

"Don't be like that, Will," said Cynthia. "Let's all have a glass of wine together and relax, and you can tell us more about this Italian business! You're hiding from the press? Something about some broken engagement?"

The young man relaxed under his mother's questioning, his shoulders drooping to betray his weariness.

"Just another beat-up," he said, accepting a full glass from Émile with a nod.

He launched into a story about a string of parties and the daughter of the Italian opposition leader and what a scream it all was; how next thing he knew the press were following him and the three of them were on the front pages and popping up on everyone's phone, and her mother told him they'd be marrying.

Émile let the words run over him. Who were these Huntleys? He hadn't recognised either of them, but then gossip columns weren't his thing. He must google "Will Huntley" the moment he had a chance.

"It was all her mother's idea, not ours," said Will. "We were only ever in it for a fling, for the fun of it. It's all so silly, really."

"Exhausting, I'm sure." Cynthia turned to Émile. "Poor Will's been hounded by the press since he left high school. Bad choice of first girlfriend; a very bitter young journalist whose father owns a lot of media. Very bad combination."

Émile swallowed his tongue. If Will treated the media the way he'd treated him, he wasn't surprised he received negative press. Didn't Cynthia understand the man was grown up now, and not a child to be coddled? Still, he was in no position to lecture anyone on child rearing. He really should just go.

"So, where did you and this dream French lover meet, Mum?"

"Oh, we're not lovers. Émile's just the handyman! He's been fixing our beds."

110

Just the handyman? As if the terms "lover" and "handyman" were mutually exclusive. What was he doing here, with this spendthrift Australian woman and her rude son? Émile pushed away his glass.

"Pleased to meet you, Will. It is time for me to go now, Cynthia. Thank you for the beautiful food."

He stood and walked to the door.

"No, Émile. Please. Won't you stay?" Cynthia's face fell. Were all men so possessive of their mothers' attentions?

"I work again tomorrow, near Nice. Until next time."

Will's eyes bored into him as he took his departure. Fine. Let the young man imagine what he wanted. Émile barely knew himself what to think about his relationship with the beautiful Australian woman.

The worst of it was, he'd like nothing more than to be Cynthia's lover. Will's words struck a truth for Émile. They deepened his conviction. From the moment she'd stood up for her right to buy the chandelier, she'd haunted him. Plucky. Articulate. Sure of her rights. Tiny yet strong. And the more he saw of her, the more he wanted her.

That charade at the markets today, pretending to want the beds for the two of them—that was less of an act, and more reality. That he'd managed to carry it off was a major coup. Her delight made his heart and soul soar like never before.

And the meal she'd cooked him as he pieced together the beds was magnificent. It was delicious, but the fact she'd dashed back and forth to consult him about it as she'd cooked it so carefully for him, had made it something to truly savor. His own meals had become hasty things in the past couple of years, urgent transactions with his stomach. He knew food shouldn't be like that, but he'd become a wanderer, with no fixed address, and though the region had become his home, and his loose group of fellow tradespeople and market acquaintances his friends, he was virtually homeless.

It was meals that made a place a home. It was the coming together at the end of the day to trade stories and hopes and disappointments, and to laugh together and fortify your mind and body for the challenges ahead, and to toast the joys of the moment with those you loved.

He missed that about his childhood and his early years with Bertha, before her expectations and disappointments became an ever wider wedge that shattered their little family and drove him south.

This fresh beginning of a better life, with Cynthia, was such a fragile thing, such a first step in a repair of such intricacy he barely dared imagine it. And now Will had arrived to drive him away, with Nathan doubtless soon to follow.

It was a bitter way to end a triumph of a day, with a jealous son protecting his mother. Why did he bother? The thing was, he didn't bother. Not usually. But Cynthia was special. He couldn't keep away, and he wouldn't keep away, if Cynthia invited him back, whatever her obnoxious son might say.

Chapter 12

And then he was gone. Cynthia's heart fell as Émile left so abruptly. It was true Will had been less than friendly. She'd been so sure he and Will would get on; that they'd enjoy each other's company. The room was colder without him.

Still, she was thrilled to see Will, though he was unusually ragged.

It was more than six months since he'd brought his little red Alpha down to her garage in the Southern Highlands, before he'd gone away on the extended sales trip, to help to market Huntleys internationally.

Serious James, her eldest, had been sceptical. "Spending spree more like," he'd said. "Selling himself maybe. No joy for Huntleys, you wait and see."

"No, darling. Will said Jim suggested it."

"It was only because he's no use at all in the business in Sydney," said James. "Will's never here. He's always out partying or sleeping in. Jim and Nicole and I work hard, but Will won't pull his weight. Never did."

"Yes, dear." Would the squabbles between the children never end? She'd tired of them long before Jimmy's diagnosis, and then she literally had no time at all for mediating their endless disputes. Running the business took every bit of her energy and time. It was all a blur until she handed over financial control to James and threw herself into building her Southern Highlands home.

Thankfully, Nicole and James cooperated and complied, but it was true Will was a wild card. Yet she adored him, her youngest surprise, a cherub so divine he could have modelled baby products.

That they were both in Europe at the same time thrilled her, particularly now he'd taken time to come and visit her.

She sipped at her wine and laughed as he described the round of parties in Italy and polished off his dinner. She wouldn't ask him about what he was doing for Huntleys just yet. She hated to nag.

"So, do you like my chandelier?"

"Glittering, like you, Mother."

"Oh darling, Stop it."

"Truly, Mother. You're looking well. French life suits you. So. What's the story with Émile the mystery lover?"

"Oh, he's lovely but not my lover. That was very cheeky of you to call him that. I actually have him to thank for the chandelier, and for the beds. They really would just be a pile of bits and pieces if he hadn't helped. Once he stepped in to secure them at the markets, he spent all day piecing them together and making them the right size to fit standard, modern day mattresses. The man's a genius. Émile's exceptionally good at fixing things. And he's fun. And I enjoy his company."

"And he appreciates you."

"Well, yes. He does. He's attentive, but no more, not that the nature of our relationship beyond friendship would be any of your business, and besides, how can you talk, my dear, with so many girlfriends now we've all lost count."

"But you loved Dad."

"We all loved Jimmy. Such a tragedy. You lost a father and I lost the love of my life."

Cynthia stared into her glass of wine. It still hurt, even after so many years. Jimmy had been her best friend and her only love, and he hadn't deserved to wither away and die. He was a kind man, a good father and the only man she'd ever wanted in her life. She sighed deeply and hauled her mind back to the present. Jimmy had given her three fine children, and here was one of them, right in front of her.

She forced herself to smile at Will.

"Besides, raising you children, seeing you through school, keeping the business afloat, there was never any time for dating. And more recently, well, it's all been rather awkward, with my well-meaning tennis friends thrusting single men at me. You can't imagine how difficult it is to say 'no' to a friend's friend. It insults everyone. Most unpleasant. I'm so glad Nicole suggested I come to France after all."

"Where nobody knows you and you can have as many affairs as you like?"

"Will, you're sounding like the press you so despise. My affairs are really my affair, not that I've had any. Nor do I plan to have any. As I said, Jimmy was my one true love, and I'm far too busy fixing this place up."

"With your French handyman."

"Émile is very helpful, yes."

Will raised his eyebrows suggestively, drained his glass and yawned. "Great meal, thanks, Mum. Might get some zeds. See you tomorrow."

Cynthia shook her head and smiled. She was glad he was here, even if he was incorrigible. She hummed to herself as she washed up. Three plates in the rack. She liked it.

Chapter 13

Next morning, Will slept late. Who knew what timetable he was on. Had he flown from Milan? One never knew with Will.

He rose around midday, plunged a fork into some leftover casserole and chatted with Cynthia as he ate.

"Pretty quiet around here," he said.

"I like it quiet. I'm used to it. Minette keeps me company. Did I tell you Émile rescued her? She'd been run over by a tourist bus, well, not entirely as you can see, but badly injured. You'd never guess it now, would you?"

"Generous Émile."

"He is generous, yes. How did you sleep in the bed he made for you?"

"I get it. I'm being ungrateful."

"You are."

"Thought I might go and check the Côte d'Azur while I'm here. Want to join me?"

"I thought you were laying low for a while."

"I did."

"For one night? No, I won't come today, thank you. I'm going to make up the other beds and rearrange things. Another time perhaps. How long are you staying?"

"Not sure yet. Is that a problem? You booked out here?"

"No. Of course not. You're always welcome."

He rewarded her with one of those smiles the press loved to capture, the kind that made hearts flip the world over, that opened doors, that made Italian mothers dream their daughters were finally about to be engaged, that made her simply glad to be alive.

"Great to see you. Love the place, by the way. Bit of a find, really. Suits you."

She smiled back, up into his blue eyes that reminded her so much of Jimmy's.

He flung his jacket over one shoulder and reached a hand into the back pocket of his jeans, bringing it back empty.

"Got any spare Euros?"

Cynthia sighed. She was never surprised by his consistent request. In all the years, it never changed. She knew she should be firmer with him. He was no longer a boy. Surely he'd learned to budget by now.

"Don't you have a wage and expenses account from the business?"

"I used it already. I had to get here, remember?"

"I'll lend you some, but this time I'd like you to pay me back, please, Will."

"I can always count on you, Mother."

Will barely made it out the front door and down the street when Cynthia's phone rang. At first she thought it was Will, planning to ask her for more money, or maybe to pack him a lunch, but this time it was James. Unusual.

"How are you, Mum? How's France?"

"I'm loving it, thank you, James. Will's just turned up."

"Is he there with you now?"

"He's just left. Off to do some sightseeing I suppose. He's probably finding it dreadfully dull here, after the bright lights of Milan, but I love it here. The place is beautiful. I can't wait to show it to you. I'm doing it up of course, but there are proper beds here now and lots of furniture, and I actually have some cutlery and crockery and saucepans, not like when I first arrived. It's been huge fun, starting from scratch. The prices over here are unbelievable. Everything is loaded with character and it's a fraction of what we pay back in Australia. I'm having a ball. Please plan a visit. I do miss you, my dear."

"Ah, look. Glad it's all going so well for you, and yes, I'd love to visit some time, but look. This is going to sound severe, Mum, but Will's expenses are out of control, and perhaps you'd better start pulling back a bit, too."

"Oh."

"Don't get me wrong. I want you to be happy, and unlike Will, you've certainly earned the right to spend some of the money you've made over all these years, building the business and keeping it strong."

"Yes, James? But…"

"But things are a bit tight right now. I don't want to worry you, but there's a lot of competition. Our solid customers are starting to retire now and not spending as much as they used to."

"You've rung about the finances."

"Yes, Mum. You're not the main problem. It's Will. His spending is all over the place. It makes it so hard to budget and manage cash flow. His wild spending has to stop or we'll all go broke."

"Harsh."

"Well. I don't want to alarm you, but you need to know. Can you talk to Will about it? How long is he staying with you? Tell him to ring me, not that he's likely to, but can you at least ask?"

"Of course, darling. And I'll cut back. Living expenses over here are very low. There's such beautiful fresh food and it's all affordable; I still need to pick up a few things, but the beds were the last major purchase, and I've been very lucky with them. I've already sourced lots of beautiful antiques, and Émile, a friend of mine, is a handyman. He's helped make some repairs."

"Great. Thanks for agreeing to talk to Will. He never answers my calls. He doesn't get it. If the whole Huntley ship goes down, his spending will be curtailed anyway."

"I'll try to explain. He's not an unreasonable person."

There was a silence before James continued. "You and I might not agree on that, Mum."

"Quite right, James. It's my job to think the best of you all, and I'm always hopeful. You all make me very proud in different ways."

"I love you, too, Mum. Are you happy over there?"

Cynthia thought back over her evening, of Émile in the candlelight with his clever hands and manners, his eyes so appreciative of her invitation, of her company, of her. She remembered the fun she and Émile enjoyed at the markets, pretending to be lovers, and chuckled.

"Do you know, James, I believe I am happy."

"Glad to hear you're making friends, and I'm really sorry to clip your wings like this..."

"I do understand. I only worry I've made you worry! I remember what it was like, balancing the budget, trying to work out when to order fresh supplies and when to hold steady. Nicole rang with a very sad story about a PR stunt that failed. That was bad luck, wasn't it?"

"It was. Nic's idea was brilliant. Shame about the movie star getting distracted by the other jeweler, though her work is really rather good."

"Pardon? You're saying the other jeweler's product was better than Huntleys?"

"Not at all. It's completely different. She sells low-cost costume jewelry, though very well designed. Stella just happened to be in the right place at the wrong time for us."

"Stella?"

"Yes, her business is called Stellar. She's really very talented."

"Is she just? I don't suppose Helene's contacted you?"

It slipped out before she could stop herself. Cynthia squeezed her eyes shut in fury at herself.

"Oh, and how is Jim?" Maybe if she changed the subject quickly he wouldn't notice. It was outrageous Helene had poisoned her eldest son's heart. In a world with so many kinder young women, people with joyous and generous hearts, why had he set his own on Helene so early in his life, Helene, so selfish, so greedy... When would James move on without her? She'd certainly left him behind, taking up with his university friend, of all insults to the lot of them.

Would none of her children settle down and give her some grandchildren?

"Grandpa Jim's great, thank you, Mum. Going strong. He's become a bit interested in social media. He's incredible, really. Nic's interviewing him once a week for her new Jewel of the Week podcast. He's a natural. You know Jim. He understands our trade backwards after all these years. I love to listen. There's so much to learn. I'll send you the link and you can explore our new website. Jim's workroom is the jewel at the top of the building. You just click on it and he shows off a jewel, talks about where it's found, how it's cut—that sort of thing."

"Astonishing! And how's my place?"

"I was down a couple of weeks ago, giving the cars a run and it looks absolutely fine. A big storm went through while we … while I was there, but there was no damage to the roof. It's good and solid. You built quality, Mum."

"Good to hear." Did he say "we"? Was someone there with him? Cynthia hoped so. He was a fine young man. If her sons would only stop playing the field and settle down they'd be amazed at all life's other riches.

She'd given birth to James while very young, and adored all her babies. Certainly they changed your life, but she wouldn't have traded those magic moments for anything; their chubby little elbows and toes, and their soft skin. Sometimes holding Minette she'd recall the joy of a child on her hip, and she'd stop what she was doing and give the moment over to the richness of the memory. No. For all the frenzy and lack of sleep, they were precious days, now gone.

She wanted to ask who'd spent the weekend with him in her house, but remembered her slip at mentioning Helene, and bit her tongue. He'd tell her in his own good time and not before. That was alright.

"And the car?"

"Yours is fabulous, Mum, going strong. Will's is a heap. Well, you can imagine how he used to drive it; so it plays up. It's a total nuisance—keeps breaking down."

"You're very good to look after our cars for us while we're away."

"I am. You're right. I don't mind helping you out, Mum, of course not, but I do wonder why I raise a finger for Will. He wouldn't do the same for me."

"You were always the responsible one, James. We all love you for it. You'll be rewarded, I know. You'll find a lovely young woman and …"

"You don't change, do you, Mum, whatever continent you're on."

"Or a lovely young man, I meant to say."

"No, I'm not gay."

"But if you were…"

"You believe in the best for us all, Mum. I'm not looking for love right now."

"We never are, but sometimes love is looking for us."

"Right, well now, I'm looking for bed, and that's only so I can get some sleep, before you ask. I wanted to catch you at a reasonable time, but it's been a long day at the books with Scottie. Thank you for taking my call."

"Of course, darling. I'm always here for you."

"It's not just that. I mean thank you for listening—for reminding Will that the wild spending has to stop."

"I'll try, dear. You're doing a fine job, you know."

"Thanks. I try—for Dad's sake."

"I promise I'll chat to Will when he gets back."

Cynthia placed the phone in her back pocket. James was such a worrier; the studious one, always so responsible. If only she were able to give James more of Will's sense of fun and spontaneity, and give Will more of James's stability and serious nature.

She shook her head as Minette found her and jumped up on her lap, arching her back as Cynthia stroked her sleek black fur. The kitten had staged a full recovery. May James's heart and the Huntley bank balance do the same.

Her eldest son was too good to her. She might have been a bit rash. Furnishing an entire house all these weeks may have been irresponsible, even though each particular item was a bargain. She'd cut back. The place was full now anyway. She'd still need to engage Émile to fix a few things. Like the lock on the front door at the very least, and the plumbing and the power.

She grabbed Minette and slipped upstairs to her bedroom, with its glorious new antique brass bed. When she ran her hands over its whimsical heart shaped curves she knew she was happier than she'd been in a very long time.

"It's just as well Will turned up at the right time, Minette," she told the cat. "Or I might have been tempted to invite Émile up here to try out the springs. That's a joke," she added, when Minette stared at her with her golden eyes. "I'm not interested in that kind of relationship. Émile and I are simply good friends. No need to complicate things between us."

Minette didn't blink.

It was Will who'd called Émile her lover. Silly idea. She shivered as she turned off her lamp. Nathan Carmichael was arriving next day, so she turned her mind away from the intriguing scar on Émile's cheek that made him quite dashing when he smiled—and contemplated instead what to wear to lunch with Nathan.

Chapter 14

Émile tested the plumbing at the villa he was renovating and inspected the fresh tiles, but memories of Cynthia and her obnoxious, handsome son haunted him all day.

It was all very well the young man joking that he was Cynthia's lover. The worst part was that he wanted to be, but was that what Cynthia wanted, too?

She'd described Émile as her handyman, and while there was some truth to her statement, he'd hoped for something a little less ordinary. It wasn't as if she paid him for his services.

He did a stock take of their encounters, each time becoming more annoyed. He'd removed Cynthia's sign, brought her the chandelier she'd clearly coveted, then given her the kitten, though maybe her accepting the damaged animal was more of a favor to him. He hated to see creatures suffer.

He'd stepped in and secured all the brass beds she'd wanted, and then assembled them for her, all at no charge.

In return, she'd smiled at him as if she wanted to kiss him. As he strode up the new staircase, running his hand along the new balustrade to ensure it was smooth, he laughed at himself. Cynthia made him feel young again. Adding up all he'd done for her was wrong. He was behaving like a besotted teenager. His friends were right to rib him about the petite Australienne. She had him around her little finger, simply because she was beautiful and slightly helpless.

He'd told her he only wanted to see her smile, and she'd obliged, but surely she wasn't merely acting, to abuse his good nature. Surely her smiles were genuine.

But she'd shrunk away when he'd tried to greet her in the usual manner. Did touching him repel her? Was his wife, who'd rejected his advances for years, correct about him and his scar? Was he just a too-nice but repulsive guy?

He put down the hammer and covered his cheek with his hand. The mark was the legacy of an attack in his family's shop when he was in his teens. A crazed intruder had demanded cash. The scar stayed red and angry for years. If he and Bertha hadn't met in a dark nightclub, perhaps she never would have fallen for him. Then again … He picked up the hammer.

Usually he kept his mind on his work. He took pride in the way he transformed places to match and surpass his clients' wishes. But was that enough in life? He wanted more. He wanted Cynthia Huntley; couldn't get her out of his head, the way she moved in her jeans, the way she stroked Minette and smiled at him.

And when her son described them as lovers, she'd blushed in the candlelight. Was there a chance she felt the same way about him?

When he finished inspecting each of the refurbished windows and doors, making sure the seals would keep out the winter winds, Émile took a break.

He wasn't proud of himself, but he did it anyway. He googled "Australian architect Nathan Carmichael." There he was—suave and distinguished in front a dozen of the world's most famous buildings—an expert on architectural detail. In a different pair of glasses with round frames in every shot—with quotes on art deco, art nouveau, streamlining, Edwardian—he looked nothing like Émile—a man who simply repaired things for a living.

Émile remembered again how Cynthia had introduced him to her son—as a handyman. He wasn't ashamed of his vocation, but now? The time had come to show Cynthia there was more to him than his ability to fix things, especially before Nathan Carmichael turned up with his wavy hair, a distinguished grey at the temples, and those creative round glasses. He clenched his fist. Why had he suggested the wine co-op? She might be there with him now, for all he knew.

How Émile longed to show her he wasn't just "handy." He was a man—a man who was fast becoming intoxicated with her.

As he relived each of their exchanges, he realized he almost always offered to fix something for her.

Émile packed up his tools, locked the villa and strode to his van, racking his brain. That evening, an answer arrived in the form of an emailed invitation—to a ball at an estate in the Loire Valley he'd helped restore. The owner, an American, had kept in touch, even though he'd departed after completing repairs of the chapel and had continued south.

If he were to invite Cynthia to the ball and spend some time with her away from her property, she might begin to value his other attributes. When he finished preparing his invoices at the end of the evening, he was in a better frame of mind—a man with a plan.

...

When Will appeared again at the House of Clubs, in a rented deep blue convertible, Cynthia convinced him to take her back to the big antique markets where she'd bought the chandelier and beds. Maybe those champagne glasses would still be available, and Will might enjoy exploring more of the district.

As they zoomed through the scenic villages and countryside, Will regaled her with tales of his travels.

"It was Jim's idea," said Will. "He practically threw me out; insisted I come and see a bit more of the world. Told me I wasn't doing anyone any favors, partying."

"He's probably right, dear," said Cynthia. "You've never been known for turning up on time."

"And what have you been up to?"

"I had lunch with an old school friend, Nathan Carmichael."

"The architect?"

"Yes. How do you know about Nathan?"

"You hear about Aussies when you're out and about. He's in Cannes for that architecture conference."

"That's right. Nathan told me all about it." And all about his life of travel, to one conference after another.

He'd been enthusiastic about the restaurant. Just as Émile had described, customers brought in jugs and carafes and bottles to be filled with their favorite drop for the week, while those who dined sampled the varieties with a range of foods.

The meal took hours. Nathan called on her to translate the whole menu, which was challenging because the font was so small, and then he'd laughed. It turned out he had more than passing knowledge of restaurant French, being so well travelled.

"This part of France supplied the Roman empire with wine," he said. "They've found amphorae as far away as Africa and analysed traces of the residue right back to Provence."

"Amazing," said Cynthia. If she'd taken care with her appearance, so had Nathan. Dressed in a white suit, he looked more like an Edwardian Englishman than an Aussie, but Nathan had always had flair.

He rustled around in his leather satchel, drew out a small case and presented it to her.

"What's this?"

"Please keep them. I pick up a fresh pair every time I'm in Oslo. There's a little pharmacy near where I stay that has them in every color."

The scarlet glasses exactly matched her jacket. Better still, they made the menu legible.

"I'm sorry to hear about you and Greta," she said, but he'd only laughed.

"It was time, dear Cynthia. Believe me."

She didn't like to probe, although she wanted to.

"The lunch was fun," Cynthia told Will. "I heard all about belvederes."

The market was crowded as ever, but Will managed to squeeze the car onto a bit of sidewalk. They couldn't open the doors, but he leaped out and helped Cynthia clamber over the side. She laughed. There was no one like Will to remind you to enjoy life.

"Right, let's snaffle up those champers glasses you told me about," said Will, and Cynthia led the way, but the merchant shrugged. They'd been sold weeks ago.

"Too bad," said Will. "Should have bought them the moment you saw them, Mum."

"Maybe we'll find some more."

"Meet you at noon, or message me? I suspect we'll want to look at different things."

"Of course." Typical Will. Probably off to the nearest tourist information booth to find some Swedish backpackers.

She wandered, and on the spur of the moment bought some potted sunflowers. When Will returned three hours later, they laughed as they tried to find spaces for them behind the seats where they wouldn't tumble and lose all their dirt.

"What's with the sunflowers, Mum?"

"Why not? The plant seller gave me a special deal. I'll adore this shot of gold every day—sunflowers with sunshine in my beautiful south-facing windows."

As he drove, she told him of her conversation with James and their need to reduce spending.

"Whatever," he said. For the first time, she glimpsed James's frustration with him.

"James means it, Will. I mean it."

Will just shrugged, but back at the house, he helped her arrange the pots along the shop front walls and water them.

Then he jumped back in the car and gave her a big wave as he sped away. That was Will; a free spirit.

Chapter 15

Cynthia pottered, enjoying the spaces in her house, rearranging the furniture and watering her sunflowers.

She spent the next day wrestling with the plumbing in the upstairs bathroom. The tap continued to drip, however hard she turned it off. The drip created a stain on the basin, but worse, it kept her awake at night. Minette loved it, often jumping up to lap at the splash, but she was determined to fix it.

She chastised herself for always buying decorative items at the markets, and nothing remotely useful like a hammer or a spanner or pliers.

A knock on the door caught her attention. Maybe it was Émile. That would be convenient. Had he brought his van? There was bound to be the right kind of tool inside. Or maybe it was Nathan! She checked her hair in the mirror and ran down the stairs.

It was Will. She was glad to see him again so soon, though he was uncharacteristically tired, his shoulders drooping as he banged on the front door. She'd have to give Will a key. Émile was also a locksmith. She'd add it to her lists of requests for him.

A whiff of alcohol greeted her as she swung the blue door open. Was Will hung over? Worse, was he still drunk? It was nearly eleven o'clock in the morning.

Will pulled her close, lifted her off her feet and kissed the top of her head. Cynthia thought her ribs might break. He'd always been affectionate.

"Hello, Will!" Did she want to know where he'd been? Yes, but it might have to wait.

"You look hungry. Coffee? Snack?"

"Always so lovely, my mother," said Will, following her into the house. "I got you a present."

"I'm sure that's not necessary." Had her chat with Will about money even registered? Maybe after coffee and some food Will would be open to discussing it. He clearly wasn't quite with it yet. She'd need to make sure he understood this was serious; not just general conversation.

When she turned back towards him after putting on the kettle, she nearly jumped in surprise. He'd reached into his jeans pocket and held out a gold bangle studded with tiny diamonds, holding it in front of her eyes.

"Will!"

"Thought you'd love it!" he said. "It has 'classy Cynthia Huntley' studded all over it. Here, let me try it on you."

"I love it, Will, but I'm not sure that it's very wise. In fact, you might need to take it back."

"Why? Oh, and here's that cash you lent me the other day. Every note of it."

"Oh." She refrained from saying "first time for everything."

"Why thank you, darling," she said instead.

"In fact, I'm in a position to give *you* a loan this time."

"Well that's thoughtful, Will, but no. I don't really believe in borrowing money. 'Live within your means,' Jimmy used to say. James ..."

"Oh. Dreary. Let me guess. 'Tell Will to stop spending.' He's like a broken record. He's always in my ear about it, but you've got to spend money to make money."

"I'm not sure I understand you." Was Will dealing drugs? Something wasn't right.

Cynthia pushed the mug of instant coffee towards him.

A knock at the door caught her attention.

Through the kitchen window, Cynthia noticed Émile's van and her heart lifted. She rushed to let him in. He was carrying a heavy and shiny box covered with switches and dials.

"I am too late," Émile said, glancing at their full mugs.

"Émile, this looks like something from outer space."

"It is Italian; a coffee machine. My clients in Nice wanted 'all new' for their kitchen so it was going to be thrown away. I thought you might like it."

"That's so lovely of you. Thank you! I'm so glad to see you, Émile. I really do want to ask you for a quote for the plumbing and electricity, and maybe the locks. Do you have time today? I need to ask your advice. But perhaps you'd like a cup of coffee with us first?"

"*Un cafe, oui*. Yes. Please. Let me show you how this works. And I have something to ask you, also."

"I'm intrigued." Cynthia was thrilled to see him. As he set the heavy machine on the kitchen bench, she was glad Will was with her. He could find out for himself what a fine friend Émile was; so generous and capable.

"At last. A decent coffee," said Will. "These are amazing, these machines. I totally miss Italy just for the coffee."

"Can you work this?" Émile asked. "You can be the barista."

"Is that wise?" said Cynthia. "All that hot steam. I'm not sure Will's entirely sober. Looks like you need a degree to operate this thing. Where did you learn how?"

Émile shrugged and set to work, steam rising and the aroma of rich coffee filling the small space.

"Let's go into the front room and be comfortable," said Cynthia. The chat with Will about finances would have to wait.

"Beautiful bracelet," said Émile.

"Will just gave it to me," said Cynthia. Émile's eyes widened. They exchanged a glance. Had Émile noticed the smell of alcohol on Will, too? Still, the French were also known to have a drink or two ...

"We're all jewelers," said Will, executing his own shrug. "I'm scouting for trends while I'm in Europe. It's my job to seek out beautiful jewelry. What do you think of this?"

"Exquisite," said Émile.

"Exactly," said Will.

"I'm talking about your mother's wrist, not the bangle."

"Stop it," said Cynthia, thrilled at the compliment. She thumped Émile on the arm and he caught her hand in his and brought it to his lips.

"I mean it," he said. His expression gave her a rush of joy, even though they were just friends.

"Smooth," said Will. "Could use that line myself some time."

"Well, Émile, I was just telling Will it's too expensive," said Cynthia. "Gifts like this are not necessary." She had no idea where he'd found the money.

Will shrugged again and sipped his coffee.

"How are you?" said Émile, his eyes taking in her frame, making her heart race. "You're really settling in, I see. All those sunflowers!"

"I love them; that great wash of gold. You're right. I'm trying to settle in, but I have to admit I've been fighting with a dripping tap in the upstairs bathroom and it's defeating me. And now I'm mad at myself. I'm as bad as Will, buying impractical things when what I really need are essential supplies for fixing ancient French buildings that need repairs. May I borrow a spanner, please? Or pliers. Or whatever is needed?"

"I will fix this tap for you." Émile bit his lip and she raised her eyebrows. "But. Cynthia. I have something to ask—of you."

"Oh." She stopped stirring her coffee and turned to give him her full attention. He leaned forwards, fingertips together. Was he nervous?

Even Will had stopped peering at his phone.

"I wish to issue you with an invitation," said Émile.

Smiling, Cynthia leaned forwards and nodded to encourage him to continue.

"*Il y a un* ... how do you say ... *un bal*, in the Loire Valley."

"A ball!" She clapped her hands together. "Oh really, Émile! When?"

"It's two weekends away. Are you free? It's in a chateau. I helped to renovate the chapel when I was travelling south. The owner is celebrating completion of a major part of the project."

"What fun! I'd be delighted to join you!"

"Brilliant," said Will. "I'd love that."

"Unfortunately, I can bring one guest only."

Will shrugged. He plucked a grape from a bunch in a glass fruit bowl, throwing it up in the air before catching it in his mouth with a satisfied grin.

Slightly drunk or not, Will was fun to be around. She loved having him here, but this new idea, of going to a ball with Émile ... She was delighted, even if Will was less than impressed.

"Will, my dear. Could you stay and feed Minette for me that weekend, please? How long will we be away, Émile?"

"I will pick you up on the Friday morning. We can stay in a place I know in Angers then arrive early in the afternoon of the party. We will stay that night, too and return after breakfast, back late the next day if you wish."

"How wonderful, Émile! Oh. What should I wear?"

"It will be formal; a long gown, perhaps. Is that a problem?"

"Not at all. Oh! I'll love it. I mean it." If Will wasn't there she'd have hugged Émile for the joy of it. Émile's pleasure at her reaction mirrored her own.

Just then, Minette rattled the back door, her way of asking to be let out.

"Excuse me," Cynthia said. She left the men in the front room and took the corridor to the rear, setting Minette free.

It was only as she returned that she overheard their conversation, and slowed her steps.

"... make a move on her, then?" said Will, his tone protective, with a hint of aggression.

"What is this 'make a move'?"

"You know what I'm talking about."

"We are not children."

"Oh, so it's 'we' now, is it?"

The two men stared at each other, fists clenched.

Cynthia forced a smile and cleared her throat as she entered the kitchen. It was unusually thoughtful of Will to look after her interests, but surely he knew no one would ever replace his father in her affections. Besides, she wasn't looking for love.

"Émile, do you think you could make a little door for Minette, please?" She changed the subject immediately, as if she hadn't overheard.

"But of course."

"Guess I'll be off then," said Will, his face dark.

"Oh, where are you going, Will? You've only just got back from wherever you were before."

"I wanted to give you the bangle."

"Don't go yet. Tell me more about it. Where did you find this?"

"On the Riviera."

"Wait. Are you going back there?"

He nodded, standing.

"Perhaps you should have a rest, first. I'd love to come back to the Riviera with you. I'll need to find a ball gown. I don't suppose you saw any while you were there, did you? I do love our local shops. They're excellent for cheese and lavender soaps, but ball gowns are thin on the ground."

"Sure. Tomorrow then." Will yawned. "A rest might not be a bad idea."

When he was out of earshot, Cynthia spoke to Émile.

"I do worry sometimes that Jimmy's death affected the children more than they let on at the time. Jimmy was so proud of Will. They were very close. Will puts on a brave front, but do you think he might still be hurting?"

Émile reached out to hold her hand. His touch was calming. Steady. Helpful, his expression gentle.

"What can I say? Death is hard. And I am in no position to discuss the behaviour of children."

"Oh?" She squeezed his hand. "Tell me, Émile."

He shook his head.

"I can fix broken things. But broken people? No."

He let go her hand.

"But I will fix your tap."

"Oh, please do; while you're here? I do have a list of jobs for you if you're interested."

"I'm sure you do," said Émile, smiling. "But I will take you to the ball only if we do not speak of any repairs while we are away. I am not just a handyman, Cynthia. I can also feed cats. How about I check on

Minette while you and Will are in Nice? I like to visit Jacques now and then."

"She'd love that. Thank you. But you don't have a key."

"Would you like me to cut one?"

"You can do that?"

"I learned to cut keys when I was a child. I come from a very long line of locksmiths. That was our family's original business, before we went into hardware shop ownership."

"Really?" How little she knew of this man. He sat straighter when he spoke of his family's trade. "How interesting, Émile. I suppose our family trade is jewelry. My eldest son is James Huntley the third. How many generations of your family have been locksmiths?"

Did Émile flinch? He played with his coffee cup, and then he looked her in the eye.

"I am from the Nation of St John, represented by parliament for at least 600 years. We were the blacksmiths, the tinsmiths and pan smiths; the farriers, cutlers and watchmakers. We painted, we worked with gold and blew glass, we made saddles and harnesses, turned wood, worked with plaster and stucco, thatched and wove baskets. But mostly, in my family, before the hardware store, we were locksmiths."

Cynthia clapped her hands. She couldn't hide her admiration. She'd never traced her own family tree, but she doubted it would match Émile's.

"No wonder you're so handy, Émile. I'm astonished. I love these ancient streets, and the way the French preserve them. It's why I'm here. In these old villages and in Paris, every bridge is beautiful. Paris took my breath away, but even to walk down the street here, I can't help but admire the stonework, the fountains, the ornate bird baths and wrought iron. Everything was made by human hands and valued and preserved. And now you tell me that the skills were passed on from family to family. Of course they were, but I never thought of this before, nor of the line of skills that continues. I suppose your father gave you his tools and showed you how to use them. How precious! How special!"

Émile smiled, but looked down at his hands and spread his fingers.

"The workers of the French Revolution did not agree with you. They believed we were too privileged; we were officially the bourgeoisie. They ransacked our guild houses, and we were humbled. And since the industrial revolution, it is machines and factories that carry out our work, and the young, they are not interested. So many of my family's old tools are no longer needed, but I treasure them, and sometimes they're the only useful thing for an odd job." Émile stared at the dregs of coffee in his cup, excused himself, rose and rinsed the cup in the sink, all action.

So, the conversation was closed. Cynthia wanted to ask him more about his own family, but it was clear Émile had other ideas.

"Will you copy my key then, please? It's very unusual. I haven't seen one like it in Australia. Look at this beautiful top. It's the shape of a clover, the same as the carvings on the door."

Cynthia had tied a purple satin ribbon around her key. As she handed it to Émile, their fingers met with a buzz. She suppressed the urge to grab and admire his fingers, to imagine the skills passed down through the centuries from parent to child, embodied in his hands.

It was on the tip of her tongue to mention her thoughts, but Émile's lips were tight, his expression guarded. Did he have children? Had he passed on his own skills?

Instead, she opened the back door so he could reach his van.

"May I watch you, please? Oh, and we'd better have another spare if possible, please. I'll give Will a key so he can feed Minette when we're away at the ball."

Émile nodded and opened the back of his van and stepped in. First, he brought out a small crate.

"For you to sit," he said. So considerate. He followed it with two sawhorses and a workbench, solid, much-used.

Cynthia ran her hands over it. What did they call it? "The patina of age," she said out loud.

"It was from our shop. They gutted it. I saved it just in time. I found it in the dumper bin and hauled it out. I use it almost every day."

Émile brought out a heavy machine, pale green, like something from the 1950s, and clamped it onto the board. Cynthia loved the way he moved inside the truck, each motion sparse, as if he could find everything blindfolded.

He rustled in a couple of drawers on the right hand side of the truck, drew out a handful of old keys and spread them on the bench.

"Can you find anything similar?" he said. Cynthia laughed.

"You sound a bit like Jim in our own shop," she said. "Although my job there was to find matching sizes and shapes and colors of diamonds and other gemstones."

"Different, but the same. A treasure is that which you desire."

He held Cynthia's gaze, his eyes intense, until she broke the spell and looked away. Why was she blushing? He carried on talking about keys, as if he hadn't noticed.

"It is becoming more and more difficult to find these old keys," he said. "The blanks, they are not manufactured any more."

"Oh? That's a shame. They're beautiful."

"Are you sure you don't want me to replace the whole lock?"

"I suppose it'd be much easier, but I'm partial to this particular key. It's the clover shape of it which matches the carvings on my front doors. Perhaps you noticed them?"

He nodded. "And I know how attached you can be to things that catch your eye."

"Like chandeliers."

"Exactly. You might want to wear these ear muffs. This will make a big noise. New machines are probably quieter, but this one really does the job. Now, what have you found?"

She held up three keys. None with the clover top—that was a shame—but all were similar in size.

"You have a good eye for this. These shafts are the correct diameter."

"Judging people's ring sizes for thirty years probably helps."

"Yes."

Their eyes met as Émile settled a pair of earmuffs on her head and that spark ran between them again, but he turned away, intent on the job. He protected his own ears with a matching pair, added some clear goggles and switched on the machine. Real sparks flew as the grinder struck metal, and in no time at all, Émile switched off the machine, flipped up his glasses, filed the edges and handed her the two spares and the original as she handed back the earmuffs.

"You must test them before I pack up, in case there's a problem."

She closed her fingers around the new keys, warm from his hands.

Cynthia sprinted around the corner, confirmed the keys worked and ran back, giving Émile a thumbs up.

He packed the mobile workbench away, along with the grinder, and locked the back of his truck.

As he turned to her, she handed him back one of the keys.

"You are sure you wish to give me this?" he asked.

"I might as well. You've got all the tools you'd need to break in if you wanted to, anyway, and you'll only be feeding Minette, won't you?"

Did his eyes stray from the key to her body and to her lips and eyes, as if to show he appreciated her? She blushed. Was she making a mistake? No. She felt safe with Émile. She wasn't even going to be here when he used the key. They were talking about the cat; nothing more.

"Thank you," he said, suddenly sincere. "You trust me."

"Of course," she said. "Why wouldn't I trust you, Émile? You've been nothing but helpful." What was this uncertainty, this lack of confidence on his part? Had somebody hurt him? And why had he closed his store if he'd loved his work so much, and was so good at it? She longed to ask, but held her tongue. He'd tell her in his own time.

As he drove away she already missed him. She'd been fine on her own for years, but he was such good company, with his lanky frame and ready good humor. And there was no question he was handy. Imagine being able to cut keys and who knew what else?

She was intrigued by his conversation about his family's traditional skills and all the tools they'd known how to use. Sometimes stalls at markets had tools for sale. She'd never be drawn to those displays, but now, she'd look more closely; perhaps pick up a few items for Émile if they were particularly interesting. Why not?

Chapter 16

With Will fast asleep in one of the spare beds, the evening was far too quiet, but just as she was getting ready for bed, James phoned again.

"Darling?"

"Will's been at it again."

"Has he? He's asleep now. Upstairs."

"Can you keep an eye on him, Mum?"

"In what way?"

"Has he been with you this past week?"

"Not exactly. He set off for the Riviera soon after he arrived, stayed for a few days and came back earlier today, but he's very keen to go back there. I suppose this place is too quiet for him. I love it, but he probably finds it boring. You know Will—the life of the party."

"That's exactly what worries me."

"He's been his own person for a long time now, James. You're not boys anymore."

"I know that, but it's my business literally, Mum. He's so erratic, and I'm the one left trying to balance the budget. We've spoken about this. Are you still lending him money?"

"I do, from time to time. I would always help out you or Nicole, too, if either of you asked."

"This isn't about jealousy. Don't lend him any more, Mum. Please."

"Alright then."

"Thank you. What else is news?"

"I'm going to a party in a chateau in a couple of weeks."

"Wow! Is this one of Will's capers?"

"No. I'm a bit old for his crowd, don't you agree? A friend invited me. I'm excited. I'm going with Will to Nice tomorrow to buy a gown."

"Enjoy yourself."

"I hope you'll come and visit me too, James, and Nicole, too, and Jim if he's up for it. I'd welcome all of you, any time. How's Jim?"

Next morning, in the kitchen before heading for Nice with her, Will spun the spare key around his finger a few times before pocketing it.

Cynthia dressed up for the outing, ditching her now customary jeans and t-shirt for a pencil skirt and ironed linen blouse. She enjoyed packing for her day or two away from the village.

She swept Minette off her feet, flipped her upside down in her arms and tickled her tummy until she purred.

"You'll enjoy a day or two on your own, too, my Minette. Bonus crunchies! Don't eat them all at once."

The trip to Nice was fun. Will drove, allowing her to enjoy the sights— the purple hills of lavender, small vineyards and more villages with their churches and stone-walled houses.

As they neared the coast, the glimpses of shining sea enticed her.

In Nice, Cynthia had booked the same hotel she'd stayed in when she first flew into France.

As Will carried in their luggage, the receptionist's eyes widened. Will gave her a half smile, and she blushed. Cynthia had forgotten what it was like to go anywhere with Will. He was a magnet.

The young woman scrutinized Cynthia. Did she imagine he was her toy boy? She smiled back and the woman glanced away.

"What time do you finish?" Will rarely wasted a moment.

"Ten," said the receptionist.

"Perfect," said Will. "You can show me all the best places, but first, where can my mother find a ball gown?"

The receptionist tore a map of Nice off a pad under the desk, grabbed a pen and circled a few locations, a practised gesture, given most of her attention was on Will.

Cynthia smiled and thanked her. She guessed, correctly, she wouldn't be seeing much of her son, but she was content to browse on her own, loving the opportunity to find out what was in fashion and explore many brands with which she was unfamiliar.

Many of the boutiques carried excellent end of summer specials, but most of the outfits were holiday clothing, with a distinct lack of grand ball gowns.

She fortified herself with some coffee-flavored gelato. Tourists from all over the world promenaded. She tried to guess their nationalities.

Best of all she stumbled on two streets of vintage clothes, in rue Droite and rue Benoit Bunico. Now, surely, she would be in luck. While one specialised in outfits from the 1960s, bright miniskirts and oversize sunglasses, the second store held more promise, especially the section up some stairs at the back.

A formal sales person sitting at a desk and sewing a pearl wrist button onto a pair of long black gloves peered at her over the tops of her glasses, sizing her up as she took the stairs.

She asked Cynthia if she would like to make an appointment to try on one of these valuable dresses. She'd used plus-perfect tense. Highly formal. Expensive.

"*Mais oui.*" Of course Cynthia would like an appointment, if that was what was needed to view the gowns. She found a rack of several which interested her, all in the tight-bodiced full-waisted 1950s style.

"*Maintenant*? Now? *S'il vous plaît*?"

The assistant made a grand show of consulting her book and her watch, sighed and nodded, lips pursed.

She flicked a tape measure and stared at a corner while Cynthia came up the stairs, noticed her glittering engagement ring and diamond bangle and then became very helpful.

"Madame is very slim."

Cynthia smiled.

The woman brought out two of the gowns which had caught her eye, one emerald green and the other a deep red. She hung them in a large change room with an ornate gold mirror and dimmed warm lighting, then gestured for Cynthia to enter.

"*Nos robes sont très précieuses, vous comprenez,*" she said, stating the obvious. Of course the dresses were precious. She stayed with Cynthia, glancing away as she undressed. She drew on a pair of white gloves then helped Cynthia lift the emerald green gown over her head.

148

The silk rustled and swished as it swept past her ears, and Cynthia imagined the parties it had witnessed. The assistant pulled up the old metal side zip and hook and eye and stood back, appraising the effect.

The color was joyous and Cynthia twisted from side to side, making the gown dance. Why had fashion ever moved on? She felt like a goddess in this creation, but the assistant frowned and tutted and shook her head, pointing at the waistband, which sat a little low, and motioning for her to come forward and be unzipped again.

The red dress was a better fit, though Cynthia found the cap sleeves a little bare, and in the dim lighting, she spotted a stain just below the waist on the left hand side and pointed at it, shaking her head.

The assistant sighed.

"I have one other in your size, but it is very special."

"These are all very special."

"Yes, but this is an original Jacques Fath."

"Well, it might not even fit."

"We will see. One moment, please."

The woman returned with a gown in a long zippered bag. Cynthia drew in a breath as the assistant drew the gown out of the bag. The soft pink material glowed in the subdued light, like a pale rose in full bloom in the moonlight, the folds of the fabric calling out to her fingers to feel their weight.

"Ah, non," said the assistant, holding up her hand and reaching for some white gloves for Cynthia to slip on.

"Maintentant," she said, and she lifted the gown over Cynthia's head.

"Un moment." The assistant tightened the bodice behind her with laces, and the gown fell perfectly from her waist. It held her curves like it was made for her.

The drapes of the skirt were echoed in a swathe of fabric at her décolletage which swept across the tops of her arms.

She twisted sideways to view the back, and the assistant returned with an elegant hand mirror, holding it so Cynthia could admire the way the ruffled swathe draped over her shoulders, around the tops of her arms, meeting in the centre at the back.

It was flattering in the soft light. Time to retrieve the glasses.

It wasn't that Cynthia was vain. Dressing well was an observance; a careful habit she'd never broken. Since coming to France, she'd been less obsessed with the finer details of her appearance, with magnifying mirrors and concealers for freckles and tiny veins. Here in France, she'd let herself take a step back, to focus more on what she saw than on how she was seen.

Working with rusty window boxes and cleaning dusty pieces of furniture called for jeans and t-shirts rather than the latest fashion, and she loved the freedom of no longer being in the spotlight in the shop and in meetings with customers and suppliers. Was she letting herself go? Perhaps, but Émile's glances told her she was still attractive, and she was strong and fit.

But now? A ball was a formal occasion where it was all about dressing well. She wanted to appear her very best, and that meant not wearing a dress more suitable for a much younger woman.

She slipped on the glasses and studied herself. The glasses themselves were hardly glamorous; still, she wouldn't be wearing them at the ball. Her hair was more silver now than blonde.

The sales assistant read her mind.

"This color is sublime for you, madame; very flattering."

Cynthia brushed her fingertips across her neck where more wrinkles had formed than she would have liked, but strangely, the material, perhaps because of its crepe texture, complemented her skin tone, and the draping of the fabric across the tops of her arms hid the puckers of time, as if the designer understood the fears of older women and how to allay them.

Unlike the red dress, this one had no holes or stains, even at the very ends where it might have swept across lawns and courtyards at previous parties.

The natural fabric breathed, even in the warmth of the summer and humidity of the coast. It was as if it was made for her.

"I'll have it," she said, and the attendant nodded.

Euphoria washed over Cynthia. She longed to be able to look her best at a ball in the Loire Valley, in a chateau, no less. She might not have particularly skilled ancestors in her pedigree, like Émile, but she would polish up alright.

She surprised herself how much she wanted to impress him. She'd dressed to please customers and to please herself ever since she could remember. Now she wanted her French friend to be proud of her when he introduced her to his friends. She'd studied French interiors and French history all her life. Now she'd be walking in the footsteps of the fallen aristocrats, though not to the guillotine, thank goodness, and just for one magic night. She couldn't remember ever being so excited about an event.

It was only as the attendant wrapped the gown in tissue paper and began writing out the sales slip that Cynthia even thought about the price.

"Et, ça fait trois mille euros, s'il vous plaît, madame."

Cynthia made a quick calculation. Nearly five thousand dollars? Impossible. Surely there'd been a mistake.

The assistant pushed the bill towards her, turning it so there was no doubt. Cynthia, to be sure, retrieved her glasses.

At any other time, the amount would have shocked her. It was ten times what she'd expected to pay, but this was a respected salon, not a market stall.

The argument in her head was invisible but she hesitated.

"*Vraiment?*"

"*Madame, on pourrait trouver cela dans un musée.*"

A museum piece? True. If only James hadn't asked her to watch her spending. The timing was dreadful.

She was about to leave the shop when she remembered the notes Will pressed on her when he gave her the diamond studded bangle.

"One moment." She reached into her purse and retrieved them. She hadn't checked them when he'd handed them over; thinking they were three fifty euro notes. She took a step backwards. Instead, each was for five hundred euros, certainly enough to bolster her buying power, and she stepped forwards again, brandishing a mixture of credit card and cash. Thank goodness!

Off the hanger, wrapped in paper and settled into a bag, the gown was less substantial, but she knew it was just right for the event. And if the price ended up posing a problem, perhaps the shop would accept it back again.

It was the kind of thing she'd wear again, of course, to her children's weddings, perhaps. She couldn't wait to show Will. Always one for living in the moment, he'd surely agree with her decision to seize the treasure.

She brought it back to the hotel room. The afternoon radiated heat. Cynthia was glad she'd packed her bathing costume. She slipped it on, added a light frock, borrowed the hotel hand towel and took herself for a stroll on Avenue les Anglais. How much had happened since she'd flown in two months ago! Her resolve to take a celebratory dip deepened. Not a great fan of the beach in Australia, always wanting to protect her skin and with so little free time, it had been ages since she'd swum, and with summer coming to an end shortly, now was as good a time as any.

She hobbled her way over the stones, almost changed her mind, then plunged in, swimming a short distance, then floating and peering up at the sky with its high white haze and dappling of clouds, so different to Sydney's deeper blue.

Stumbling back up the stones, she longed for Australia's golden sand for a few brief moments, and then laughed. The dip certainly cooled her down. It was part of the adventure of the whole free and easy weekend, along with the shopping, extravagant and fun. It was something to tell Nicole next time she rang.

Back at the hotel there was no sign of Will, so she headed out by herself again to enjoy a bowl of mussels.

He was still missing when she returned to their room, not that they'd made any particular arrangements, but when he wasn't around the following morning, nor answering his phone, she began to worry.

"I need to go back to Minette," she texted. "Are you coming back with me?"

Nothing. Half an hour later, she paid the bill and headed out, shrugging. He was a grown man after all. He'd never been particularly communicative. Once again there was a different receptionist. Maybe the one he'd hit it off with was part of the weekday crew or was with Will somewhere.

"May I leave a message for one of your guests, Mr Will Huntley, please?" she said, and the receptionist placed some hotel stationery and an envelope on the counter.

"Sorry. Went home. Ring me, please, Will. Mother."

She crossed out the "sorry". Why was she the one apologising, here? Should she be going to the police? It wasn't really a police matter, surely. Maybe he'd run into some friends.

She screwed up the note. He'd have to check out himself and work out how to return to her place himself, but he'd been managing on his own for a decade now. Why was she fussing?

She glanced at the robe bag across her arm and smiled. It was really better not to think about Will.

Instead, as she hired her own car, drove out of Nice and wound her way back to the village, later than she'd originally planned, she turned her thoughts towards the ball.

She was so grateful to Émile for giving Minette an extra feed. She smiled. Émile was something. He was warm and generous and fun. Could he dance, too?

For a moment she worried she should have spent less on the gown and more on other items. Would they share a room on the Friday night? It was possible. Did she want to buy a sexy French negligee? Did she? She laughed at herself.

They were just friends, weren't they? Let Émile make the first move. Their weekend away would be extraordinary enough without it being a date.

Chapter 17

Émile pondered how to travel to the chateau. Any number of his friends would have loaned him a car, since the motorbike and van were clearly unsuitable.

But to impress Cynthia, he hired a car. He selected a top line Citroen, stylish and spacious, so Cynthia would glide in comfort and enjoy her views of the French countryside. There'd be plenty of space for his suit to hang, for his dress shoes, and for whatever she would bring.

This trip was important—a chance to show her he was more than a handyman. Though he mixed easily with all kinds of people, he was rarely invited to parties, and this would be one of the few times a client had invited him back for a formal celebration.

A small voice warned him that the motives of the host, a rich American divorcee who owned the chateau, might not be entirely pure. She'd crept up on him a few times as he was packing up after a day's work, offering him a drink. Once, when he'd accepted, thinking she was being hospitable, she'd let her hand rest on his bicep a touch too long and he'd stood and made his excuses with an apologetic shake of his head. He wasn't interested in casual sex. It complicated things.

That Cynthia had accepted his invitation for the weekend thrilled him. She was great company, vivacious, good humored, and beautiful in her petite way. He loved that she listened to him with care.

Émile chose his clothes carefully for their weekend. Cynthia had only ever seen him in his work attire—thick, protective boots, a dark blue shirt and dark trousers.

As well as the evening jacket and white shirt, he'd bought some casual shirts for their adventure, a pair of black lace-up shoes, casual trousers and a leather jacket. The new outfit made him feel different, and the truth was, he *was* different around Cynthia. In her company, he was happy. He felt strong and capable, his skills like superpowers.

He'd taken his own skills for granted. Fixing things was a way of life. As his hands and skills had grown to match his grandfather's and father's, they were merely something expected. In the hardware shop, customers took his knowledge and advice for granted, and his clients paid for him to get things right, but Cynthia celebrated his expertise. She was particularly delighted, always grateful for his contributions. She treated him like a hero and he lapped it up. It made him want to do more for her each time.

One evening he pulled out some tools and crafted a clover shaped top for the key she'd given him for her House of Clubs, and he smiled to imagine her surprise.

Her house was full of projects. She hadn't mentioned heating to him, but she'd soon discover Provence often plunged to zero. She'd need the old heating system to work, or to replace it. He knew how to install air conditioning—efficient for her spaces, particularly if he repaired the window seals for her and added insulation above the ceiling.

He was getting ahead of himself. She hadn't even shared her plans. Her village property might just be a folly—a wealthy woman's amusement like Angelica's chateau—and she'd be back on the plane to Australia. It was best to keep their relationship light. It wouldn't do to make too many assumptions or place too many hopes on it, however attractive he found her. And he *was* attracted to Cynthia. Every time they were together he was more intrigued by her blend of strength and vulnerability. It was courageous to make a future in a strange land. He admired her.

Yes, the weekend would be a chance to see Cynthia in another light, an opportunity to have fun, as well as witness all the progress at the chateau since he'd moved on, and to catch up with the other contractors.

But mostly he anticipated the time alone with Cynthia. He loved that she'd trusted him to feed Minette while she was away. Her house was strangely soulless without her. He'd missed her. If he hadn't had this weekend together to look forward to, it might have worried him. He was self-sufficient. He wasn't seeking love. His life was full enough, wasn't it?

All week he laughed and smiled more often. He hadn't told his Nice contractors his weekend plans, but his plumber friend, Jacques, in the village suspected something was happening in his life, especially when he was in town again to feed the cat, and they'd had lunch together.

Émile was pleased Jacques asked him about himself, a sign he may be emerging from his haze of grief. At first his friend made much of the invitation the American had sent, implying there might be something between the two of them.

"Me and all her other male friends," said Émile.

"But you, my friend; look at you. There's something different about you. Haircut. New clothes. You plan to enjoy this trip, no?"

"That's true. We'll enjoy this trip. It will be a change of scene."

"'We?'" Jacques repeated, his old face crinkling into a smile.

"Yes. I'm taking Cynthia, the Australian."

"Ah! The little Australian; the one who bought the corner shop," Jacques said. It was a rare joy to see Jacques smile. Since his wife's death, his steps were slower, his head heavy and the creases in his face deeper than ever, his mouth downturned. But now he held up his glass.

"Yes."

"Ahhhh. Émile." Jacques laughed and clinked his glass against Émile's, then shook his head.

"What."

"Falling in love again," Jacques sang in English with a heavy French accent.

"No, Jacques."

"'No, Jacques.'" Jacques clapped Émile on the arm and then on the back. "Have fun, my friend."

And now, as Émile entered the rental car branch, he chuckled to remember Jacques' smile.

The attendant was apologetic. "Welcome, sir. I apologize. We were unable to procure your exact car, sir, but we do have a Citroen."

He recognised her smile. It was brave. She knew she was about to be blasted. He felt for her. He'd been in business long enough to guess that whatever was about to happen was not necessarily her fault.

"I did request your car, sir, and the depot assured me it would be here, but then unfortunately, the other customer changed their plans. I can, however, offer you a half price discount."

"I don't care about the discount," Émile said. "I really wanted the larger car. Is there nothing else you can offer me?"

"*Malheureusement, Monsieur* ..." Unfortunately, indeed.

His heart sank as she brought out the keys and paperwork and asked him to sign on the dotted line.

"I'm sorry we only have C3s available, but they are all Citroens and quite new, and there are three colors to choose from."

What choice did he have? There was no other car depot anywhere nearby, and time was running out.

He loaded his gear into the back of the white one with a hot pink roof and drove to Cynthia's.

She was strangely preoccupied when he arrived. Was she disappointed about the car? He squeezed her bags into the rear seat space and laid her garment bag across the lot, but she remained concerned.

She dashed back to the house and returned five minutes later, still distracted.

It wasn't how he'd imagined their special weekend would begin.

"I'm sorry about the car," he said.

"Sorry? The car?" She slipped in beside him, and clicked on her seatbelt. In her pale pink pedal pushers and slip-on shoes, her ankles were distractingly beautiful.

"I ordered a larger one, but only this small car was available."

She turned sideways, noticed his frame folded into the seat and smiled.

"Oh, Émile. I don't care about cars, although you are a little cramped there. Should I drive?"

"No. It's fine. The van was not suitable. I wanted to transport us in some elegance. This is not what I planned."

The tiny engine whined as they reversed. The little tyres and suspension transmitted every bump. His head hit the ceiling a couple of times.

Cynthia rested her hand on his knee.

159

"Relax about the car," she said. "It's funny, really. I love the hot pink roof."

"I hoped this. There was also a grey one, but I worried we'd be invisible; this thing is so small."

He was rewarded with her laughter, but before long it was clear she was troubled.

"Something is worrying you," he said.

"Yes," she said. "I wasn't going to say anything. It's Will. I don't want to bother you about my family."

"I'm happy to listen if it helps," said Émile.

"James has been telling me for months that Will's behaviour is increasingly odd, and I've been making excuses for him. I know I have. Will is my baby. He was hardest hit of the three of them when Jimmy died. And he's so much fun. You've met him. He's … different—but in a good way, a great way. The world needs people who are different, don't you think? How boring if we were all the same."

Émile nodded and she continued.

"Will's fun. He appreciates the moment, like children do. Most adults lose that ability, but Will is special. James thinks Will is hopeless, and there's definitely some sibling rivalry. Am I talking too much?"

"Not at all."

"But lately… and now, especially just now…"

"What's happened?"

"I lent him some money, and then you were there when he gave me the bangle, and he also gave me some notes. It's true I've been lending him money over the years, and he insisted I have some of that cash back, so

160

I took it; and I spent it last weekend, on my gown actually. I was grateful. In Nice, when you cared for the kitten for me. Have I thanked you for that?"

Émile nodded. "It was good. I took Jacques to lunch. He's more his old self."

"You're such a good friend; a great person, Émile." She squeezed his thigh and he almost drove off the road. She removed her hand. It was wise.

"But that weekend, Will didn't come back to our hotel in Nice, and he didn't answer my calls, so I left him there, wherever he was. It's not like he's a helpless little boy any more. You've met him. He's totally independent. So I left him in Nice. And Émile, I was so worried he wouldn't turn up this weekend as planned, to care for Minette, but he arrived on Thursday, and everything was fine for a while. But then he asked for the cash back, and of course I didn't have it, because I'd spent it on this gorgeous dress. I can't wait to show it to you."

Émile turned and smiled at her. He was so glad to be with her.

"Go on."

"Well, he stayed around yesterday and played with Minette—he's lovely with the kitten; well, she's a dear—but then last night he up and left again. He didn't say goodbye. He didn't leave a note. I went back and checked his bedroom and he's not there. He's left a few clothes."

"Maybe he ducked out for a run? Did he know what time you were leaving?"

"Maybe. I hope that's all it is. But there's something else."

"Yes?"

"I wanted to wear my new bangle to the ball, the one he gave me when you were there—the one with the diamonds in it."

Émile nodded again.

"I can't find it. I was sure I put it in my bedroom, on that beautiful old dresser with the big round mirror, opposite the window. But I can't find it anywhere."

"You worry Will has taken it?"

"Well… you didn't notice it on the dresser when you were there last weekend, did you? I didn't think about packing it until earlier today, so it might have been missing all week, but you're the only other person with a key."

"You think I took your bracelet."

"Oh no, Émile. I didn't say that. But do you think Will could have … stolen it?"

Émile gripped the wheel tighter. What did he know of Cynthia and her family? What right did he have to comment on their relationships, particularly when those with his own family were so strained he'd simply left them behind for his life on the road?

Worse, he wasn't impressed with Will, though Cynthia clearly adored and indulged him. The man was handsome, but he was utterly selfish and spoiled. Nothing he could say here would help. That Cynthia worried that Émile himself might have stolen her bracelet offended him. He would give her back her key.

"What can I say, Cynthia? I do not know."

She sighed and admired the scenery. He wished she'd put her hand back on his knee. The driving position was cramped. He needed to stop and stretch. He would call in on another depot and insist on a swap.

They made their way north west, the little car engine screaming on the main highways as they drove at 130km an hour.

"We will swap the car in Limoges," he said, after a long silence.

"Limoges! How exciting. Can we see some of their porcelain, please?"

"It's a big city, Cynthia."

"You'd rather we didn't see the porcelain?"

"I didn't say that. I'll be glad to stop and walk around. We can stay the night there if you wish, though I was going to take you to Angers."

"Angers?"

"It's closer to the chateau. We will be able to walk and explore the area together a little before the party."

"Oh, I'd like that."

"But you'd like to see Limoges." He gave her a huge grin and was rewarded with her laugh.

"Émile, you are talking to a Francophile. I love all of France. I want to see everything—superficially and up close. I want to go into every church and museum and walk every cobbled street; to go to every market and sample every croissant; and especially to talk to every Frenchman in French."

"*Every* Frenchman?"

"And especially to you, Émile. Tell me more about this chateau we're visiting."

The distance disappeared as he described the chateau, originally built in the 1700s, extensively remodelled in the 1800s, and renovated by an American in the past year.

"I worked on the chapel, repairing the leadlight windows and fixing the roof."

"What an enormous project!"

"Oh yes, my role, it was small. There are eighteen bedrooms. I could have stayed and worked on more windows, but it was time to move on."

"You prefer to move on?"

Was it a loaded question?

"I did, then." He didn't want to talk to Cynthia about the client's expectations that he provide more than repair services. He'd been flattered, but the time had not been right.

Émile kept an eye on the fuel gauge, eager to unfold his frame from the small driving space; but despite the distances they were travelling, it stayed remarkably full. That was one advantage of these smaller cars.

"Can you find a museum or shop you wish to visit in Limoges?" he said. "I will drop you there while I swap this car for the one I ordered."

"Dear Émile," she said, placing her hand back on his leg. "So kind."

She did some research on her phone, found an outlet and he drove her there, extricating himself from the drivers' seat for a few minutes before heading for the nearest car rental depot.

"I can't tell you how excited I am to see what's inside," she said, smiling.

"One moment, Cyntia."

"Oh?"

Her attention made his heart race, but he'd determined to do this. He pulled from his pocket her house key, and held it out to her in the palm of his hand.

"You are amazingly clever," she said, her eyes alight with joy. "I can't believe you did this! How?"

She took it and turned it over and over, smoothing the new, clover-shaped top of it with her tapered fingers. He shrugged. He'd enjoyed the work.

"But you should keep this, Émile. I already have one. I'd like you to keep it." And she handed it back.

He searched her face. Was this significant? It was to him. He closed his fingers tight around it.

"*Merci.*" He thanked her. For more than a key.

She dropped her eyes at his gaze, but maybe it was just because she couldn't wait to enter the shop. She practically skipped inside it as he drove away, and he allowed himself a smile as she disappeared from his rear view mirror.

Chapter 18

Cynthia was waiting with a big smile and a large, heavy box when Émile pulled up in the elegant new car, shiny black with silver trim.

"Success," he said, as he swung out of the driver's seat and opened the boot for her. "Fortunately, there's still plenty of room for your shopping."

"I couldn't resist. James might not be happy, and my friend Kath will think me a fool to acquire more possessions, but with your superb coffee machine, I wanted some matching cups. These were a bargain. I want to remember our trip, Émile. This is special. How beautiful is this car!"

The luxurious smell of leather pervaded the interior as Émile closed her passenger door. The suspension and quiet ride encouraged conversation.

"Tell me about Angers, Émile. Where will we stay?"

"It's the closest town to the chateau. I spent some time there at the hospital and afterwards, after I fell from a ladder, working on the rose window."

"Oh no? What happened?"

"I broke an arm, but the break, it was complicated. It's a small hotel but the people were kind to me. I stayed there during rehabilitation and a couple of times when I went back for checkups, and they remembered me."

"You're a loyal person, Émile. You're a good friend to Jacques who lost his wife; you cared about the kitten, and now you're bringing your business back to this little hotel."

"Who are we, if we don't live by our values? I believe this very strongly, Cynthia. It has caused problems with my family."

"Oh?"

Surely he would tell her now about his family. Was he a widower? Was he divorced? Surely he'd tell her now. But Émile said no more.

The sun was beginning to set, draping long shadows across the fields and lighting Émile's face with gold.

"Angers," he said, after a long silence. At twilight, they entered the outskirts, crossed the river and purred into the small streets. Émile pulled up beside a wedge-shaped five-storey building right on an intersection.

"*Et voila.*" He turned and smiled at her, and she leaped out, eager to help transport their bags inside and ready to stretch her legs and explore.

"Émile, *bien venue*," said the receptionist, and their conversation continued in French. "We were expecting you. How is your arm? Shall I help you with your bags? You have your favorite room, as requested, and the other one."

"I'm better than ever, thank you, Marie. We'll be fine. This is my friend, Cynthia."

"Good evening, Cynthia. Émile will explain, but breakfast is here in the morning from seven o'clock. She gestured behind her at a room with windows on three sides.

"Lovely, thank you."

Émile stood back as Cynthia stepped into the small lift, and she pressed against the mirrored wall to make space for him and their bags.

"I will take the stairs," he said.

She reached across the bags and pulled him in by the arm and they laughed like children hiding in a cupboard.

They emerged a couple of floors later onto plush red carpet and a corridor of white and gold wallpaper.

"Lead the way, won't you?"

Émile took them to the door at the very end, above the breakfast room. Inside were French doors set in three walls, hung with red velvet drapes. Each led out onto a tiny balcony. The middle pair overlooked the intersection and a jumble of interesting old buildings in the distance.

There was a double bed with a lush velvet cover to match the drapes, a small desk, and plenty of hanging space. The bathroom was small but tasteful, with bevelled mirrors on three sides, indirect lighting, a marble vanity and matching floor.

"This is beautiful, Émile."

"It's small but comfortable," said Émile, and he shrugged. "I will be in the room next door. We can stay here tomorrow night as well, or stay at the chateau if we wish."

"I'll take an overnight bag in the car tomorrow just in case. And now?"

"Now I would like to walk. We can find a restaurant for dinner if you like."

"In Australia we say we like to 'stretch our legs' after a long drive."

"Oh yes. I would like to stretch my whole body."

"Thank you for this adventure, Émile. Will it get cold?"

"Not very at this time of year. You might need a light jacket. I'll see you in the foyer."

Cynthia was delighted with the room. She pulled back the curtains and examined the tiny balconies, enjoying the views of two and three storey buildings in the roads leading to the intersection, and many diverse rooftops.

She freshened up, brought out her favorite jacket, a pale blue velvet, and flung it over her shoulders.

It was a luxury to have Émile walk beside her, a friendly presence; and a relief to be out of the car after the long drive. It was the first time they'd walked together anywhere. Most of their exchanges had been in her house, where there was a job to be done.

Now, the distractions were all around them, beautiful French buildings, small boutiques and residences with ornate front doors and window shutters and climbing roses and only the pleasant challenge of finding a suitable restaurant. They wandered through the streets, past the cathedral to the river, stopping half way along the bridge to admire the lights of the town reflected in the quiet river.

When a slight breeze ruffled the water, Émile helped Cynthia put on her jacket. It was so long since anyone had done that for her, she shivered, and Émile placed a light hand on her shoulder, drawing her closer to his warmth.

It was compatible, a friendly gesture, and they walked on together in step, remarking on the huge moon rising over the rooftops.

As they turned back towards their hotel, the glow of candles on white tablecloths at a restaurant beckoned them, and they entered, greeted by the aroma and sizzle of meat on a griddle. Émile pulled out Cynthia's chair and studied the wine menu while she took in the cosy scene and was astonished to see the chef cooking meat on an open flame in a chimney.

"This is extraordinary," she said.

"What's that?" Émile looked up from the wine menu and smiled.

"That chef is barbequing—inside."

"But this is normal."

"No, Émile. Australians are experts at barbecues. It's one of our national pastimes, and nobody ever does it indoors."

"But this is the most ancient way of cooking. How do you think food was cooked in castles before electricity and piped gas?"

"I suppose so."

"This is a cheminée restaurant."

"Chimney? Oh. Well, it smells delicious. I can't understand how doing nothing all day but staring out the windscreen has made me so hungry!"

…

How long was it since Émile had taken a beautiful woman to a restaurant? He couldn't remember. The candlelight caressed Cynthia's soft cheeks and chin. It fell on her delicate cheekbones, on her neck and shoulders and all her delicious undulations. She was enchanting.

The flame made her eyes sparkle as she explained how Aussie men all gathered around the sizzling steak and sausages on the "barbie" while the women fussed with salads and desserts in the kitchen. They'd meet around the table once all had full plates, and slap mosquitoes while they "passed the sauce."

"It's a ritual," she said.

"You miss Australia?"

"Not at the moment, no. I've been there and done that. France is far more exciting for me, full of surprises, and this, for example. Such a treat, Émile! I'm so glad you thought to invite me, and I love it that it's not too rushed. Staying tonight to break up the travel, we'll be fresh for tomorrow's party."

"Tomorrow we can see more of Angers if you wish. There's Château D'Angers with a Neolithic tomb and other archaeological remains, and the medieval Apocalypse Tapestry; and the Château de Brissac. We call it 'the giant.' It has seven floors and more than 200 rooms. We could have booked a room there for the night ..."

"Oh no, I'm very happy with your choice."

"It's modest."

"It's delightful. Truly."

"And there's the cathedral and some beautiful gardens, some medieval architecture and quite a good museum, de beaux arts, not too big." Was he talking too much? Being face to face with Cynthia was making him nervous.

In the car, with his focus on the road, their conversation had ranged easily from French history to contemporary politics, different translations of various French and English sayings, and even philosophy—unlike Bertha, who shut him down when he tried to discuss his beloved Jaspers' meditation on the paradigmatic individuals—Cynthia had been fascinated. She'd laughed and questioned him about Confucius, listened carefully and debated the points gladly. There'd been no awkward silences.

And here in the restaurant, she was charming; more beautiful than ever.

"Lovely!"

They chatted easily, about food and wine and aspects of their childhoods. He successfully skirted questions about the recent past; his life before he headed south in the repair van. Instead, there were plenty of stories to share about the many tiny challenges he'd been able to solve for his clients.

Cynthia asked him more about his time in Angers. He told her he'd stayed in the hotel for several weeks while having physiotherapy. The team at the hospital repaired his broken elbow, and the time away from work, wandering the streets and gardens, gave him time to re-examine his past. It was a lucky recovery. Had he fallen a little further to the left, he might have cracked his skull on the edge of the altar.

"I was very fortunate," he said, staring at the candle.

"Oh?"

"I could be dead. My client took full responsibility; paid for my medical care; ensured I underwent full rehabilitation."

"Well, you need to use your arms for your work. Did you have insurance?"

"Yes, as did the client. I am grateful."

He didn't add that the time in Angers not only healed his body but also gave him a chance to consider his future, to reach a decision for the time being.

Coming back to Angers with Cynthia was significant to him.

Cynthia insisted on paying. After their meal, the fresh air outside was cooler still, and Émile held out his arm to Cynthia, inviting her to snuggle closer as they walked together in step, their appetites sated, pleasantly relaxed by the good wine.

Inside, he walked Cynthia to her door. Would she invite him in? She hesitated, eyes on his, and on his lips. He leaned forward, but she fiddled with her key, all bright thanks.

"Such a beautiful meal, thank you, Émile," she said, and covered her mouth to yawn. "What time will we meet for breakfast?"

"Come down tomorrow when you are ready. I will wait for you in the breakfast room. I will work through emails and invoices. There is no hurry from my point of view, but I will be glad to be your guide for the day."

"Thank you, Émile." She reached out and caught his fingers, squeezed them, then dropped his hand, entered her room and closed her door.

Chapter 19

Cynthia's heart pounded. Why hadn't she invited Émile into her room? He'd been nothing but kind to her; nothing but a careful driver and host, and their conversation and laughter at dinner had come more easily than ever. Her body buzzed with joy, remembering his warmth against her as they'd walked, so tall and strong—and that was exactly why she'd left him on the other side of her closed door.

She loved Émile as a friend. He was excellent company, and there was no question she was attracted to him. But why complicate their relationship with anything physical? It had been more than a decade since she'd had any interest in such things. That side of her life was long gone, with Jimmy's death. She shivered, then stared at her surroundings, bringing herself back to the present, to this plush room with its accents of maroon and cream and gold. She ran a hand over the pleasing velvet of one of the cushions and smiled.

The weekend was young. She entered the bathroom and admired the marble and gold fittings. The French really knew how to make interior decorations special. She drew herself a long bath with the fragrant oil, and luxuriated in the new surroundings. Émile was attentive to her and a perfect gentleman. She appreciated everything about him, including the fact he'd made no demands about their sleeping arrangements. He probably wasn't interested in her that way. For all she knew, Émile was gay.

Next morning, downstairs, she searched for his familiar face in the breakfast room. His back was to the entry area. Sunlight flooded in through the windows, lighting up bowls of oranges, jugs of fresh juices and shelves of marmalades and jams. They glowed like jewels.

Cynthia crept up behind him and placed both hands on his shoulders.

"G'day stranger," she drawled.

"What's this?" he said, catching both her hands in his, before letting them go.

"Incognito, I see."

"Oh yes, my sunglasses. It's very bright here."

"It's beautiful! What a wonderful room!"

"You understand why I staged a full recovery at this hotel. It is easy to stay."

A waiter hovered with pots in each hand.

"*Café? Thé? Croissants?*"

"English Breakfast, please. *Un croissant, s'il vous plaît.* Delicious."

Their day of sightseeing passed rapidly. Cynthia read out historical facts, while Émile laughed at some of her questions.

"Be kind, Émile. We didn't all grow up in France knowing everything. I'd like to hear you give an acknowledgement of country in Wiradjeri, not that I can do that either yet, actually. Or to name the northern rivers of New South Wales. That's a better example."

"What's that?" he said.

"Exactly."

"I do not mean to make fun, Cynthia. I'm glad to share our history. I learned so much on school excursions. I act like the teacher, but I commend you. You actually know a lot of our culture already, much more than most tourists, and your pronunciation is almost perfectly Parisian."

"So I've been told. Will I fool them tonight?"

"Let's see."

"*On verra*, indeed."

They returned to their separate rooms at four o'clock, planning to meet in the foyer an hour later.

Cynthia lay on the bed, ready to rest her feet, and closed her eyes for a moment.

When she awoke and saw the time, she was mortified. Only fifteen minutes to prepare! She snapped to attention. She splashed cold water on her face, twisted her hair and secured it with an elegant new clip, dabbed perfume in all the right places, then slipped the gown over her head. Oh no! She'd forgotten she needed help to do up the ribbon at the back.

She quickly sent Émile an SMS: Help.

Moments later, Émile knocked on the door, his white dress shirt open and only partially tucked into his slim black trousers.

Cynthia was unprepared for his appearance. He smelled of aftershave. She couldn't keep her eyes off him.

Her own gown, not yet fastened at the back, gaped at the front, and she pressed a hand to her cleavage against the soft silk, stepping back to let him in the door, which closed behind him. She promptly turned her back to him.

"Would you please do up the back, Émile?"

"I'd rather not," he said. "But of course. I joke."

"Ha ha. I'm so disappointed. I wanted to surprise you with this dress."

"You certainly did surprise me."

He was warm behind her. He was gentle with the fabric, drawing it together as he pulled it closer around her. His fingers brushed her bare back, soft as a whisper.

"I suppose I pull on these ends of the ribbon."

"Yes," she said, certain that a man who could repair anything on earth could work out the mechanism. "It's like a shoelace."

"It is most definitely not like a shoe."

"Is that a compliment?"

"It is." As his fingers tugged at the ribbon, drawing the bodice in closer around her body, the warmth of his breath beamed down her neck like sunshine. Time stopped. She longed to lean backwards into him, his bare chest against her back, to let his hands find her body, and embrace her, cherish her …

No, she didn't. Émile was just a friend; a very good friend, but nothing more. And their relationship must stay that way, lest things become more complicated than either of them might want.

They were off to a party.

"How's that?" he asked, hands now at her waist, testing the tautness of the fabric around her.

"Yes," she said. It was difficult to concentrate so close to him. If she didn't pull away, they'd never get to the party. She rushed to the edge of the room and turned back and waved to him.

"Go, go. I'll meet you in the foyer."

What was that smile of his? The smile of a Frenchman who knows how to please a woman? How many women had Émile pleased, perhaps in this very room? She shook her head. Why was she even thinking this way? Émile was her friend and nothing more.

No one had touched her like this since Jimmy died. There'd been interested men, of course, but she'd been distracted by her children, by the business, by the sale of the family house and the division of all the assets, and then by the creation of the Southern Highlands house that now lay empty, a premature retirement home.

Her life was here and now, in France, where the gorgeous Émile was about to escort her to a party in a chateau. How lovely to have a friend like Émile.

She glanced at her reflection. The gown was everything she'd hoped it would be; elegant and understated. The color and cut suited her. Eyes already bright and cheeks pink with excitement, she needed no makeup, save for a smidgeon of palest lipstick.

She hesitated as she went to slip her wedding and engagement rings back on. For the first time since Jimmy died, she placed them on the ring finger of her right hand.

A frown crossed her face. Where *was* that bangle Will had given her? It would have gone so well with this outfit this very evening. She'd rarely been cross with Will, but she was deeply suspicious he'd pocketed the bangle, perhaps needing to pawn it for cash. No matter. Tonight was for living. Émile had told her he'd found her wrist exquisite, not the bangle. She smiled and bit her lip, then grabbed the key and ran to the lift.

Émile was waiting for her in the foyer, adjusting his cufflinks, every bit the debonair gentleman. Evening dress suited the tall Frenchman so well, for a moment she was shy. Every impression of him as the hired help disappeared out the three huge windows. Émile was devastatingly handsome. Perhaps her attraction to him *was* more than mere friendship. She banished the thought, but it returned again. Émile the locksmith had created the key to her House of Clubs. Did he own the key to her heart?

What were these ridiculous thoughts? She was behaving like a love-struck teenager, as if intimacy was right there in the ether for them to claim, as if they were living within the pages of a romance novel, when everyone knew it was something far more complicated, a bond forged between young people for the rest of their lives. Jimmy had been the love of her life. She felt for their old engagement ring, still so solid on her finger after decades. She was fine. This strange longing would pass.

As Émile turned at her footstep, his eyes caressed her—the tight bodice and bare neck, her waist above the flowing gown, and she shivered—then he sought her own eyes; in his gaze—a hunger.

They moved towards each other in slow motion. Every cell in her body was on high alert. She wanted to press closer to him; but she was all self-control.

Émile was the same with her—exceedingly formal—as if handling dynamite.

Next thing she knew they were in the car, gliding out of town and into the countryside. After a day of chatter and discovery and easy banter, there was no small talk.

Lightning illuminated a pink and grey cloud on the far horizon.

They slowed as they approached an ornate stone gate. Other cars were ahead of them on the long driveway, and still more followed them in.

Guides in dark clothes pointed torches, guiding them to park in a field and follow a series of lit banners towards the extraordinary building, its multi-turreted facade spotlit in the twilight.

Blazing sconces lit up the waiters who circulated, their sleek trays laden with champagne, while other waiters pressed *hors d'oevres* towards them on long silver platters.

The outfits were stunning—gowns which would not have been out of place at the Oscars, and black suits of every kind, some men and even women, wearing tails. A couple of young men were dressed in harlequin costumes, balancing on stilts and juggling fire sticks.

A man with a black mask and Dracula teeth lunged towards Cynthia's neck and she shrieked and rushed into Émile's arms.

"Roddy, you've changed!" Émile said, clapping the man on the shoulder. "I could have sworn the invitation said 'formal' no 'fancy dress,' but that's our Roddy—dramatic flair personified. Meet Cynthia. Cynthia, this is Roddy, Angelica's stylish stylist and antiquities consultant."

"Of course," she said, finding her wits and holding out her hand politely.

"Delicious," said Roddy, eye-catching in his black cape, white face, red lips and those fangs. "Émile. We thought we'd lost you for good! We missed you at Ommegang. That's another dress-up occasion, of course, but fangs aren't welcome there. Where else would I ever have the opportunity to wear *this*?"

"You do look frightfully magnificent," Cynthia said as he and Émile shared a French double kiss welcome and then shook hands. The champagne wobbled in their glasses.

"I missed Ommegang, yes. Still on the road," said Émile.

"Ah, the life of freedom is good, then?" Roddy said.

Émile nodded and laughed.

Freedom from what? Cynthia felt disoriented, alien. So much about Émile remained a mystery. When she'd dubbed him a "rolling stone" it hadn't mattered, but the more she learned about him, the more she wanted to know. Who would have imagined he'd polish up so well? While handyman Émile was endlessly useful, suave Émile was what Nicole might call a silver fox. She smiled at the image. Just as well she had no intention of becoming his prey, despite the way he moved around her, so aware of her, as careful as if she were made of delicate glass, or of wax, and he, the flame.

On the far side of a reflection pond near the main doors of the chateau, a tall woman in a floaty red gown with a stiff, high collar greeted them. She was all flashing sequins and bangles. "Darling, Émile," she said in an American accent. She threw her arms around him and ruffled his hair. "How's your arm?"

"Perfectly repaired," he said. "All thanks to you."

"'Repair man, repair yourself,'" she said, laughing loudly at her own joke. "And this is?"

"Cynthia."

"Oh, how lovely. I didn't think you were looking for love, Émile. As you know..."

"Cynthia is a client, Angelica," said Émile. "From Australia."

Angelica's eyes sought Cynthia's with a knowing smile. She'd noticed her flinch at being described as a mere client.

"Oh?" said Angelica. "And you never mix business with pleasure, of course."

Didn't he? That would be a shame. Tonight, Cynthia hoped otherwise. Didn't Émile find her attractive enough? Was her own gown too insipid? Cynthia took a large swig of champagne. Why all these useless self doubts all of a sudden? What did anything matter, anyway? She was at a French chateau! In a ball gown. And she was with the most handsome man at the ball, even if the hostess imagined he was free game.

"It is good to see you again, Angelica," said Émile. "So good of you to invite me. The place is sensational. You are sensational."

"It oughta be sensational, this place; it's eaten up millions, Émile. Millions. But worth it. Just wait till you see inside. There's a live band; and dancing—cheek to cheek. Be sure to save a dance for me, Émile."

At a huge whoosh and bang, Cynthia cowered beside Émile, who put his arm around her. Above them burst a flood of light as fireworks exploded across the whole sky, and reflected in the pond. As each thud resounded in her chest, the colors charged to the limits of her vision, shooting and radiating bright blues and greens and scarlets and orange and gold—celestial sunflowers.

Suddenly, Émile swept her into his arms, closer and closer. His lips tasted of champagne. The fireworks swept from her closed eyes to the tips of her toes.

"Don't mind Angelica," he said, breaking away. He murmured into her ear as the fireworks cartwheeled around them. "I couldn't resist you any longer, Cynthia. I've been wanting to kiss you since we fought over that chandelier months ago. And that charade when we purchased your beds, that was but a promise."

She closed her eyes again and pulled him closer. Who needed a multimillion dollar French chateau and a whiz bang party when all you needed was to kiss Émile?

Angelica, beside them, had a painted-on smile. Cynthia covered her throat. If Angelica had Dracula teeth, she'd be in trouble. Awkward.

"Yes," said Angelica. "Well, I guess that answers my question. When you said you were coming to my party, I kinda thought you might have reconsidered our arrangement, Émile. Clearly you have other ideas." She clinked her glass against Cynthia's then downed the rest of her own champagne. "Brava, little Cynthia. Bon chance."

She sashayed away in her red dress and chrome high heels, plonked her empty glass on a tray and collected a full one, greeting one guest after another.

"Should we leave?" Cynthia said.

"Don't mind Angelica. She has a very open attitude to sex. She might have expected me to have an affair with her, but she has them with everyone. I said 'no' but she doesn't really hold a grudge. She loves a party. She loves everyone."

"Except me."

"Shall we go in and dance?"

Cynthia nodded and they swept up the grand staircase and into the ballroom, past statues and armor and deer mounts.

The worn tiles of ancient black and white marble made the room into an enormous chess set. Which pieces were she and Émile? Were they even on the same side? Was he the black king and she the white queen? She shook her head, trying to banish the idea of Émile sleeping with Angelica.

The band, on a stage at one edge of the huge room, struck up another number when Émile took her in his arms again and led her out into the room.

"You're very beautiful," he said in her ear. They danced together well, as well as Jimmy ever managed. Why was she comparing Émile to Jimmy? It was decades since they'd danced at their wedding, and she'd rarely danced since, and never like this, in the arms of an attentive Frenchman who wanted to hold her closer.

She loved Émile's strong arms around her; the way she could trust him to twirl her ever faster as the room spun around them; the way he caught her. They spun together so fast the only things not moving were his eyes on hers and his smile and the bond between them, invisible yet as strong in time and space as the forces between celestial bodies. She and Émile were twin stars in this universe, bound together in the music.

They danced number after number, until Émile was so warm he removed his tie and loosened his collar. As he tied the tie around her wrist in a big bow, his lips brushed the inside of her wrist.

The bliss of it ricocheted through her. Dizzy with champagne, she giggled like a teenager. Émile was so much fun when he pretended to be so romantic.

"There is your bracelet," he said, bending down to her. His pulse was beating in his neck. Suddenly she wanted to play along, to kiss him back, close to that little scar. She threw back her head and stood on her toes, but before he could lean closer, Angelica appeared beside them, her arms up.

"May I?"

"Of course," said Cynthia, yielding, backing away. She could hardly deny the hostess of the party a dance with her favorite former tradesman. He was the most handsome courtier in the grand ballroom, and Angelica most striking, the queen of her castle.

Cynthia made her way to the side of the hall, beside a wall of swords and three full suits of armour.

She admired Angelica. She'd dealt with tradespeople herself while building her Southern Highlands home. Imagine directing a chateau's worth. Was there a project manager, or did Angelica mastermind the whole thing? It was mind boggling.

Her eyes were drawn to the striking couple in the centre of the ballroom, Angelica's red dress a flash of fire. They danced well together—too well, though why should Cynthia care that Angelica was fond of her workers, fond of Émile at least. Too fond.

Émile kept his distance from Angelica, his back straight. Had he danced the same way with her? She didn't think so. Surely he'd drawn her closer. They'd danced so well she'd barely noticed the mechanics of it. They'd floated, soared and spun, at one with each other and the music.

But what if she tried to cling to him, as Angelica was doing? Angelica was clearly being very fond of him now, as well as when he'd been on staff. Was that why he'd hit the road again? Did he resist being claimed? Was that what Roddy meant by Émile enjoying his "freedom"?

With a sudden certainty, she knew she didn't want Émile to keep moving on. Did she want him in her life; in her future? Yes. On their long drive yesterday, and this morning, sightseeing, and every time she saw him, for that matter, he'd been such interesting and fun company. And who would have imagined he'd polish up like this, so dapper. Émile was devastating.

How long would he and Angelica dance together?

Roddy sidled up to her with a satay stick and glass of champagne. Beneath his black cape, he'd stowed his teeth in his top pocket.

He followed her glance and shrugged. "Strange. Impossible to eat with fangs," he shouted leaning closer to her to be heard, in a fog of peanut sauce. "You'd think the opposite."

She giggled; his charm was infectious. He followed her gaze again, this time to Émile and tall Angelica, impossible to miss.

185

"Where did you meet my friend?" Was Roddy checking her out?

"In Provence. He helped me."

"That's Émile; the kindest person I know."

"He is; very generous, and clever."

"You're Australian?"

She nodded. Would he say something about kangaroos?

"That's a long way south," he said, his smile warm.

Where was Roddy's partner? Did he bring one? He finished his satay and placed the stick in the steel fingers of the closest panoply.

"Would you like to dance, Cynthia? Fangless?"

"Oh thank you, Roddy. I won't; thanks anyway. I'm parched."

"More champagne?"

"Water, but please don't worry. I'll go."

Just then a waiter glided past and she selected a cool, sparkling mineral water.

"Been together long, you and Émile?"

"Three or four months, I suppose." Was that true? Were they actually even "together"? Did she want to be known as Émile's partner? Oh yes. She did want Émile. For herself.

"And you?"

"I've known Émile forever," he said. "He is like a brother to me."

The number finished, but Émile and Angelica remained in the centre of the floor, her arms around his neck as the band struck up a slow dance.

Cynthia gripped her glass tighter. Roddy's glance slid from her face to the couple, and back to the grim set of her lips. Noting his stare, she cleared her throat, softened her lips and patted the back of her hair. She placed her glass on a ledge in the stone wall and held her hands out to Roddy.

"Dance, Roddy?" He agreed, and she led him into the centre of the floor, right next to Émile and Angelica.

As they approached, Émile removed one of Angelica's arms from around his neck and opened their stance to include the newcomers. As he kissed the back of Angelica's hand and bowed to her, Cynthia found herself clenching her fist.

Émile locked eyes with Roddy, who dropped Cynthia's other hand and took Angelica's, and Cynthia grabbed the hand Émile offered her, joy rocketing through her.

Claiming Angelica for himself, Roddy swirled his cape and spun her away, while Émile held Cynthia close and closer as the music swelled, so closely she was unsure where her own body stopped and his began. He smelled divine. No wonder Angelica wanted him for herself— Angelica, and how many others? Did it matter to her? Yes, said a small voice inside. It did. But if she fell in love with Émile, would he leave her, as he'd left Angelica, Angelica who clearly still wanted him.

She broke away.

"Enough dancing, Émile. Will you show me your work? Can we see the chapel?"

"Of course."

Chapter 20

Outside, with the melody and beat of the music fading behind them, Émile led Cynthia up the stone path past a bank of formal hedges and into an enclosure to one side of the chateau. He held her hand lightly but tightly, his fingers interlocked with her smaller ones.

"The stables," he said. "The coach house." Each building was substantial. "They were going to turn them into guest accommodation. So! They've completed that work. He has been busy, Roddy. This way …"

They rounded another formal garden, a huge fountain in its centre. Effort and care had been lavished on the gardens. Versailles came to mind. Behind was another high hedge and beyond that, the stone building; small, with stained glass windows. They entered the rear door, thick, hand hewn. Timber like that no longer existed in France. In the semi dark, they made their way up the aisle, between the ornate wooden pews.

How long since he'd been here? Nearly a year had passed since the accident, and this was the first time he'd set foot inside. His steps slowed, and he stopped before he reached the altar, his body suddenly freezing cold. It was as if he were in a tunnel, alone in this space. Cynthia's hand dropped away. He stared at the rose window, now complete.

It all came back to him. He'd been working on the top right hand side of the rose window—intricate work, painstakingly replacing stained glass damaged during the French Revolution when the chapel became an armory. He'd carefully recreated the pattern by studying and repeating the designs of undamaged sectors.

That terrible day, he'd been totally immersed in his work, and unaware Angelica had entered. She must have been watching him for some time before he noticed.

She'd taken a special interest in his work, and in him. Every few days she'd stop by and quiz him about his progress. On one previous visit, she'd invited him to dine with her. He'd been eager. Her meals were legendary. She'd updated the huge kitchen first, and forged an arrangement with a local catering college to let the students use her state-of-the-art appliances. Her only fee was that they leave some of the food they prepared for herself and any guests.

The meal was delicious. In his new life of balancing all day on narrow boards and climbing up and down ladders with glass pieces, lead and a soldering iron, he was always hungry. Food kept up his strength and concentration.

It was precise, precarious work, at altitude, and the old stone floor was less than even—a hard landing should he fall. To relax and eat delicious food at the end of an exhausting day and discuss American history with his charming client was an unexpected joy. He'd stayed later than he'd intended, and drunk far too much of her good wine.

"I must go, Angelica," he'd said at the end of their meal.

"Oh really?" she'd said, and she'd leaned closer to him, close enough to kiss him.

"Yes." He stood to leave.

"Perhaps you'll dine with me again," she'd said.

That very next day, he'd been busy up the ladder. Once again, her approach took him by surprise. It was when she'd slipped her fingers up his trousers and grabbed his ankle that he'd lost his balance and fallen.

He'd thought through the accident many times—on the way to the hospital, and throughout his recovery.

It wasn't that he was a particularly religious man, and he didn't judge Angelica for her own behaviour. Plenty of people had affairs. But the truth was …

Suddenly Émile remembered Cynthia was by his side in the chapel. Back then, he'd known Angelica was not for him, but Cynthia? He was more than fond of Cynthia. She kept wanting to pay him for his gifts and efforts, but he only ever wanted to do it all for nothing, for the pure joy of being with her. She brought out something different in him. He loved to make her smile.

Tonight, back in the chateau, on the dance floor, with her beautiful body in his arms, there was nothing he wouldn't give to have Cynthia come to him as Angelica had done, offering him her love. There. He'd been truthful with himself.

But nothing was changed about his circumstances. In the long weeks of recuperation he'd told himself he must never mix business with pleasure. And if Angelica expected he'd change his mind and accept her advances once he was fully recovered and back on the job, she was wrong.

The first thing he'd done when he left Angers, fully recovered if a little weak, was to find her, up in her tower room, and busy checking fabric samples for a set of twenty four dining chairs. He offered to pay her the full costs of his medical care. Without pausing, he explained he was leaving her project for others to complete, and he'd head south once more.

"Oh don't worry about the money," Angelica said. "And you tell me if you ever change your mind about my company, Émile. You'll be welcome."

"I can only wish you the best of luck here, Anglica."

She'd stood and come to him. She'd placed her hand on his damaged arm, gently.

"Émile, you're really gonna leave me?"

He'd nodded, packed quickly and headed south again.

While accepting Angelica's invitation to the ball had been about impressing Cynthia, the pull of the chapel was strong. Only here could he confront his demons and test his resolve. Angelica meant nothing to him romantically, though he still admired her energy and confidence, and her generous mission to restore the chateau.

But Cynthia. She sat quietly on one of the pews, regarding him. How long had they been there while he'd traced the arc of his fall with his eyes, and stood over the place he'd fallen? Was she remembering her wedding, her husband's funeral? Chapels were sacred spaces, away from the world. This was one of the oldest parts of the estate. He and Cynthia spoke easily together, but they hadn't discussed spirituality, nor religion. There was so much about her he did not know; that he wanted to learn.

As she sat, alone on the pew, he came and sat beside her, and she leaned her head against his shoulder.

"You're troubled, Émile. I don't want to probe, but if it helps you to talk, I'm here for you." She brought his hand to her lap and stroked his fingers.

Why did he hide his feelings and his past? She was a gentle person, so different to Bertha with her never-ending demands.

At a great clap of thunder, she gripped his fingers hard. This time it was real fireworks. As the storm arrived, lightning flashes illuminated the stained glass windows to jewels. Rain pelted down, smashing and spattering off the stones outside. A wild wind whipped at the trees outside the door. The temperature plummeted as they clung to each other.

Émile placed his jacket around Cynthia's bare shoulders. When he passed his arm around her waist, she nestled closer. A shiver ran through him; nothing to do with the weather.

Cynthia was not Angelica. His attachment to Cynthia was becoming serious. Long-term serious. Coming here and discovering the depth of his attraction to Cynthia would mean another confrontation was needed—this time with his more distant past. All these months he'd travelled steadily southwards, escaping the wreck of his past life. But now? It was time to travel north again.

She reached for his hand again, and he gave it to her, her small fingers igniting in him a fierce protectiveness. He squeezed her hand and she squeezed it back at every flash and clap of thunder.

They waited at the doorway until the rain stopped. The fragrance of late lilacs, bruised from the battering of rain, was intoxicating. Raindrops on every petal shone in the lights from the chateau.

She hesitated at the threshold, pulling up the hem of her dress, assessing the puddles. As he swept her into his strong arms, cradling her above the mud, she laughed, locking her fingers around his neck.

"Will we go back to the hotel?" he asked.

"Oh, yes. Angelica won't mind?"

"Angelica will party all night, and she has plenty of friends to keep her company."

This time, Cynthia invited him into her room.

"Is this just so I can help you out of your gown?" he asked.

"Yes," she said, but something had changed between them. She took his serious face in her hands and pulled him closer. She brushed her thumb across his scar and he turned away.

"I am ugly," he said, and turned his face away, though her touch was a magnet.

"Nonsense. There's barely a mark. Besides, most of us carry our scars on the inside."

When he turned back, he searched her eyes, then bent his head to hers. The brush of her lips against his sent his pulse racing.

"Stay with me tonight," she said, as he undid the lace of her gown. It fell loose, revealing the sweep of her waist and hips.

Had he heard her correctly? He stood, transfixed.

"Stay with me, Émile?"

Only then did he press his lips to the back of her neck, exactly where it became her shoulder.

A great rush of heat engulfed him. Slowly, he eased the dress down, then turned her towards him, and—at last—a real kiss.

Chapter 21

Morning in the hotel with Émile was luxurious, a tangle of limbs in a tumble of bed clothes, and no need to rush. Bits of their clothing were draped all over the tiny room.

As Émile slept again, Cynthia traced the scar on his cheek with her finger. She resisted the urge to kiss him. Why wake him too soon? This opportunity to study his eyelashes and the way his dark hair swept across his brow was precious. His shoulder and collar bone, the texture of his skin—all were usually hidden. Émile was a Greek or Roman statue, draped with the hotel linen, except he was French.

She smiled as she mused on their night together—the otherworldliness of the party, the power of Angelica's personality and her incredible chateau; and the eruption of jealousy that told her with certainty she was serious about this man. Émile's loyal friend Roddy; the bliss of moving to the music with Émile for hours, dance after dance; and their time in the chapel, where Émile had retreated deep into his own thoughts.

She'd tried to reach him there, but then the storm struck. What secrets troubled Émile? He was so kind, so adept, and yet there was a sadness there, some streak of doubt etched deep into the lines at the corners of his eyes.

No one aged without some worries, but troubles shared were troubles halved weren't they? He'd assisted her so much, in every way. Until that flash of lightning in the chapel, illuminating Émile's anguish, Cynthia had thought only of her own needs. Only then had she become aware of Émile's. For the first time she genuinely cared for him. Was there some way she could help him in return?

Yet every time she asked him about his past, he ducked and wove and changed the subject. That was fine. She didn't need to pry, but surely as their friendship grew, he'd relax with her, and trust her not to hurt him; instead perhaps to help him.

He'd been so quiet in the chapel, before the storm. Maybe that was common. Many French people were deeply religious. Or was it to do with the accident? Had it triggered difficult memories?

In the flashes of lightning, she was sure she'd seen the shine of tears, yet he'd remained so silent. Fortress Émile.

And now. Was it fair to observe someone as they slept, defenceless? Yes. With love. After Jimmy, she never thought she'd care for anyone. In sickness and in health, alright. Émile wasn't sick, was he? Was that the secret he was guarding? That wouldn't frighten her. In fact, she was better qualified than most women to stand by him until the end, if that was his problem.

Did he think her too weak to deal with such things, that she only cared for the good times? People often made that mistake about women, but most were stronger than men. Stronger in childbirth; then steady, the glue in their families, able to take on any worthwhile tasks they chose. Well, it helped to hire people who knew what they were doing. Angelica was onto something there, and Émile was clearly a treasure if you were renovating anything, but without Émile in her life, she'd simply hire any help she needed.

With certainty, Cynthia knew she wanted more than a handyman. She wanted company—Émile's company—every day and every night.

She wondered again at his past as she gently brushed a stray lock of hair from his forehead with one finger. His dark eyelashes fluttered and his eyes focused on hers. She smiled and he caught her finger between his teeth. She snuggled in close, safe and cherished in the circle of his arms, and they made love again, Émile so tender she laughed and cried. Afterwards, they fell asleep, wrapped in each other's arms.

Émile was up and dressed and packed when she awoke again. She sat up groggily as he entered the doorway, balancing a tray of coffee and croissants.

"Room service!" she laughed. "Is there nothing you can't do?"

"They were about to close the breakfast bar. Sorry if I disturbed you."

"Disturb me," she said, lying back, arms open, her whole body an invitation to him.

"Really?"

He left the tray on the tiny desk and sat on the edge of the bed until she pulled him back towards her.

Later, their coffee was cold, but she munched on a corner of a croissant.

"Can we stay another few days, Émile?" she said. "I'm loving this, loving being with you. It's like a honeymoon. Let's go visit some chateaux. When did you last have a holiday? Can we keep this room? Will we move your things in here with me?"

He'd been peeping out between the curtains. When he turned, his face was dark, troubled. Why?

"But I must go away, Cynthia."

"Well, that's alright. As long as you promise to come back to me." Lying on her side, resting on her elbow, languid, she teased him.

"'Promise to come back to you.' Do you mean this?" Émile snapped to attention, alert, then paced and turned and confronted her.

She sat up and stared back, equally serious.

"Yes. Exactly that," she said. "Promise to come back to me."

"This is why I must go away."

"You are really not making sense, Émile."

He turned away again and paced. He ran his fingers through his hair. Again he turned and stared, as if she were a wall that required repairing, as if she'd offended him, as if she were trifling with him. Had he lost respect for her? Had she ruined their friendship by taking it to the next level? Surely he'd been a willing participant. Yet he was so serious.

"You know nothing about me," he said. "Yet you say you want to be with me. What if it is only the idea of me you like; not the real me."

Cynthia furrowed her brow. Her conversation with Kath about French philosophers came to mind, but she banished it, to better focus on Émile. She took a deep breath.

"Okay, Émile." She swung her legs off the side of the bed to face him, the sheet across her torso. "The only reason I know nothing about you is because you keep dodging questions about your past. Is there something I should know about you? Are you a convicted criminal, hiding from the law? Are you an axe murderer? You're a complete mystery, Émile. You've told me almost nothing about your life. And what on earth is Ommegang?"

He'd gone silent on her again, striding to the French doors and opening them to the street, as if he wanted to fly away from all her questions.

When he turned back to her, he was angry. It was the first time she'd seen him like this. Had she touched a nerve? She'd asked lightly, with humor, but the truth was she really did want to find out more about this mysterious Émile. She was falling in love with him, she knew. No man had come so close to her but Jimmy, emotionally or physically. She had no idea what the future might bring, and she didn't regret their night together. She wanted more nights together. She and Émile knew how to be happy.

197

"Émile? Have I asked too much? Is it unreasonable to ask you to tell me about your past?"

…

They'd been doing so well. Cynthia's company was a joy. She made him laugh. He loved to be with her. She respected him and clearly enjoyed his skills and his presence. That they made love so well made his heart soar and his whole body sing.

He longed to go to her, to kiss away her questions and make love to her again. Why did she have to talk, to force him to dredge up the painful past?

If she wanted to go there, he'd take her, but first, he had to go there himself, and confront it fully—his unfinished business.

"I must pack," he said, more abruptly than he'd intended.

She flinched. He hadn't meant to sound so gruff. He didn't do casual sex. He cared about Cynthia and had no wish to hurt her. But sightseeing with her today would not be possible; not while she was asking about his past like this. The trouble was, she was right to ask. His past was a problem—unresolved. How could he move forwards with Cynthia, with his past still such an open wound?

"Alright then," she said, suddenly prim and businesslike. Ten minutes earlier, she might have thrown a pillow at him and they could have made love again, but now? It was as if an invisible barrier had risen between them, a sheet of cold glass. Behind it, on different sides, they were polite strangers.

"You go," she said. "Go then, and do whatever it is you have to do." She grabbed her nightgown and stood behind it, dignified, then dashed to the bathroom. She put her head around the door.

"I will stay here and explore the sights by myself, Émile. I will pay our hotel bills, and I will travel back by train or bus. I'm fully accustomed to being on my own. I managed perfectly well before I met you, Émile, and I'll do it again."

"I did not mean to offend you …" Her tone was so prim. Had he done this to her, with his ill-chosen words and his worries? Now more than ever, he was determined to solve his past, so that they need never have this confrontation again.

"Thank you for a fine weekend," she said, all firm politeness, the barricade of her expression formidable as the solid door. "You're free to go, Émile. You owe me nothing. I'm sorry if I hurt you in some way."

It was clear he was being dismissed. Had he blown it?

"You do not understand…" He tried again to bridge the aching gap between them, all the deeper for the fact they'd just been as close as it was possible to be.

"Oh. You're quite right about that," she said, her tone brisk. "There's plenty I don't understand about you, Émile. Forgive me for trying to find out more, to alleviate my ignorance, for trying to get to know you a little better, to discover more about the man behind the handyman."

He moved towards her, trying to appease her, trying to recover their easy way of being together, to reconnect. He reached a hand out to stroke her shoulder behind the door but she shrank behind it; now only her chin and eyes and forehead on show. And her lips. He stooped as if to kiss her goodbye.

"No. Not now. Thank you. Go. You may go now. Leave me. Leave me alone."

So, Cynthia had pushed him away. And so she should. Why hadn't he finalized matters sooner? As urgency gripped him, he left her room, packed his bag and returned to knock on her door.

No one answered. So. She was either avoiding him, or she'd already left for her day of sightseeing, without him.

Regret squeezed his heart. He'd far prefer to stay with her, to defer the matters he'd been avoiding, not to mention all his work commitments. He'd love nothing more than to have a holiday, to accompany her to all the castles of the Loire Valley. But that was not the honorable path.

He tried her phone, but she didn't answer.

Would her anger dissipate? Should he wait for her return this evening, and ask to accompany her again?

The truth was, he wasn't yet willing to tell her about his past, because it wasn't totally in the past. Not yet. It was suddenly urgent he relinquish every hold Bertha had ever had over him. Only when he'd cleared up his past could he be truly free to claim the future.

Life was so much more than making a living. It was about belonging, and sharing things with those you loved. As he knocked again on Cynthia's hotel room door, he closed his eyes and let himself remember Cynthia's body so close to his, the deliciousness of her in his arms as they danced at the ball, and later, in bed, as they'd made love.

Émile wanted to be with Cynthia every day and every night—to repair her home with her and share her life. And if she was open to the same idea, if she'd ever give him that chance—that was a future worth fighting for.

But none of that was possible without a clean break with his past. It was time to complete the process he'd begun when he'd headed south nearly eighteen months ago. It was time to free himself from Bertha for good. Only then might he approach Cynthia with open arms, an open heart and an open future, and find out if she would have him.

He took the hired car north on the fastest freeways, speeding past towns and districts he'd spent weeks and months in, making his living, forming new bonds with other builders, going about his work as generations of his family had done; while burying his feelings about his life and his wife far, far from reach, so far behind him that he'd never needed to confront them—until Cynthia had turned up, so likable, alluring, captivating—until she'd started probing.

He wasn't angry with Cynthia. She'd been right to ask. The problem was, he was ashamed.

Three hours later he was on the outskirts of Paris—the city of love—but he skirted it and headed further north, back to the centre of all his failures.

Chapter 22

Cynthia went through the motions. She phoned Will, who promised he'd keep feeding Minette. She booked another two nights at the hotel, then took a trip on a tourist bus to visit the great chateaux of the Loire Valley—Chambord, Chenonceau, Cheverny and Amboise. She viewed tapestries and gilding, chandeliers and marble, turrets and tiling, four poster beds and fountains.

She picked up plenty of decoration tips for her French property. Would she add trim and panelling? Should she apply some gilded plaster to the ceiling of the front room, and a rosette ceiling mounting to the chandelier?

She refused to think about Émile and their row. Each time his face came to mind—his hurt reaction to her dismissal of him—a flash of anger flared in her and she pushed her chin up and her shoulders back.

She would have loved to have shared her reactions to all she was exploring with Émile, but he'd insisted on disappearing, so instead she shared them with fellow tourists. No matter that most were in pairs—the honeymooners inseparable—and most spoke other languages. A smile or two and nod of agreement from strangers had to suffice.

She found a small supermarket in Angers and bought cheese and bread, a punnet of strawberries and a small bottle of champagne. She picnicked on her balcony each evening, alone, and told herself she was content.

"Let him go," she said to the intersection, holding up her full glass, offering "cheers" to the view. From here she witnessed snippets of the lives of the neighbours, a blind drawn or a coffee cup left on a shelf by the window. Was she lonely? Did she long for a face to come to a window and give her a wave? Down on the street, everyone was going about their lives.

Leaves on trees in the distance were turning gold. Was autumn almost upon them? What would her new home be like in this cooler season? In winter? Was she ready to shiver? Should she fly home to Australia, to bake in the summer heat? That was ridiculous. She was overacting. The presence or loss of Émile in her life— one moody and mysterious Frenchman—was neither here nor there.

In fact, she should call Nathan Carmichael. The internet reported he was guest lecturing in architecture in Washington, London and Sydney. He looked exceptionally well. Those glasses suited him. She flicked through his achievements and credentials. There he was in Spain with a purple pair, in Venezuela in an orange pair, and on the contact page in cream ones. There was an email address. Her finger hovered over the button.

"Just saying 'hi,'" she keyed in.

Her phone rang moments later.

"Cynthia! Marvelous to hear from you. I'm in Tokyo."

"That sounds interesting."

"Oh, it is. Are you still in France?"

"Yes. I've been to a ball in a chateau. And I've just decided to go to Paris." Had she?

"Ah. Paris. I was there in April. I delivered the keynote for the European Awards. One never tires of Paris."

"Never."

"Must go. Great to chat. See you next time I'm in the south of France."

The chateau tour business offered two-day trips to Paris. She booked, finally ready to revisit the past.

The coach traversed the distances, and from her seat high above the traffic she enjoyed excellent views of the French countryside. As yet another enchanting chateau and village and church steeple flashed by, Cynthia remembered her first and only other trip to Paris.

Chapter 23

1986

Rain thundered down outside Huntleys. For the third time, Cynthia mopped up the water in the entrance foyer and around customers' umbrellas.

A week after the date with Jimmy, Cynthia conceded he was right about the weather in Paris. She didn't even own a proper coat. A few more months of work would hardly go astray as she set out into the world.

Eleanor's Asscher-cut diamond in Jim's special setting was a beacon on the dark day, a spotlight. The customer in the trench coat thought so, too.

As Cynthia re-entered the showroom, their conversation was clear.

"It's on the front of your catalogue, here," he said, pulling the folded flyer, slightly soggy, out of his pocket and pointing at the ring.

"Yes, but these things don't come out of thin air, sir, and this particular one is not for sale," Eleanor said. "However, Jim, the goldsmith, would be delighted to speak with you about your needs."

"I need this one," he said. "And I need it now. Not in two months."

"The rings inside the catalogue show prices. This one, sir, does not."

"'Priceless,' eh? Everything has its price. What do you want? That one's three thousand. I'll give you four. Five. Five thousand dollars."

"Sir, my husband gave me this for our anniversary."

"And now I need it. Six thousand."

Behind the customer, Cynthia gestured at the intercom and pointed up. Should she summon Jim?

Eleanor shook her head, but beckoned her across.

"Have you met Cynthia, sir? Cynthia models our rings. I'm sure she'd be glad to show you some more. While we don't have another Asscher at the moment, we do have other rare cuts—a very large pear, for example. Cynthia, please prepare the VIP room for this customer. Ask Jim to bring out the special ones."

Cynthia ran to the top of the building, switched on the lights to the VIP room, noticed a leak running down the inside of one of the windows and hastily mopped it with a towel from the bathroom.

Then she ran up the spiral staircase at the back of the building, her heart pounding. She hesitated as she went to knock on the door. Jim hated to be interrupted. With so many orders, he worked from dawn to dusk, but Eleanor had told her to do it. She wrapped her knuckles on the dark old wood.

A sulphur smell greeted her as she entered the strange circular room. Jim was at the centre of his curved bench, surrounded by tiny files and pliers of every size and shape, and blowing on the flame of the blowtorch. The tongue of fire shrank as he looked up and pushed up his eye protection.

"Yes? What can be so important?"

"Sorry, sir. Mrs Huntley has a very keen customer. She's asked if you could please bring the 'special selection' to the VIP room."

Jim twisted a couple of knobs, hung the torch on its bracket, sprang from his stool, removed his apron and pulled a key from his pocket.

"I'll see you in there," he said.

So, he didn't trust her enough to let her know where he kept his "specials." That was alright. Cynthia didn't take it personally.

She hovered near the door to the VIP room, then moved to the lift, ready to greet Eleanor and the customer as the doors opened, but had to dash into the tearoom where the new intercom was ringing. Cynthia lifted it.

"It's okay. He's gone."

Cynthia rushed back to the VIP room where Jim was waiting with the case on the circular marble table.

"I'm sorry, sir. Eleanor says the customer has already left after all."

Jim sighed deeply, nodded, picked up the case and returned to his lair, leaving her to turn off the light in the VIP room and close the door. The room smelled damp. Was the whole building leaking? Was that why Jim was so remote? Was Huntleys less prosperous than it appeared?

Downstairs, Eleanor was her usual bright self, bustling about. Was it a forced cheeriness? She was no longer wearing her special ring. Cynthia was going to ask, but bit her tongue.

Jimmy asked her on other dates, to two old French movies at an art house cinema in Paddington, *Monsieur Hulot's Holiday*, and *Mon Oncle*, and they laughed and kissed in the dark, his arm around her as if it belonged there.

After another date, to a French crepe restaurant in Mosman, he caught the train with her all the way to Woy Woy, where her mother insisted he stay the night and have Sunday lunch with them. She made up a bed for him on the front veranda.

She baked him a pavlova for dessert the next day.

"Lovely manners," she said, when he thanked her and asked for a second helping. She nodded at Cynthia. Cynthia hadn't told her about the proposal. It was a warm secret she held close, warmer than the way Jimmy held her hand deep in his coat pocket on cold days.

When he took her to his own home the following weekend, Jim and Eleanor barely waved. They were watching television with dinner on trays on their laps. In the flickering blue light, Cynthia could just make out their furniture, big old brown pieces she liked. Beyond them, the lights of the harbour were mesmerizing. Jimmy linked his fingers with hers and tugged on her arm. He led her down the stairs to his room under the house, with its own tiny kitchen and bathroom.

Later that next week, despite the rain, Jimmy asked her on another date, to a surprise destination.

At the end of the block, an orange car waited, its headlights making scintillating beams through the rain. The engine idled roughly. Jimmy opened the passenger side door for her, and Cynthia slid onto the bench seat amid a smell of oil and deodorant, glad to escape the rain. The man at the wheel sprung out, but not before introducing himself.

"Hi," he said. "I'm Scottie, Jimmy's mate. Gotta run."

"Thanks, Scottie!" said Jim, revving the throaty engine a couple of times. "Great mate from school. Like our car? We've been doing it up."

So this was the source of the oil on Jimmy's fingers his father had complained about; Jimmy's weekend project, the mighty old Ford, his pride and joy.

Jimmy patted the wheel, wrestled the gear stick into first and jerked away from the kerb.

His patter didn't mean a lot to Cynthia, but his enthusiasm was infectious.

"It's the 1971 model, the Ford XY Falcon GT-HO Phase III, fantastic on the open road," he said, changing gears up and down in stop start rush hour traffic. "Scottie's father found her. One of his clients had to sell. This is the 351 Cleveland V8, up to 380bhp."

Despite the car's obvious power, Jimmy was a careful driver, though when they reached their destination, there wasn't much to see.

"Sorry about the rain," he said. "And the dark. It's La Perouse, the most French place I could find in Sydney. Scottie packed our picnic. I hope he got everything on the list. Back in a sec."

Jimmy dashed out to open and close the back of the car, and brought back a box. He drew out each item.

"Veuve Cliquot," he said, flicking the light on top of the cabin interior so she could study the orange label.

"*Méthode traditionnelle*," she said.

"Even I understand that," said Jimmy, as he pulled out camembert cheese and crackers. "Translate the back while I fish out the glasses. No. Looks like Scottie forgot them. Oh well. Let's share a mug."

Delighted, Cynthia read out details, then turned off the light. As their eyes adjusted to the darkness she saw silhouettes of trees beyond the raindrops rolling down the windows.

"What are we celebrating?" she asked as he called out "cheers" and held the mug to her lips.

"Oh, I almost forgot!" he said. He handed the mug to Cynthia and felt in his trouser pocket. "It wasn't going to be like this. I was going to walk you along the beach and ask you under the moon and stars, but I can't wait any longer. Will you marry me, Cynthia?"

He handed across a Huntleys ring box, its gold HHJ lettering glinting in the dark.

The ring picked up the light of a couple of streetlamps, and sparked out five flashes of light as she turned the box in the dark interior.

"Oh Jimmy," she said. "The marquises."

Jim and Eleanor would know about this. This was serious. Speechless, Cynthia sought Jimmy's eyes. She let him take the ring and place it on her finger. She turned her hand in the faint light and let it sparkle as he squeezed her other hand. His touch was warm and delicious. Her heart raced. So, this was love.

"There's more," he said. "I've been dying to tell you. They've agreed. I can take you to Paris for our honeymoon, and we'll come home via Antwerp. We'll go to the diamond markets. We'll be able to pay our way with the savings we'll make."

His kiss tasted of French champagne.

Their wedding was a small affair, held on the lawns of the Huntleys' Point Piper home Eleanor inherited from her parents. Jimmy was born there, and Cynthia and Jimmy were going to renovate and redecorate a floor of it for themselves when they returned from Europe.

Three weeks later they were on a plane to Paris.

The city of light was everything Cynthia dreamed it would be. Emerging at Charles de Gaul, she and Jimmy took a taxi to their tiny old hotel, dumped their bags and walked for hours as the sun slowly set through a tangerine haze, reflecting off domes and steeples and apartment buildings ornate as wedding cakes. The Eiffel Tour, the bridges, the Seine, Notre Dame, the Arc de Triomphe, the Sorbonne— familiar as old friends, yet thrilling in their novelty. They attended a baroque concert in Sainte Chapelle on the Île de la Cité that evening, surrounded by ancient stained glass set in stone.

"We're inside a jewel," Cynthia whispered to Jimmy. Enchanted, they emerged hand in hand and ate coffee-flavored gelato to stay awake, lovers in a city of lovers, in love with life.

Cynthia's French was serviceable, though the slang and speed surprised her. Discovering the city day and night with Jimmy and exploring each other's bodies in their tiny ornate room—she'd never wanted it to end.

Chapter 24

2018

Cynthia alighted from the coach. The centre of Paris hadn't changed. The glass pyramid under construction on top of the entry to the Louvre when she'd been there with Jimmy was now complete.

There were more people, and the fashions were different—hair less bouffant, more sleek, and no outrageous shoulder pads—but Cynthia easily found the coffee shops where she and Jimmy had sat and held hands, and restored their energy after hours of making love.

Returning to the Luxembourg gardens made her heart ache for him so much she sat and wept for the loss of him. She lifted her head. Three well-dressed children raced model sailing boats on the pond. How similar they were to their own children, James and Nicole and Will, now all grown.

One child clambered in to push his boat faster. That would be Will. She laughed and dried her eyes and wandered on. She bought a warmer coat for the approaching winter. Here in Paris it was already cold. Would Provence also make her shiver?

Memories of Jimmy kept flooding back. Would she ever be able to walk across the Pont Neuf without remembering him? No, but that was good. It made her smile, as if he were still with her, tucking her hand inside his coat pocket to keep it warm. She smiled in the mild afternoon and walked on. It was impossible not to notice couples staring into each other's eyes. Paris pulsed with romance.

Eyes were on her, too. The French knew how to walk and admire each other. A walk was so much more than a way to rush from A to B. It was public, a performance. They even had a name for someone walking in Paris. She was a *flaneur*, enjoying the sights. She didn't need a partner. She adjusted her scarf and set off again.

In the distance, a man in a dark coat approached and her heart quickened. Was it Émile? He was making eyes at her. Was it the cut of her new coat? She stopped to window-shop, hoping for a closer peek without him noticing. She slipped on her glasses but by now it was clear he was a complete stranger. He showed interest in her, but she turned away and pretended to check her phone.

Further along, she thought she saw Émile again, this time at the back of a bookshop, but when she entered it was someone else, and she left immediately.

She lifted her chin. She didn't need Émile's company in Paris. She was a strong, independent woman.

A shoulder bag in a window display caught her attention; sleek and black, with a sensible strap and a beautiful buckle. Nicole was always complaining she couldn't find a bag large enough to hold both her laptop and her lunch. Cynthia entered and explored the whole range, but ended up buying the initial one. Dear Nicole. Her own sense of fashion had somehow bypassed her daughter. She'd post this gift to her as soon as possible.

Maybe one day the two of them would wander together through Paris and she'd help her select some new outfits. She messaged Nicole an invitation, with a photo of the corner of the Boulevard Saint-Germain and three stylish dress shops in a row, with a shoe shop on the corner she really should examine. Shopping in Paris was a joy.

Later, from the post office, where she'd overheard some Aussies discussing the Jardin des Plantes, she made her way there. To go somewhere new was only sensible. One could spend a lifetime in Paris and never see all its treasures. Paris held her past, and it did—all those memories of Jimmy and her younger self—but it also held the present. She was glad to be here again, wasn't she?

The rambling gardens were so much wilder than the Luxembourg ones, she immediately felt at home. The wandering paths, edged with a range of plants which sprang up of their own accord—they reminded her of wilderness, of abundance, of the fertility of the planet beyond mankind's imaginings.

She longed to discuss her thoughts. Jimmy had been right beside her as they'd discovered Paris together, and they'd chattered nonstop. Now she was alone. Silent.

Oh, where was Émile when she needed him? She reached for her phone, but remembered his expression as he'd extricated himself from Angelica's arms around his neck in the middle of her dance floor. He didn't like to be crowded. If he wanted her—Cynthia—he'd come back to her. Wouldn't he? Oh, people were far too complicated. Their love making had been a total mistake. Try to tell that to her body, awakened again after all these years and hungry Émile attentions.

She shook her head and wandered on, admiring the sculptures and reading the plaques on the bases of the giant trees. There was so much history here no one could hope to absorb it all.

As she rounded a corner she came face to face with a great stand of sunflowers, their joyous mix of yellows and golds so extraordinary they took away her breath.

Perhaps she should return to her home in Provence tomorrow. She longed to see her own sunflowers, and little Minette.

She wandered on. As night fell and the lights reflected in the river, their beauty haunted her. She wanted to point them out to someone. Jimmy was gone; and Émile was … who knew where; immersed in his own mysterious life.

She pushed her cold hands into her own pockets and walked on, determined to enjoy her evening no matter what. She and Jimmy had caught the metro everywhere to save money, but now she needed to stay on the surface, not to miss one glimpse of this magical city.

She pulled her scarf up high around her collar and selected a restaurant beside the river. She ordered a cold white wine and a bouillabaisse in perfect French and watched the *bateaux mouches* slide up and down the river, with their commentaries in every language. The sweet wine and rich aroma of the soup mollified her.

The waiter was efficient and she was glad she came across as French, perhaps for the first time. She wanted to talk to someone, but the waiter was too busy to chat. If Émile were with her, he might have shared the history of the soup, and some stories about the river and Notre Dame. They might have held hands under the table like the older couple in the corner. Not that she missed him. Not at all.

She phoned Will but there was no answer, so she phoned Kath.

"Cynthia! Aren't you in France?"

"I am. In Paris!"

"Wonderful. And is it everything you dreamed it would be?" Was she being cynical or sincere?

"Of course. I love it."

"Is anything wrong, Cynthia?"

"No. I was just thinking of you. How's the downsizing going?"

"Driving me crazy. It's hot over here, and there's stuff jammed everywhere, in the roof, at the top of cupboards. I can't believe how much junk we've accumulated. What temperature is it in Paris?"

"Cooling off. Not as cold as when Jimmy and I were here, but I had to buy a coat."

"Did Nathan ever get in touch?"

"He did! We had lunch in the village."

"And?"

"Oh, you know Nathan. He's more in love with his itinerary than ever, though he did give me a pair of his famous round reading glasses."

"I thought you and he …"

"Nathan has a very full life, Kath. He's in Tokyo now."

"And you're 'not interested,' I know. You think I don't listen to you, but I actually don't want you to be lonely for the rest of your life. So how is Paris, really?"

A few seconds passed. Another boat glided past, lighting up the nearby bridges and ornate tops of the buildings, commentary blaring. It gave Cynthia a moment or two to frame her next sentence. She *was* lonely. Suddenly. But not for Nathan. Only for Émile.

"I met someone, Kath."

"That's exciting, Cynthia. Tell me."

"Oh, but we're not seeing each other. Well maybe we are, but he's not here. We had a kind of a row, and now he's disappeared. We get on so well. Really. I really enjoy his company. In every way.

"In 'every' way, Cynthia! But that's marvellous. That's special. Does this 'someone' have a name?"

"Émile." Just saying his name made Cynthia grip the edge of the table. The romance of the chateaux, her revelation in the chapel that she could make him happy, and the pleasure of their passion that night … She wanted him right there beside her now. What a shame her wine bottle didn't have a genie inside it. She'd ask it to make him materialise, warm and welcome. How much wine had she had? What was this new clamouring inside her, this hunger for Émile?

"But that's perfect! Come on, tell me everything."

"He's a handyman and a locksmith and he's very generous. He has many skills."

Kath's deep laugh carried a hint or two and Cynthia cheered up. The waiter refilled Cynthia's glass, and she told her friend all about the chandelier and the kitten and the beds and the coffee machine and the ball at the chateau, and how well Émile danced, and how he'd gone very quiet in the chapel. She sipped more wine, avoiding sharing the most delicious intimate moments, then skipped to their morning argument.

"Was it an argument or a misunderstanding?"

"I hope it was just a misunderstanding."

"About …"

"He's always been a bit mysterious, which worries me. I know almost nothing about his past, and the morning after … Well, after the ball, he told me he had to go away. He said he had 'unfinished business' but he didn't share any details. He hasn't told me anything about his past life, beyond about eighteen months ago. Oh, he's told me he's from this something or other St John and that his family goes back six hundred years or so. Fourteen hundreds and the French Revolution? Fine. But try to ask him anything about more than a year or so ago, and zilch."

"Is he married?"

"I didn't ask. But he almost had a fling with the woman who owns the chateau, but he didn't."

"Maybe that's a clue. Maybe he's commitment phobic."

"Why didn't he just tell me he's not looking for a long-term relationship then? Why did he sleep with me if it doesn't actually mean anything to him?"

"Cynthia, I hear your pain. You know why men do that."

"But …"

"I don't suppose you could just pick up the phone and ask him, could you? You're always so together on the outside. If you spent half the time on your inner life as you spent on your appearance and decorating home interiors, you wouldn't need to ask me if you like this guy. Don't get me wrong. I love you exactly the way you are, but I really can't make this decision for you."

"I don't want to go begging him for information. Men hate needy women, don't they? Nicole's always talking about it. And Angelica, who owns the chateau, was all over him, and he resisted her. If he doesn't find me irresistible, then I don't want him at all. I wasn't looking for that kind of relationship anyway. No one can replace Jimmy in my heart. Émile was supposed to be a friend."

"You really like this Émile, don't you?

"I guess I could phone him. But then, he could phone me, too, don't you think?"

Cynthia asked Kath more about her own life, about her work and the children and the small apartment she and her husband bought, a world away from Paris. Kath raved about her new lifestyle; how she could play golf and tennis all day if she wanted, without having to worry about any housework; how she and Bob caught ferries everywhere and went to shows and had dinner outside in the balmy evenings, and how beautiful the city was at night, with all the lights reflected in the harbor.

Cynthia was pleased for her, but did it make her want to return to Australia? Not really. Not yet.

Chapter 25

It was dusk by the time Cynthia made it back to Provence the next day, foot weary and dragging her wheelie bag. She'd expected her heart to lift at the sight of her new home. But as she reached her corner, instead of the row of golden blooms she'd anticipated, her cherished sunflowers drooped their heads. Summer had ended, and, sadly, the blooms she'd loved had died along with the long days of light and warmth.

Normally she'd have cheered herself up by imagining what to plant in their place, but this evening, her spirits were low. Maybe she just needed to eat something. She felt for her key in her coat pocket, the clover-shaped key she'd fallen in love with, and stared at it glumly. That was her problem, she surmised. She placed too much importance on things, and not enough on her friends and family. Was that true?

What was true was that she missed Émile. Why hadn't he phoned her?

Inside, Minette did not rush to greet her. She treated Cynthia's return with disdain, placing one rear foot in the air and licking it, then disappearing towards the kitchen.

"Come on, Minette! Okay, I abandoned you for a few days, but I'm sure you're well fed. There are plenty of crunchies in your bowl. Am I really so bad?"

Will, of course, was nowhere to be found. He'd left no note.

The house was cold. The front room as night fell was eerie, the chandelier glittering like icicles. What was she doing here, so far from her Australian family and friends? Was her French property simply another expensive folly, like her Southern Highlands home? What kind of fool was Cynthia Huntley?

She walked through the house, stared at the jumble of furniture in the back rooms and shook her head. She'd gone wild at the markets. James was right to remind her not to spend too much. She really should stop wasting money. She sighed. At least she'd only bought the coat and bag in Paris. Could any other tourist who'd been in Paris say the same?

As she wandered among her market finds and thought again about how to place them to best advantage in each room, the loneliness stalked her. What was that saying from the Bible? "Do not lay up for yourselves treasures on earth, where moth and rust destroy and where thieves break in and steal, but lay up for yourselves treasures in heaven, where neither moth nor rust destroys and where thieves do not break in and steal. For where your treasure is, there your heart will be also."

Where was her heart? When it beat for Émile, and it did, did that mean he was the true treasure?

She peered into a cupboard and the empty fridge. How long had she been living on her own? Long enough to understand that if she chose to live alone, making her own meals was her own responsibility. She should have thought to stop at a restaurant or supermarket, but now she was too tired to step out again. She found an egg in the door of the fridge. A boiled egg would have to be enough.

She carried her suitcase upstairs and began to unpack. She pulled out the carry bag for the gown and unzipped it. The soft silk brushed her fingers and wrists as she took it from the bag, and she buried her face in the folds, inhaling, remembering.

Already the ball at the chateau had taken on mythic qualities, with its dramatic setting, Roddy and Angelica larger than life, and Émile so chivalrous at her side, so attractive and attentive, the ideal companion, and afterwards, the perfect lover.

She remembered his strange behaviour in the chapel, and the storm; a portent of their argument and separation.

She hung up her gown, the beauty of the lustre of its silken folds now bitter sweet. Why did she waste so much money on it? What a folly. Who was she to tell Will what to do with money? Still, perhaps she'd wear it again. At least it had been ideal for the occasion.

She sighed, remembering how Émile had swept her into his arms to save it from the mud—so caring, so considerate. So what? The very next morning, after their night together, he'd turned tail on her and run away. Did he not cherish their love making as she did? Did their intimacy mean nothing to Émile? He was French after all. Maybe that was what all Frenchmen did—made love then disappeared, as casually as finishing a cup of coffee.

She turned from the gown, hands on her hips. What now?

There was still no sign of the bangle on her dressing table. Perhaps Minette batted it off the edge and it rolled under the bed, but she searched everywhere, to no avail.

She shivered. The temperature kept plummeting. It wasn't just Paris that was cold at this time of year.

Downstairs, Minette showed more interest, wending her way around Cynthia's ankles, and she swept her into her arms and sank her fingers into the soft fur of her tummy until she purred loudly. She pushed her face into her softness and smiled. Who needed a man's kisses when you had a cat? She suppressed the reality that Émile had given her Minette. Who cared?

That there was no sign of Will didn't surprise her. He lived his own life.

She boiled the water and placed the smooth egg into its turmoil of splashing steam, snapping her fingers away from the heat. She mused at her half-stocked kitchen. It was all very well buying silver napkin rings, but she could do with a slotted spoon. Fortunately the local markets were on again next day. Stocking her home with small things would surely be alright. If she listed the place on AirBnB, the tenants would need these things. She could fly back to Australia tomorrow, if she wished, but wasn't she still living the dream?

A phone call from James cheered her up.

"James, darling."

"Mum, how are you?"

"I've been in the Loire Valley. It's more beautiful than you can imagine; all those chateaux. No wonder it's such a popular honeymoon destination. And I've been in Paris."

"Great. Good to hear. Listen, have you heard from Will?"

"He looked after Minette while I was away, but he wasn't here when I got back, and he's not here now. Why?"

"I don't want to worry you, Mum, but his expenses are more random than ever, and as usual, he's not answering his phone. Apart from the fact it's completely selfish and impacts on the health of our business, I'm seriously worried about him. It's getting worse. Is he on drugs? What's going on?"

"To be honest, James, I'm also worried about Will, but you remember how hard he is to contact. I'll try. I promise. I'll be back in touch if I have any luck. Thank you for everything you do. Is everything else okay? How are you?"

"I'm fine, thank you, Mum. Things could be better with the business, as you know. Profits are never high enough, and there's more competition than ever, but I'm hopeful. We're trying some fresh ideas and Jim's podcast is developing a following. Nicole's on top of all that."

223

"That's exciting, James. It's always been the way. Business is always changing. You've got to keep working hard at it all and trying new things. As for Will, I'll try to find him. I'll try him right now."

Cynthia left fresh messages for Will: "Thank you for looking after Minette."

"When will we see you again?"

"Are you still in France?"

Nothing.

As she ate her egg, she wondered what Émile was having for dinner, and was tempted to send him a message, too, but she'd heard nothing from him, and perhaps she never would. Hadn't she dubbed him a rolling stone? Perhaps he'd rolled right on back to Angelica after all.

Next day, restocking food supplies, she ran into old Jacques at the *boulangerie*. He gave her a friendly nod and they swapped standard greetings.

"*Ça va?*"

"*Bah oui, eh vous?*"

"*Très bien, merci.*"

She shivered as she made her way home, and wished she'd thought to pack more of her warmer clothes when she'd first set out. The days were becoming shorter, and the nights increasingly cold. She loved the changing golds and oranges and reds of the leaves of the trees in the village, the smell of firewood on the breeze, the different calls of birds, but how she missed the warmth of the summer!

By day, the sunlight flooded in through her south facing windows, but all her windows needed repairs—the cold wind was like icy fingers down her neck—and she'd no idea how the heating system worked. She'd just decided to contact the real estate agent from whom she'd bought the place when she ran into Jacques again in the town square. Both hunched in their coats.

"I don't suppose you know of any other handymen?" she said.

"Ah, Émile. He is still in Belgium?"

"Belgium?"

"*Mais oui. Il est belge, n'est-ce pas?*"

Belgian? She obviously didn't know the first thing about Émile. She smiled and nodded at Jacques to hide her shock. So! So much for Émile being her "fabulous French lover." He wasn't even French. She tucked her baguette under her arm again and headed back to her house, crushing the autumn leaves in her path.

"Belgium. 1986. Disaster," she told Minette, pacing her front room. "So, Émile is Belgian! What a liar!"

Belgium. The name of the place catapulted her right back to her time with Jimmy in Paris. Afterwards, they'd travelled to Belgium, to buy diamonds at the diamond markets of Antwerp, a disaster of a trip that only caused problems for the whole family.

Chapter 26

1986

High on each other's company and their carefree honeymoon days and nights wandering through Paris and making love around the clock, Jimmy and Cynthia had phoned home.

Eleanor, overjoyed to hear from them, was quick to explain she'd already begun the renovation of their section of the house. She said she was pleased for them and looked forward to their return. Jim kept his comments short, grunting about being short staffed.

On the train to Antwerp, they picnicked on cheese and biscuits, then they dozed and stared out the window, Cynthia's head nestled on Jimmy's shoulder, their arms and fingers intertwined. Fields of tulips sped by, the landscape so flat Cynthia imagined they were traversing the pages of a book.

Antwerp station was lofty, a great dome built at the turn of the previous century.

"I need to find a ladies' room," she told Jimmy.

He was waiting for her as she emerged.

"Sorry. Jimmy, I'm feeling weird. Maybe I ate too much cheese. Do you think it could be food poisoning?"

Jimmy navigated them to their hotel, even smaller than their Parisian one, not that Cynthia expected anything grand. The trouble was, it seemed to have been partitioned off from a larger room, with a thin panel, and noisy neighbors next door.

"I'm still off color, Jimmy. Maybe you go and find where you need to be tomorrow. I'll stay and rest."

Rest was impossible that evening and for most of the night, with her frequent trips to the bathroom and a crowd of young men next door playing drinking games and singing loudly, mostly in Dutch. It was a misery.

She'd hoped to accompany Jimmy to the diamond markets and their series of meetings, but couldn't stray far from the room, she was so unwell.

"We need to move hotels," said Jimmy.

"No. Don't waste the money. It's only one more night. I'll sleep on the plane."

He brought her citronnade and bottled water and crackers, and all she could do was press his hand in gratitude.

When he curled up around her she tried to block out the noise of the revellers. She loved it that Jimmy tried to comfort her in her misery. She'd married a treasure.

She saw nothing of Antwerp and Belgium but the blurred grey street as they waited for a taxi. She shivered in a wind so icy it blew through her gloves and under her coat collar. Still unwell, only dreams of Paris and the sunny garden in Sydney sustained her. A distaste for Belgium took root in the back of her mind.

Eleanor was delighted to welcome them back to Sydney and even more excited as events unfolded.

James Huntley the Third arrived seven and a half months later, born to Cynthia with those blue, blue eyes.

But not all was well. Jim and Eleanor had agreed Jimmy and Cynthia should bring back more Asscher-cut diamonds and some standards. Unfortunately, Jimmy had lashed out and bought other unusual shapes and cuts in Antwerp while Cynthia was confined to their hotel room.

"We're unlikely to be back this way in a hurry," he told Cynthia. "Consider it an investment in the future. Those Belgians have treated me really well. They know I've come a long way, and they've brought out their best gems for me."

Cynthia was alarmed at the amount he'd spent, but Jimmy was adamant. Fresh up on theory from his studies, he'd figured that unless Huntleys imported cheap pre-mades like everyone else—a race to the bottom—they'd never be able to survive. He believed that with Jim's skill to create unique pieces they could add great value to every single one of the unusual diamonds. Not only was it impossible to compare the value of an extraordinary ring with a mass produced one. Its very rarity was bound to make it more valuable.

He might have been right, but most Australians were conservative at the time, and there was no market for the unusual diamonds. Jim shook his head and eventually gave up displaying those he'd set. Then he refused to set the remainder, muttering something about throwing good money after bad.

The expensive French honeymoon, the home renovations and the large diamond purchase sent the Huntleys into debt just as interest rates soared, and with Cynthia busy caring for first baby James, then Nicole and then Will, she was unable to provide free labor in the shop.

Tensions simmered between Jim and Jimmy, who worked harder than ever. It was Eleanor the peacemaker who brought them all together on Sunday afternoons to forget their disagreements and admire the babies' gummy smiles. Eleanor never failed to remind them how lucky they were. The children made old Jim smile like no one else, and Eleanor, who'd confided she'd always wanted more children, was ever willing to mind them when Cynthia was ready to help in the business again.

She spoiled young James, then Nicole and Will with books and trips to the zoo and special food, and quietly placed her hand on Jim's any time he tried to complain about the noise they made or the financial worries of the business.

"Life is short, Jim. We're rich," she'd say, and for a while, Cynthia's sense of guilt about the expensive honeymoon, and especially the days afterwards in Belgium which had been such a failure, began to fade.

If she hadn't been so in love with France, they'd never have planned such an indulgent honeymoon. If she'd been well and right beside Jimmy during the meetings in Belgium, instead of desperately ill in their charmless hotel room, he may never have overinvested in the special diamonds.

Over time, her guilt simply morphed into bad memories of Belgium, while France, where she and Jimmy had been happiest, remained a blissful dream.

Alas, Eleanor's pronouncement they should count their blessings became too true. Jimmy was diagnosed with cancer, and they had a new set of worries to contend with.

Cynthia's love for her growing children and Jimmy and her passion for France helped keep her sane.

Throughout all the tests and treatments and Jimmy's dwindling health, Cynthia dreamed of France, an alternative reality, and when Jimmy died, closely followed by Eleanor, they'd had no choice but to sell the Point Piper waterfront home to bail out the business.

Building her French-style home in the Southern Highlands had been a compromise, and now she was living the real dream, a dream which excluded Belgium.

On one level, she knew her negativity about Belgium was irrational and unfair. Jimmy pointed out they made the best chocolates in the world, and the two of them had laughed. And once, when they'd been invited to a barbeque with neighbors and a couple of Belgians, he'd pointed out they were perfectly normal, and Cynthia could find no fault, other than the fact they'd refused to speak French with her.

"Maybe they're from the Dutch speaking part," Jimmy had said. "Let it go, my love. It's verging on prejudice. You can't blame the Belgians forever for selling me those diamonds. I was the one who bought them, and frankly, I still believe they were a great buy, even if Jim will never agree."

But even if nationality had nothing to do with it, why hadn't Émile told her where he was going, nor kept in touch?

She should never have accepted Émile's help with the beds, she told herself, as she grabbed her pillow, turned it over and punched it, particularly this silly master bed with its oversized love heart made of bronze. It was far too big for one person.

And as for that extravagant gown, and the whole trip to Angers and the chateau—well, Angelica was welcome to the mysterious Belgian.

It was all very well her inviting Émile into her bed that night of the ball, but what did she really know of him? Could he have been the one to steal her bangle? He'd cut those keys pretty swiftly. He probably had master keys to everywhere.

She sat up in bed. Émile still had his key to her place. What if Émile broke in while she was sleeping and made his way to her room? She shivered and imagined him slipping in beside her, and her heart quickened. No. Yes. No. Yes. She turned on the light.

The point was the key. Should she get the locks changed again? Or maybe she should return to Australia after all; forget this stupid French folly that brought bad luck all her life.

Speaking of which, she'd promised James she'd keep trying to reach Will. She pressed his number again. No answer.

She'd try again in the morning. A freezing wind whistled mercilessly around the eaves. Autumn had arrived with a vengeance and she was cold. She pulled up another quilt and snuggled lower in the bed, forcing a memory of Émile's warm arm around her and his thorough attentions as far away as possible. Forget it. There were other ways to keep warm, and she vowed to pick up some pine cones and set a fire in the hearth of this beautiful bedroom next time she went out.

In the morning, frost on the window looked like Jim's tiniest diamonds. It disappeared as the sun hit it and she felt more optimistic. She just needed to buy more warm clothes before winter really hit. Maybe Jacques or Nanette or Inès would feed Minette if she took that trip to Lyon.

She tried Will's number again out of habit and sat up so quickly when he answered that Minette fell off the bed.

"Sorry, Minette!" she said.

"Hello?"

"Will, it's Mum. Don't hang up."

"Why would I hang up on you? What's up?"

"Will, you never return my calls. Oh. Never mind. Where are you? How are you?"

"Chill, Mum. I'm okay."

"Where are you?"

"Vegas."

The bottom fell out of her stomach.

"France was getting me down. Thought I'd try my luck over here."

"What do you mean 'try your luck'? And did you take back the bangle you gave me?"

"Don't worry. I just borrowed it. I'll buy you a better one. I was a bit short of cash."

"Will, we're all worried about you. You're always short of cash."

"That's not true. Remember the cash I gave you?"

"Yes, and it came in very handy at the time, thank you, but I'm not really interested in money. I'm interested in you. How are you?"

"I'm okay. Why the sudden interest?"

"Don't hang up on me."

"I'm here, okay."

"Good. That's good, Will. Tell me. Is it drugs? It's alright if it is. We'll work through this together."

"No. So maybe I drink a bit too much sometimes, maybe all the time, but I don't do drugs."

"Then what is it, darling?"

"I've just hit a streak of bad luck."

"All this talk of 'luck'. You're not gambling are you?"

"So? It's something to do. Don't stress. The Riviera was great. Met a couple of English girls."

"Were they gamblers? Did they take you there?

"We enjoyed the casinos, yeah—fantastic jewels on show in the casinos, let me tell you—but they left me once I started losing."

"So now you're in Vegas?" She strained to keep the panic out of her voice. Gambling was trouble. How could she keep him on the line? It was essential he begin to understand. Dread slushed in her stomach like molten lead. Why hadn't she seen the signs sooner? How bad was his problem? Gamblers rarely acknowledged their addiction. They lied to themselves as much as they lied to everyone else.

"Yeah, but I'm alright. If you can lend me a bit more money, I'll be fine."

"Listen, Will. There's no such thing as a streak of luck, good or bad. The only way to 'win' in this life is to stay out of those places, and don't you dare start betting on those apps. I know. I had an uncle who liked the pokies, the one-arm bandits, and it kept him poor his whole life. He couldn't say no. He'd go into the club and only leave when he'd lost everything. Sometimes we didn't see him for months. He never managed to have a normal relationship; never married; used to tell lies. The way you took that bangle? Will, technically that's theft—to take back something you gave to me, but that's what gambling can do to a person. It makes you lie to yourself and lie to others. But listen, I don't care about the bangle, but I care about you. Nobody wins, Will. The companies that make the machines win. How else do you imagine they pay for those swanky places?"

"But they welcome me. They give me free food and drinks."

"Of course they do, a good looking young man like you, but they'll suck you dry. Do you really want to spend your life inside a casino?

Because that's what will happen to you. When did you last eat a proper meal, my darling?"

"Since when did you start telling me how to live my life?"

"I know, Will. You might not want to listen, but stay on the phone anyway, won't you? Where are you exactly?"

"I only just arrived really. That's why I need more money, so I can stay and play and win back what I lost."

"No, Will. It doesn't work like that. Don't become a cliché."

He hung up on her.

Blood pumped in Cynthia's ears as she messaged James: "You're right, James. I got on to Will. He's out of money, in Vegas."

James phoned her straight back.

"You've been giving him money, haven't you?" he said.

"Now and then," she said. "But this. I don't understand why I never noticed it before. James, I promise I won't lend him another cent."

"I knew it. I'll get on to Scottie and get him to freeze his account."

"Is that legal?"

"We'll do whatever is legal. Bloody Will."

"Don't be angry, James. It's an addiction. Maybe it's my fault. Maybe I let him down somehow. Did I do something wrong when I was raising you all?"

"Well I'm not an addict, and you raised me."

"Will needs our help, James. I think it's new. He might have caught the habit here, in the Riviera. I had no idea he needed help. Did you? I've been so blind to his needs. Don't let Scottie cut off his phone."

"I'm not convinced it's not some new ruse so he can have an all-expenses-paid holiday."

"You can't be serious, darling. The gambling explains so much. And if you feel you need help, too, then please, go see someone. Get some counselling, if you need it."

"I'm okay, thanks."

Then she messaged Will: "Love you, Will. I'll be back in touch soon. We'll find a better way."

She racked her brains, and rang Kath. They'd always turned to each other when they had problems with their children more complicated than a trip to the doctor could solve, like her youngest biting everything at preschool including other toddlers, or Nicole's obsession with eyeliner that nearly had her suspended from school.

"What's up?" Kath was short of breath.

"Are you okay, Kath?"

"Never better. Now I don't spend all my life doing housework, I've taken up running again. You caught me half way up heartbreak hill. I'm training for the City to Surf!"

"That's fantastic, Kath! Look. I need your help."

"Excellent. I've found a seat at a bus stop. I'm all ears."

"Will's been gambling." She hated her words, but naming the problem also brought relief.

"Is that a problem? Maybe he just does it now and then. Plenty of people do."

"But you know Will, Kath. He never does things by halves. I knew he had a problem with alcohol—he's the first to admit it—but this … I can't believe it took me so long to see it."

"Okay. How bad is it?"

"He's always out of money, even though he earns a reasonable wage from the business, Kath; not a fortune, but very fair, and he has an expense account. He should never be short of funds. James has been trying to tell me there's a problem for months, all year really, and I thought it was plain old sibling rivalry. I feel so stupid now."

"Gamblers can be very good at covering their tracks, Cynth."

"But I thought I knew my son. And I feel so guilty for not noticing! I guess I'd come to terms with the drinking, since he never would give it up. I put it down to it being his way of dealing with the loss of his father. Jimmy dying like that … It changed us all, and Will and Jimmy were always so close. You remember, Kath. Parents shouldn't have favourites, but everyone could see how close they were, and oh, Kath, it broke all of our hearts. But Will actually came home happy from all those parties—hung over, sure, but happy, as if he'd had a break from the grief. I couldn't afford to do that; not with the business to run, and …"

"Cynth, how is rehashing all of this helping?"

"I'm just trying to work out what I did wrong."

"Maybe you did nothing wrong. Jimmy's death was a tragedy, but you can't bring him back to life now any more than you could back then. Let's talk about the present. What can you do for Will now? Is he with you?"

"He's in Vegas."

"Oh. Can you get some help for him? Like counselling or something?"

"Will's never liked being told what to do, Kath. He'll do the opposite."

"Hmm."

"And he's completely out of money. He's lost it all again. He's on the street. I'm panicking, Kath. I had an uncle who gambled. It ruined his life."

"Are there some clinics over there, somewhere he can stay while he sorts it out?"

"Fantastic idea, Kath. I doubt he'll agree to being counselled, but he might want a roof over his head. Thank you! I'll see what I can find!"

Cynthia ignored her own needs for food, for a glass of water, for sleep. She spent the next few hours researching gambling addiction clinics. Absent-mindedly she stroked Minette, a hot anchor on her lap. She closed her tired eyes, resting them for a few moments before searching again.

Every search led to the same place—the Peters Clinic, conveniently located in Vegas. It was expensive but the success rate was excellent. Nothing else mattered.

She called Ron Scott senior back in Australia and instructed him to sell some of her shares.

"What's this about, Cynthia?" Ron tried to advise her. "We talked about this when you bought the property. You need to keep your investments to help fund your lifestyle. Once this investment is gone, it's gone."

"I can't explain now, Ron, but this is absolutely urgent," said Cynthia, in the voice she'd had to use time and again when she was running

Huntleys. Ron had her best interests at heart, but Will's future was more important than anything right now. "We'll worry about the future later, Ron. This is non-negotiable. They're my shares and I'm instructing you to sell them."

She booked the clinic for Will, and tried his phone again. He refused to pick up, or maybe he'd run out of power.

She made other calls and tried him again.

Then she texted him: "Go to the Peters Clinic. They're expecting you. Free food. I've paid."

She asked the clinic to contact her the moment he turned up—if he turned up.

Chapter 27

Three and a half hours later, Émile was on the outskirts of Brussels. The city streets were smaller and more crowded than he remembered. After the speed of the highway and the vast spaces he'd traversed, the density of the traffic depressed him.

How did so many people live here, all on top of each other? From the highway he branched off to the smaller and smaller streets, where vans and trucks and cars crawled, and sets of lights held them up for minutes at a time.

His old shop was unrecognisable; draped in the hated Quinka logo and the ugly purple and gold. The street was different. He'd become a stranger.

In his rush to meet the past and settle matters once and for all, he'd barely eaten, save for a quick burger last time he'd filled up the petrol tank. It sat in his gut like regret. The sooner he was over and done with all of this, the better.

Closer and closer he drove towards his hometown; the familiar streets, his school, like old friends, like memories, like the back of his hand, like the wrinkles at the edges of his tired eyes in the rear view mirror in the fading light.

Should he freshen up? No time would be the right time to confront Bertha. Best to simply begin and then see it through.

The entry to the apartment building was as cold as ever, the foyer that made his heart sink for as long as he could remember. With each step upwards, the joys of his day receded, replaced too soon by the recriminations that would surely come, in his home, this place where he was always a failure.

He could fix so many things, but never his wife's expectations and accusations.

As he climbed the steps, it all came back to him, the slow disaster of it.

He stood at the door to their old apartment, the key in his hand.

He rang his old doorbell, the one he'd installed himself, back when they were young. How many times had he come through this door since then? Could this be the final time? He sighed, his heart heavy.

Bertha greeted Émile with a scowl. No change there.

"You," she said, peering at him from behind the chained door. "You're back."

"I've brought you back your key."

She glared at his face, stared at the key and his heart did the old wild, tired caper. What game would she play this time? Would she flirt and try to win him back? Or yell and scream? Or cry, or nag? The neighbours had heard everything before. Whatever would happen would happen.

"How are you, Bertha?" Did he really want to know? Yes. If he'd never found the key to her happiness, he still cared about her. They'd shared a life and a child. He wanted her to be at peace without him. Content, if not happy. "How's Maxime? Let me in, please, so we can talk in private."

She shrugged. There were more threads of white in her dark hair, and it was cut short. It suited her; the curls softened her hard face. She closed the door. The chain jangled as she slid it off, the one he'd installed, and she opened it again, turning her back to him and walking away.

"You expect you can turn up like this and take up where you left off?"

"No, Bertha." Émile closed the door. The apartment still smelled of a thousand arguments, of captivity, of failure. "How have you been?"

"As good as any woman who's been abandoned."

"'Abandoned?' Please. You told me to go. You showed me the door. From all accounts you've been happy enough. I hope you've been happy. I tried to make you happy all our lives. I want you to be happy, but I don't have that power."

She shrugged and rearranged one of the cushions on the lounge. There were more of them than ever now—a whole family of soft things that didn't answer back.

"How's Maxime?"

She shrugged again. Bertha glanced up the corridor but didn't answer. Would she offer him a coffee? A glass of water?

"May I use the toilet?"

She shrugged again.

He placed the key in the middle of the table and went down the corridor, glancing in Maxime's room. The Ommegang case was still there under the window, exactly where he'd left it, but there was no sign of Maxime, the place too tidy; lifeless.

The bathroom. The cistern he'd repaired so often he could do it in the dark. The never-ending bottles of potions stacked on every horizontal surface, all promising beauty and joy.

As he left the bathroom he noticed a picture on top of the bookshelf; Bertha with several other women in the sunshine. They seemed to be on a cruise. They were all smiling, relaxed and happy. Good. She'd managed to have a holiday.

But below the picture, on the second shelf, shoved beside a book, was a pile of unopened letters.

Fury ignited Émile white hot. It curled his fingers into fists and sent him gasping. He grabbed his letters and re-entered the living room, staring at her. He pushed his fingers through his hair, fighting for control, then thumped the pile on the table.

He swallowed. Calm. Only by staying calm could he clear the future.

She stared at him.

"Don't talk to me about 'unforgivable,' Émile," she said. "What about you, your failed business, disappointing your whole family, letting Maxime down. He moved out, not long after you did."

"Where is he? Do you ever see him?"

"He's in Germany, I think."

"You 'think'? This is our son, Bertha."

"Why are you here, Émile?"

He sighed and clenched his fists and opened them again. He'd follow up Maxime later. There had to be a way.

"You were right to tell me to leave, Bertha. We were never happy together, but in the past eighteen months, I've never been happier, and you're happier too. It is true."

Would she smile at him? She flicked her eyes at him and back again, staring at a spot on the carpet. If she smiled, her face would crack. All her power lay in making him feel guilty. The realization freed something inside him and he stood taller. He could do this. He was never coming back, unless she asked him kindly, as an old friend, but never as her husband.

Did she sense it too; a new freedom in this room? She moved to the window and opened it and stared out at the lights of the suburb. A noisy bus went past. A dog yapped.

"I did the right thing by you, Bertha," he said. "When we sold up, I kept enough to buy my truck, my livelihood, and I gave you all the rest, so you could retire and live here in comfort."

She ignored him.

"Bertha, you and I married because we thought it was the right thing to do, to bring up Maxime together. And we did that, for better or worse. God knows I did my best by you both but it was never good enough for you."

"You've met someone else."

"We're still young, Bertha. The past eighteen months has confirmed for me that you and I were never meant to be together. You are well. From my point of view, our trial separation has been successful, and you look happier now than at any time I can remember. Can you put your hand on your heart and say you want me back?"

She turned away from the window and stared at his key on the table.

Chapter 28

Cynthia sighed and rubbed her toes on Minette's warm, furry body beneath the bed clothes. She was rewarded with a purr. Neither was in a hurry to get on with the day these cold mornings, so dark and grey. The house was too cold.

Maybe she should go back to Australia. What was she doing here? She'd mentioned it to Nicole the previous day, who'd told her she had to stay because she hadn't had a chance to visit her yet, and why should Will have all the fun.

"You don't mean that, Nicole," she'd said. "Will has far too much fun. He's in Vegas. We're worried sick about him. I always knew he liked a drink, and he's always been mad to party, but gambling is a terrible vice."

"I meant sightseeing in France with you, not having affairs all over the place like Will, and making horrible Huntleys headlines."

"How are things for you that way, darling?"

"Oh, Mum. You can say it. Yes, I went on a date with Scottie. A proper one. There's actually a lot more to him than meets the eye."

Cynthia didn't know what to say. James's best friend was the son of Jim's best friend. Scottie had been making eyes at Nicole since all the children were in high school. He'd given up on waiting for her to notice him, married someone totally unsuitable who'd fortunately divorced him; so now Scottie was on the loose again. Cynthia and James had discussed their hopes that Scottie might show interest in Nicole once more. She could do a lot worse than date the steady son of the Huntleys' long-term accountant who now part owned his father's successful business and worked so closely with James. So far Nicole's choices included a hopeless series of heart breakers and the last time they'd discussed their love lives, she'd told Cynthia she was giving up and becoming celibate.

"Oooh, Mum. How's that sexy Frenchman?"

"Turns out he's not even French. He's Belgian."

"Oh. But isn't that kind of French, anyway? Weren't all those lowlands under the Dukes of Burgundy at some stage, some of them at least?"

"Really?" She'd forgotten Nicole had studied history. Her own general knowledge was abysmal. She'd do a little Google search when they'd hung up.

"Come on, Mum. Tell me all about the ball at the fancy chateau. Can this Émile guy dance?"

"Well, yes. He's a superb dancer, actually. We danced for hours, practically the whole time." Cynthia smiled, remembering the way he'd held her, the joy they'd shared in the way they moved together so well, dance after dance, even though he was so tall. He'd practically lifted her off her feet in a dance she'd never danced before. A polka, he called it.

And then the way he'd swept her up to save her dress from getting wet, after the storm, as if he cherished her. She knew modern women weren't supposed to want to be protected and fussed over, but she admired the strength and skills of men like Émile. They certainly made life easier while they were around. Too bad they weren't to be trusted.

"And?"

"Sorry?"

"Well, are you still seeing him?"

"It's been a while."

"Oh." Nicole was so disappointed that Cynthia's heart fell. She knew she was angry at Émile, but couldn't quite remember why. He'd insisted he had to go away for a while, but hadn't said why. It hurt her, the way he'd announced it so soon after their love making, as if he couldn't wait to get away from her. It didn't bode well that Angelica who'd owned the chateau had been sweet on him too, and he'd clearly left her, even though she'd done the right thing by him and fixed his arm after the fall.

"Maybe he's commitment phobic," Cynthia said. Were they the right words?

"Do you want him to commit to you? You're really keen on him, aren't you, Mum."

Cynthia considered the question.

"He was very useful around the place, and we did get on, yes. I might have grown quite fond of him. Actually I do miss him, but he left me. Well, I suppose, I did tell him I could manage perfectly well without him."

"You sent him away?"

"It all happened very quickly."

"Well, why don't you phone him up and find out if he misses you, too? It's not the 1950s any more, and even then, I reckon lots of women made the first move."

"Do you think so, darling?" Making the first move hadn't been working so well for Nicole, but maybe she was right. What could it hurt to phone Émile?

First she phoned her friend Kath.

"Cynthia!"

"How's the house sale going?"

"I'm exhausted. I'm so over all the stuff. What do you do with your children's sculptures from primary school when they're all almost thirty?"

"Ask them to collect them by a certain date, and if they don't, then take photos of them and throw them out. Why do you think the skip bin was invented?"

"Genius. Thanks, Cynthia. What's on your mind?"

"Are Belgian people religious?"

"I'm no expert. Some are. Some aren't. Why?"

"Turns out Émile is Belgian, not French."

"Oh no!"

Kath knew her so well.

"Yes."

"Not that that should influence you at all, Cynthia. It's ridiculous to assume everyone who is Belgian is bad. Technically that's pure prejudice."

"I know."

"So ... Have you heard from him?"

"No. And I haven't contacted him either, before you ask."

"Well, I don't know how you expect me to know if he's religious if you don't know, given that I haven't even met the man. You could work it out yourself but you're so busy with appearances you have zero insight sometimes, Cynthia. It's astonishing."

"That's why I phoned you. Help me."

"The point is that quite a lot of French people actually are religious, especially if they live in a small village. Your little village isn't like a big, anonymous city. If Émile really cares for you, and if he's the gentleman you say he is, he'll want to protect your reputation. So don't write him off just yet. He might be doing the right thing by you. What did he tell you?"

"He muttered something about 'unfinished business.' That could be anything, couldn't it? Family duties, bankruptcy, wives in five countries? I'm beside myself."

"Why don't you phone him?"

"You're right. I should. I just…"

"What?"

"I need him to fix my windows, and I love the way he dances. He cooks. He's such great company."

"Why's that a problem? Sounds to me like you want him in your life."

"I do. I do, but what if he doesn't want me?"

"You don't want your heart broken."

"No. Does anyone?"

"You might need to take a risk. I can't do that for you, Cynthia, but what I am going to do is order that skip bin. Great idea. Good luck with that phone call. Let me know how you go. I was hoping to visit you next year on the way to Greece, by the way."

Cynthia patted Minette. She'd learned to be alone. She'd had to, and she'd been content in her own company, until she'd met Émile, so clever and kind.

Had she lost him, or was Kath correct? Was he putting things right so he could come back to her? She certainly hoped so.

...

Émile got off the flight to Berlin, took a taxi and stood out the front, contemplating the great glass edifice that had swallowed his son.

So far north already, with the business with Bertha now behind him, it was time to confront his son, though he didn't want it to be a confrontation. More a *détente*, a truce, if that were possible.

Bertha had thrown another barb at him before he'd left.

"You always think you're so good at fixing things, Émile. Fix this thing with Maxime, will you?"

"I'll try, Bertha."

How did you approach someone who never answered your calls; who hadn't gone home in eighteen months and didn't leave a forwarding address?

The trip to Berlin was a hunch. The corporation had a thousand subsidiaries. Maxime could be anywhere in the world.

He'd hired a shower at the airport, shaved, and bought a fresh shirt.

Inside the revolving glass doors was a bright yellow counter and another wall of glass doors. Well-dressed people bustled in and out brandishing key cards. He didn't have one of those.

A receptionist beckoned Émile across. Maybe she was accustomed to normal people being overwhelmed by the sheer power of this foyer.

"Yes?"

"Ah. Maxime Laurent, please."

"Is he expecting you?"

"We didn't set a specific time, but …"

"One moment please. Your company, please?"

"Emelioration. I'm Émile."

The receptionist punched some numbers into the phone and ran her eyes over Émile as she adjusted her headphones and listened.

"Yes. He's here, downstairs," she said, glancing at Émile as she gave his location, speaking into the headset.

Émile's heart raced and pounded and stopped. Would he explode?

"Maxime said he'll be down in a moment but he doesn't have very long. Please take a seat."

Émile exhaled and stared at the seat, a too-long purple plastic bench, but he could only stand, rooted to the spot, gazing at the glass doors.

Maxime gave him the veneer of a smile and pumped his hand professionally before walking him out the revolving door and out of earshot.

"I can't stay long, Dad. I have meetings."

"Of course."

Maxime took him a block away to an outdoor coffee shop, bustling, all broken concrete and graffiti, the sleek high walls of shiny glass office towers a world away.

They sat and Maxime picked up a packet of sugar. He turned it over and over. He wouldn't meet Émile's eye.

Who was this stranger with a bit of a beard, in thick-rimmed glasses and a too-tight business suit—a mix of man and boy.

As he glanced up and their eyes met, both talked at once, part guarded, part eager, and they laughed.

A waiter appeared in a hessian apron.

"Long black, no sugar, please."

"Soy mocha with two."

Émile smiled. His son still had a sweet tooth.

He gazed at the new Maxime—the business length hair, the clever hands—fidgety. The left one was permanently clamped around the latest phone.

"Yeah." Maxime stared at Émile, defensive, then thoughtful. "Will you ever forgive me?" His eyes locked on Émile's. There was a tinge of fear in them, and bravery, and defiance.

"There's nothing to forgive, Maxime." Émile laid both his hands flat on the packing crate table.

"You can't mean that, Dad. I know you wanted me to join you in the business."

"You were always your own person, Maxime. Your life is yours to lead. I wanted to give you every advantage, and if all I could imagine was a life like mine, that was my problem, not yours."

"I never expected you to say that."

"I've never stopped saying it. When you wouldn't take my calls, I wrote you letters, but they're still all there, in the apartment. Your mother…"

"I haven't been back."

The time went too quickly.

He stared at his son's tie, and closed his eyes. Quinka colors.

Maxime drained his cup and scooped out the remnants with the spoon.

"Are you coming home, Dad? How long are you here? Gotta go."

So that was it. Their reunion was over, too soon.

"You have my number, son. We could meet for a drink after you finish work this evening, if you're free."

His son stared at him, appraised his lined face and leather jacket as if he were a customer, then broke into a grin.

"Okay. I'll text you."

Later, at a wine bar, Maxime turned up with another young man. With their tight suits, BOHO ties and close cropped beards, they could have been clones.

"I'm Liam," said the stranger, leaning forward to shake Émile's hand. His accent was American and his grip, confident.

Maxime rocked from foot to foot, offering to get the drinks. Was he nervous?

"So, Maxime tells me you have beer under the streets in Brussels, like a water supply?" said Liam, making himself comfortable on the bar stool.

"Some streets, yes. In the old part," said Émile, sitting. "What's that accent, Liam? US?"

"You got it," Liam nodded with a warm smile. "Philadelphia."

Maxime returned with a small drinks tray and searched Émile's face and then Liam's.

"So, Dad. How's life on the road?" Maxime appeared anxious to fill the silence. How much did Liam already know?

"Not bad. I've had some great projects, thanks."

"Past tense? Are you done with it?" Maxime was always smart. Émile hadn't noticed himself what tense he'd used.

"Maybe."

"But you said you're not going home?"

"We don't always know what the future holds," Émile said, and Maxime and Liam nodded sagely, licking the beer froth off their cropped moustaches in unison. Did Maxime hand stray to Liam's thigh for a moment? It did. Liam squeezed it and it returned to the top of the table.

"To tell you the truth, it never felt like home," Émile said. "Your mother and I tried to make a good home for you, Maxime, but I guess I was always happiest in the shop."

"Sounds like it was an amazing place, sir."

Émile almost choked.

"Yes, but, well, Liam. Times change, don't they. No point running a relic, not with the future knocking on your door."

"Maxime told me about your truck, sir. Sounds cool."

"Thank you, but enough with the 'sir's, okay, Liam? It makes me feel a hundred and fifty years old."

"No problem."

Maxime launched in.

"Liam and I work in the same division, international accounts. We did our training together and hit it off. We're living together now. We're partners."

"Excellent," said Émile. His mind whirled. "Great. Good to meet you, Liam. There's not enough love in the world. I'm glad you and my son have found it together." He meant it.

Maxime beamed.

Was this why he hadn't been in touch? Did he fear his parents' prejudices?

He reached across the table and squeezed Maxime's hand. "I'm proud of you."

The two men were silent for a moment. Maxime broke the moment, back to his businesslike self.

"So, what's your plan?" Maxime asked.

Émile smiled as he watched the amber bubbles swirl and rise, gas escaping into the fug of the wine bar.

"South. I'll go south again. More drinks?"

Using English, so Liam could clearly understand, they talked for another hour, about the living conditions in Berlin, the extraordinary growth of Quinka as the Do It Yourself movement continued to grow in cities and towns around the globe. They discussed the rise of craft beers of the world; and Liam's life as the son of teachers; and how when he'd turned up in Quinka a year ago, he and Maxime had discovered so much in common.

Finally, they spoke of Ommegang.

"What's that?" said Liam.

"You'd love it, Liam," said Maxime.

Émile sat back on his stool.

"I thought you had ... disowned our heritage, Maxime."

Liam glanced from father to son and back again.

"No way, Dad. I've been busy, sure. And when I got this Quinka job, it needed my total commitment. It is important to do things well—you taught me this—and my work is recognised."

"He's been given two promotions already," said Liam, proudly.

Maxime smiled, then his face became serious.

"Ommegang. This is my heritage. We will go together one year, Liam. I have an idea, for Quinka, at Ommegang. Quinka could sponsor something ..."

Émile bit his tongue. Quinka had stolen his shop, his son and his way of life.

For eighteen months, Émile was bewildered, betrayed, sold out and utterly rejected; but here in this busy wine bar, in one of the world's most vibrant cities, here was his son—the young man he'd raised—healthy, full of energy, and clearly happy, with a partner to match.

"But what is it exactly?" said Liam, ordering a bowl of warm olives from a passing waiter.

"It is a parade through the old part of Brussels," said Maxime. "We wear green stockings. I am not joking."

Liam raised his eyebrows and they all laughed, but at a ding on Maxime's phone, his son grew serious.

"I am sorry. Time is up. We have to meet some suppliers this evening; take them for dinner. This has been great. Actually. Thank you."

Their eyes met, their mutual relief mirrored; magnified. His love for his son roared in his ears. It was deeper than the centre of the earth, hot and heavy and bright, tumultuous, joyous, never ending.

"Your mother might appreciate a call," said Émile quietly as they embraced, and Maxime nodded.

Chapter 29

Life in the village was colder and lonelier than ever. All the trees had lost their leaves. Cynthia pulled all the dead sunflowers out of their pots, the sun on her back lacking any real warmth.

In Sydney at this time of year, they'd be baking at the beach, sweltering, longing for the Southerly to break the heat of the day. Here, she shivered.

Jacques wandered past and stopped to talk.

"You're still here?" For the first time, he used "*tu*" with her—the close personal form of the language, reserved for friends and family.

Cynthia turned and straightened and nodded at Jacques, with his stooped shoulders. She knew what it was to lose a life partner. She leaned forwards. Would he "*faire la bis*" with her?—offer his cheek for the kisses customary among the locals? He did, and joy shot through her, warmer than sunshine.

She smiled as he began to speak, her ear now finely attuned to his local accent.

"So many visitors like you, we call them the summer people," he said in his slow way. "They are only here for the good times. They are selfish. They don't understand why we don't let them into our hearts, but there are so many strangers in our lives, the tourists who come in their thousands, never to return. As winter arrives, the people like you, they leave, as surely as our children leave us forever to work and play in the cities. Only the old folk are left, and with my wife passing, and others, we are fewer and fewer. Our village is a temporary adventure for you.

For us, it's our whole lives. If we let you into our hearts, they shrink a little with every departure."

Jacques's tone was gentle, but his words stung. She'd been so selfish and short-sighted, running around collecting French antiques, completely absorbed in her own desires and oblivious to the needs of others. She blushed hot, chastised. She'd learned nothing from her experience in the Southern Highlands building her house—so fanatical about the authenticity of its French trappings, and blind to the fears and dreams of her children. Was this when Will had taken the wrong path?

Surely by now she should have learned that life wasn't made up of buildings and furniture; nor even jewelry, her family's mainstay. The bangle Will had given her was worth nothing if his soul was in peril. Life was about relationships. How could she have been so blind?

Is this why Émile had left her? She'd never once asked him about his own needs and worries. Yes, he'd been secretive, evasive even; but she'd never even asked him why. Perhaps if she'd been genuinely open to his past and willing to confront his demons with him, she wouldn't be rattling around in her freezing edifice with only old furniture and nick nacks for company. She'd been totally focussed on what Émile could do for her.

"Oh, Jacques. Thank you for explaining. Thank you for making me feel more welcome here. I couldn't understand why so many locals refused to speak French with me."

"We like to practise our English, just as you like to use your French. At least then, when you leave, you leave us with more English words."

She laughed and held his gaze. He was in no hurry to leave, there in the sunshine. An idea came to her.

"Jacques, I'd be glad to share my English with everyone in the village. Any time. Maybe I can volunteer at the school?"

"They would love that. I will mention it at church."

"Thank you. Would you like to come in, Jacques, for lunch, for dinner?"

He smiled and shook his head.

"You are here still, Madame, but you do not understand us. How can I, a single man, dine with you, a single woman, alone?"

"But…"

"Do you want tongues to waggle all over town? In Paris, we could do this. Not here, in our village, where everyone knows everyone's business." He gestured at the sun-filled entrance to her shop. "But here, for example, if you were to put some benches, outside in the sun, you could give me coffee and we could sit and chat. And others, too."

"Oh, but that's a brilliant idea, Jacques. I'll do that. Thank you."

He cleared his throat and lowered his head. "Can I ask, why do you stay?"

"Oh." She considered letting him know she was contemplating leaving. Could he guess how she felt about Émile? How did she feel about Émile? … So she shared the general picture.

"Truly, Jacques. I've been fascinated by France and have loved speaking French since I was a girl. I love your language and your lifestyle. Look at all this beauty."

She moved to the front of her doorway, and passed her fingers over the faded blue paint and the ancient clover carving, then gestured at the street front, the stonework lit by the sun, and the shadows softened by curves in the cobbles. Could he observe the same beauty? Did he love it like she did, or was it all so normal to him it was invisible?

"But you have a family?"

"I'm a widow. My children have grown up and don't need me now, and Australians are very international. My children's generation, like your children perhaps, are living and working all over the world. We love to travel. My house here is large enough for them to visit and I hope they will, often. Maybe you met Will? And James will visit shortly, I hope. And my Nicole, too, perhaps, in spring."

Jacques nodded, his smile warm, then stooped and broke off one of the ruined sunflowers. He pinched at its centre with his thick fingers and held out his hand to her.

"These, you save," he said, and dropped a few slim black and white striped seeds into her palm. "You plant them in spring."

"Oh. Thank you, Jacques."

As he went on his way, his words rolled over and over in her mind, smooth, yet pointy as the seeds she'd been about to waste. It was true the relationships with her children were her real treasures, and her greatest fear was losing them.

As she finished her gardening, she caught a glimpse of herself in the window, and was horrified. The whole time they'd been talking, there'd been a great streak of mud across her cheek.

How was it that she could take such care with her appearance and no one said a word to her, and on the one day she looked diabolical she could have the deepest conversation she'd enjoyed in years?

She phoned the clinic in Vegas again. The receptionist apologized. Will had not contacted them. Fear gripped her again.

Cynthia was ashamed to have portrayed all her children so positively to Jacques, when Will's behaviour was more than troubling. Blind to his extreme behaviour for far too long, and too ready to make excuses for him, she was only now taking James's warnings about him seriously. If only she could reach him. If only he'd see sense and simply take himself to the clinic.

Worried sick, she forced herself to eat something while interrogating the past. If she'd stayed in Australia, she might have prevented Will from his irresponsible behaviour. Preoccupied with keeping the business strong during Jimmy's demise, she'd practically ignored her children. She'd never been tough enough on young Will, who'd acted out in so many ways. Was that why he drifted from party to party, never committing to anyone for long, always living in the moment? What should she have done differently?

She slammed a pot down on the stove. Was it too late? She tried his number again. No answer.

Cynthia heated some vegetable soup. She ate it with some torn bread, contemplating Émile's old friend's words. Was she really so selfish?

She wandered through her house, staring again at the jumble of antiques she'd collected. What was it but a pile of old, inanimate junk? She picked up a figurine and turned it over. It had given her such delight when she'd found it under a pile of rusting hinges and other metal fittings in an old wooden crate, but what had she done with it since, but stow it in one of the empty bedrooms?

But if she went back to Australia, would her life be any different? Would she build or buy another house and spend all her time decorating it, too? Was her life as empty as Will's? He flitted from one relationship to another, making headlines with his poor choices, while she flitted from object to object. Was this her legacy from Jimmy's death? Is this what Jimmy would have wanted for her?

On the edge of a plush Louis XV armchair in the cold room, her knees hard up against an ornate embroidered fireguard with a scorch on one side, she put her head in her hands and wept.

Who was she to accuse Émile of being remote and Will of lacking commitment? She'd invested the bare minimum of effort in her friendships. Not even when Émile explained Jacques's loss did she think to take him a spare casserole. She'd resented the way the villagers' behaviour towards her was so slow to thaw, yet she'd shared barely anything of herself, of her own hopes and dreams and fears and worries. If their conversations in the local shops were as shallow as the price of cheese and the weather, whose fault was that? Had she asked them about their health or their children; their memories of village life when they were young; their advice on keeping warm through the cold of winter?

But Émile. He'd been generous from the start, not simply with the chandelier and Minette, and all those jobs he'd done for her for nothing, but also with his company. How often had she phoned him unless she had repairs for him to make or some other problem he could solve?

The one thing she'd given him was her body, and to be truthful, he'd shared his own with equal generosity. Maybe more. The memory still thrilled her; the way they'd moved together in ways she'd thought her own body must have long forgotten; that ancient hungry dance that brought bliss like nothing else.

And how did she reward him for his generosity? By sending him away.

Shame and regret washed over her again. It was too late. She was destined to a life of lonely bitterness.

She took a deep breath, stood and stretched her arms out wide. She took herself to the bathroom to wash the mud off her face and splash cold water on her red eyes, gasping at the shock of it.

At a knock on the front door, she grabbed a towel and rubbed her face dry, then raced down the stairs and under the chandelier. It shot out rainbows in the last of the day's sun.

Chapter 30

Émile flew back to Provence, his heart on tenterhooks. Would Cynthia still be in the village? With winter biting early, she might have given up the dream and fled back to hot Australia, like so many other fun seekers and holiday makers before her.

He berated himself for not calling her, but there'd been so much on his mind, and until he'd made peace with Bertha and Maxime, there was nothing he could offer her, save for more minor repairs on her building and furniture. There was so much more he wanted to give her, to share with her.

He laughed at himself and shook his head. Thank goodness he had two good excuses to visit her. He lashed the box of coffee cups carefully onto the back of his motorbike. In the rush of their argument, she'd forgotten it in the back of the hire car. He'd taken it to Belgium, Berlin, back to France and now from Nice to her village. If nothing else, he'd be rid of the thing, he smiled grimly.

The other excuse was the big one. Her key was warm in his top pocket; the clover key—his key to her House of Clubs. He'd offer it back—her reaction would tell him everything.

At the very least, he'd drop in on Jacques and find out how he was faring, dear Jacques, his old plumbing friend, his knees ruined, his knuckles knotted as hickory, and his heart as big as an ocean.

There was work to do, emails to follow up, clients to call, odd jobs and offers to quote on larger projects in Nice and back towards Avignon, but first on his list and most important of all, he must see Cynthia.

Roddy had asked if he loved his life on the road and the truth was that aspects of it thrilled him—but it was lonely, now more than ever.

At first, he'd been elated at the simplicity of it, with just the radio and his slim philosophy book for company before he fell into an exhausted sleep at night, and, by day, his companionship with other contractors and the suppliers at the markets.

But now? He longed for a place to call home, and for so much more— for the love of a woman, but not just any woman. Visiting Angelica again reminded him of that. He longed for a particular woman, with her own individual vanities and strengths.

All his life he'd strived to make Bertha happy, but they'd never been suited to each other—her unexpected pregnancy tying them both to a life of duty they'd only recently escaped. At least now he knew Maxime was thriving. If happiness eluded Bertha, that was out of his hands.

He pulled up next to the curb and kicked down the stand. Cynthia's golden sunflowers were nowhere to be seen. Hope hammered in his chest that she'd still be there. Surely she hadn't returned to Australia, with or without Nathan.

He clenched his fists, then loosened them to trace a finger over the strange clover carving. There was meaning behind their distinctive shape: Faith. Hope. Love. He rapped at the door and waited.

Nothing. Through the glass window, the chandelier glinted with a life of its own.

Her key was in his pocket, but he would never enter without her permission. He waited.

His life of "freedom" flashed before his eyes, mocking him—a life of a perpetual visitor in the homes of others, of doors closing to him as he moved on from project to project, of his narrow camp bed, and hasty meals prepared from his van.

He shook his head. Even if Cynthia had gone, at least he'd go see Jacques while he was here.

Heart heavy, he was about to place the box on her doorstep and turn away when the black cat appeared. Hope rose and swayed in him like Minette's tail. Perhaps ...

Moments later, when Cynthia opened the door, she was flustered. She patted the back of her hair, as if composing herself, but strands of it had escaped. Her eyes were red. He'd never seen her so dishevelled, so upset. He longed to draw her into his arms and comfort her, but did he have that right? They'd parted on strange terms. Would she even speak to him, let alone allow him in?

"Émile?"

He stood, cradling his bike helmet under one arm and the box in the other, the clover key still in his pocket. His heart jumped. She was more beautiful than ever in an old pair of jeans—small as an injured bird, striving for dignity in her distress. Again he longed to soothe her, but the last time they'd been together, she'd sent him away. He stood at the threshold, a cold wind at his back.

Cynthia glanced from the box to his face.

"I brought you back your cups," he said.

"Oh. Those. Things. They're not important, but thank you."

...

Was this Émile's way of saying "goodbye" for good? Returning her coffee cups may be just more "unfinished business" he was dealing with, in a string of commitments across two countries.

His vintage motorbike was propped at the curb. Was he on his way south again, away from her, forever?

"Freedom." That's what Roddy called Émile's lifestyle. She swallowed.

Avoiding his eyes, she stood and stared at him, at the planes in his face, and his jaw; those lips, the little scar. Her heart pounded.

"Cynthia…" Émile broached the awkward silence.

"Émile?"

"I have secured a divorce, but …"

"But …?"

"That does not mean …"

Cynthia reached out, took his helmet from under his arm and stepped back to let him in.

"Won't you come in and sit down?" she said. "I haven't thanked you yet for that extraordinary experience in the Loire Valley. I stayed on. I saw Chiverny and Blois, and so many other chateaux, and so many moats and turrets and fancy gardens. Have you ever visited Chambord? I couldn't believe it." She was babbling, nervous, agitated.

"Do come right in, please, Émile. Do you have a few moments? Can I make you some coffee? I haven't quite worked out all the switches and dials on your fancy machine. Maybe you could make us both some coffee, and I'll unpack these beautiful cups. We could christen them together if you can stay a little longer. Do you have time?"

He followed her through the front room, under the sparkling chandelier, and into the corridor and kitchen.

"Oh, and Émile! Look; here's Minette. See how she's grown. She's missed you, Émile."

She placed his helmet on the table.

When she turned back to him, his hand was outstretched; in it, his copy of her key.

She took the key; hot with the warmth of his body, and held it tight.

"But you don't want my key any more, Émile?" Her face fell. The chasm between them was wide as ever as hope dropped away; her bleak and lonely future a certainty.

"What do you want, Cynthia?"

She stared at him, his frame so big it took up half her view—his broad shoulders and warm chest there, right there, where she could rest her cheek and listen to his heart and be held.

A coffee cup spun and almost toppled on the counter in her rush to stop fussing with it. She took a step towards him.

"I want ..." Would he run away again if she told him the truth? She swallowed.

"I want you, Émile. It's true. I don't need all these things. I don't even really need this house. But I need you, if you want me." There. Was that so hard? In the silence, she fretted. He'd go away again. She'd been too forthright, too clinging.

"You need me to do your repairs," he said, his expression impossible to read. For a moment, his eyes fixed on something behind her. He stiffened and she turned and followed his gaze, to the scarlet glasses Nathan had given her.

"I am too late," Émile said. "He is here. Your architect."

"Oh, Nathan? He gave me those at the restaurant. He has pairs in every color. He hasn't been here. He was in Japan last time we spoke."

Émile's eyes returned to hers, seeking answers. The space between them vibrated with tension.

"Émile, I do need you to do my repairs. But I need you, too. I need your company. Émile, I need your love, and I need to love you back."

As he stood, so still and serious, she raised the key. Slowly, deliberately, she slipped it back into his top pocket. She inhaled. Leather, engine oil and pure Émile. Intoxicating. She placed her hands on his strong shoulders and smoothed them downwards, pressing them against his chest. His muscles were firm under the thick winter shirt, his heartbeat strong, his warmth a balm.

Émile said nothing.

Only now did she dare look up into his eyes and see reflected in them her own sense of wonder and relief.

She reached one hand to his face and brushed her thumb across the scar on his cheek, one question in her eyes.

In answer, Émile brought his hands to her hips and pulled her gently, inexorably, deliciously, closer; and then he kissed her.

Chapter 31

Cynthia led Émile upstairs, his warmth and his tread behind hers more than welcome. When he'd turned up with the coffee cups and tried to give her back her key, she'd feared he was saying goodbye, that he'd chosen to move on from her, to leave her behind as he'd rejected Angelica.

Now he'd understand how much he meant to her.

As they entered her bedroom and he drew her close again, her phone rang.

"I'm sorry, Émile," she said. "I have to take this. It might be about Will. We're worried sick about him."

Émile nodded and dropped his arms. He made his way to the fireplace where he crouched and lit a match to the crumpled paper and pile of pine cones. It flared and lit his face. Her heart pumped faster.

"Yes? Hello?" She gripped her phone tighter. "Oh, that's the best news! Thank you so much for telling me straight away. Thank you."

The first flames began to rise, silhouetting Émile's head and shoulders as she joined him near the hearth. She perched on the edge of her loveseat.

"Will's at the clinic. He's in Vegas. He has a gambling problem. I should have seen the signs; his addictive personality, the missing bangle. James tried to tell me for months that something was wrong. How can love be so blind, Émile?"

Émile sat beside her on the loveseat as she tapped out a message to James, to let him know Will was safely at the clinic.

Émile's arm was bliss around her as the firelight illuminated his face and hands, and as the warmth began to lap at their bodies, he began to talk.

"You give them everything, and then—ffft. They are gone," said Émile.

"But you never stop caring," she said. Now would he tell her about his past? Flames rushed up the edges of another piece of wood and it ignited with a pop, sending sparks up the chimney. She nestled closer and reached for his hand.

"My son, Maxime."

She nodded as he spoke.

"I thought I would be angry, but I was relieved. He is in Berlin. I saw him just this morning. When he was born, this tiny baby and I held him, he was so trusting. He needed everything, and I gave it to him, only to have him throw it in my face. That's what I thought. But now ... I know that love is bigger."

"I couldn't be happier for you, Émile." She squeezed his hand. "I spoiled Will. Everyone did. When Jimmy died, I couldn't say 'no,' but I believe it started long before that, when Will was born. He was always Jimmy's favorite. Do you have other children, Émile?"

"No. Bertha and I … We were too young. We married for Maxime, but we were never happy. We could never talk like this."

If she stayed quiet, would he tell her more?

"My hardware shop, in Brussels. I built it up; I taught Maxime everything. It was for Maxime I worked so hard. But I could not keep it together. Bertha said I failed him, but it was not so simple."

As the warmth and light lit the room, he told her more—how Maxime was a smart boy, and, like any only child, Émile and Bertha's pride and joy and constant focus. From the time he could sit on the counter and be relied upon not to swallow nuts and bolts, the boy had joined him in the shop on Saturday mornings while Bertha slept in.

Everyone knew Maxime was born to take over the business one day, as Émile had inherited it from his father. Their customers were their friends. They marvelled as Maxime grew, admiring his curly hair and dimples, so similar to Bertha's, and how quickly he could count their change.

It hadn't all been smooth sailing with their son. There'd been that problem a few years ago with bits of hose pipe disappearing, and Maxime doing a personal trade in bongs, but he'd grown through that.

But Bertha was never happy. Since the moment she'd told him she was pregnant, it was all duty and no joy.

Émile sighed. Cynthia entwined her arm with his. She threaded her fingers through his own and held them tight.

"Going back," he said. "It was so hard to see my old shop. Quinka undercut me on every item. Even my most loyal customers could not ignore their prices. I couldn't blame them, but I was going broke. Quinka know this. They do this all over Europe, Cynthia. This is not my tragedy alone. Roddy, too. You met him. They bought his shop when he was on his knees, as they bought mine."

She could imagine it, she'd seen it in Australia, the arrival of the "super store," with its shiny promotions, the photo with the mayor on the front page of the local paper, cutting the ribbon, as if there wasn't already a hardware store or two in their district to meet the residents' needs.

"Me, I'd fixed the mayor's kettle for nothing only the previous week," Émile said. "The special prices now one else could beat, the free welcome mats in Quinka colors in households all over town, even at homes where I'd delivered goods without charge to help my customers. My days became quieter at the shop.

"At first Bertha loved it—hours off for long lunches with her single friends, but then the harping began again. Why were profits down for April, worse for May and hopeless for June, usually one of our busiest months? Of course it was all my fault. Why could I not do something? It was my job to fix everything else in our lives. Why could I not fix this?"

Cynthia heard how the Quinka representative from head office came to his counter in a suit, his smile too white and insistent. She heard about the offer to buy him out and hire him back to run a sub-branch; how he'd taken the paperwork and brought it home to examine with Bertha.

"'You're throwing away Maxime's inheritance, Émile,' Bertha told me. 'Why are you selling his future? Do something.' We'd never been happy, but this was rock bottom impossible. It was hard, Cynthia. I was so ashamed; so helpless. This was the first thing I could not fix."

Cynthia rose and moved to stand behind him as he hung his head. She massaged his shoulders till they lost their tension, until he tugged at her hands and pulled her around and sat her on his lap. She smoothed the hair back from his brow and listened.

"Only Roddy understood. He had exactly the same experience in his own suburb. He told me he was getting out, taking the money and going into renovation. I remember his words. 'I'm all for a life on the road.' It was alright for Roddy, the younger brother, who'd only ever worked in the family business, and had no partner or child to consider."

Cynthia nodded.

"I envied him, Cynthia. With Bertha so negative, I sniffed freedom. I hoped we could be happier apart. So I bought my van and left, and it's been alright, this life on the road. But the hardest thing …"

"Tell me."

Émile took a breath, his lips tight. He exhaled.

"Maxime. My Maxime. When he finished his degree …". Émile closed his eyes and turned his head away. His hands were fists. Cynthia slipped off his lap and kneeled beside him, the fire hot at her back. Gently, she placed her fingers over his hands till the muscles relaxed and he took them in his own.

"Maxime joined Quinka. He took a graduate role." Cynthia stood as he placed his head in his hands, elbows on his knees. She gripped his shoulder then ran her hand across his back, soothing him.

The fire crackled as the pine cones glowed like miniature Christmas trees.

Quinka! The company that forced him to sell his beloved shop! What could she say?

She brought her hand to his shoulders and squeezed his tight muscles again. His shadow was a leaping giant on the ceiling.

Eventually, he sat back and took a deep breath.

"You saw Maxime this morning?" Her prompt was gentle.

"And he is happy. He has a partner. Liam, from America. It is a different world. What do they say? 'Global'? My neighborhood was small. Maxime's has no limit. Quinka is international. I do not know if this is good."

"Is he happy, Émile?"

Émile stared at her, considering her words.

"Maxime had his own dreams and I was blind to them," he said. "I thought I'd failed my son, but he is well. I believe Maxime is happy. Yes. He is excited about his future."

Cynthia's voice was soft, but steady.

"Quinka. It's hardware, isn't it? On a global scale, but it's still about fixing things and making things; about tools and materials…"

"And so?"

"And so, in a way—well, of course it's different in so many ways—but perhaps Maxime has joined the family business after all."

There was deep silence. Finally Émile spoke.

"Perhaps."

She sat beside him and again she placed her hands gently over the fists he held in his lap.

"You're a good person, Émile. You did your best by Maxime. The young ones follow their own stars."

He sighed and glanced past her to the door.

"I should go."

She still loved Jimmy, but Jimmy was a memory. Émile was real, and he was here, now.

He stood to leave.

"Back on the road?" She was bewildered. "But you kept your promise to me. You've come back to me. You need to know you never have to leave, Émile. Please stay. Please stay with me. If you want."

She hated the tone of her voice, pleading. Had she no dignity? She no longer cared. She didn't want dignity. Dignity left her lonely. She wanted Émile.

His answer was a kiss, sudden and deep, and in the leaping golden light of the fire, she grabbed his arms and pulled him to her bed.

Chapter 32

When Cynthia awoke to the aroma of coffee, her first joy was to find Émile beside her, smiling, the cup steaming in his hand. He'd stoked the fire in the night and the room was warm as toast.

Later, much later, she checked her phone and found James's answering text: "Arriving in a fortnight. I'll go on and visit Will at the Clinic. Got to get our finances in order."

With Émile back in her life, the days rushed past in a blur of happy preparations for James's arrival. Cynthia washed and repaired extra quilts and linen, bought fresh pillows and made up the bed for him in one of the spare rooms.

Then she visited every shop in the village and stocked the fridge with local delicacies, as much to share her happy news as to buy their goods. It was true she loved to shop, but she and James and Émile would eat it all. Best of all, she told the shopkeepers she was expecting her eldest son to visit, and was rewarded with genuine smiles. They all knew how it was to welcome home a grown child, to swap news and share memories.

When he wasn't working on his contract jobs in Nice and surrounds, Émile made repairs on the spare bedside tables and sealed up the edges of the windows.

She cherished their moments together. She felt like a teenager, snatching kisses with Émile on the staircase, staring into his eyes over their candlelit dinners and holding him close and warm through the dark nights.

Some mornings, when he crept out of bed in the darkness to go to work, he left her to sleep. His beloved vintage motorbike spluttered to life and clattered away, its distinctive rumble diminishing in the distance as he headed for his jobs on the coast.

Filled with a new energy, she hurried through the day, rearranging furniture, planning menus for James's visit, writing lists of repairs to be done on the property. She planted tulip bulbs in the sunflower pots for spring, and spoke again to every merchant and everyone in the street to make it clear she was here to stay, and would gladly speak English or French with them, whichever they preferred.

She paid a visit to the local school and offered to volunteer as an English tutor one afternoon a week.

Again she was rewarded with warmer smiles, and a couple of locals even stopped to give her the double kiss.

When James turned up in Nice a fortnight later, she and Émile took him to lunch overlooking the beach.

But James was jetlagged, subdued and preoccupied, and for the first time, Cynthia questioned her decision to pass on the business to her children. Had she burdened their lives with it?

He nodded off in the back seat for a while, and on awakening, his attitude had improved. He praised the gently sloping hills with their vineyards and lavender plantations, and her picturesque village.

James was clearly impressed with the location of her property. He and Émile swapped tales of "footfall"—that irreplaceable bonus brought by position. People who walked past goods noticed them, thought about them, talked about them to their friends.

A good location directly correlated with turnover. It was why Quinka had wanted to buy Émile's hardware store, and it was why Huntleys, above Sydney's Eastern Suburbs, always turned over stock, every day and every week.

They talked about marketing, and how fortunate Huntleys was that Nicole had a knack and passion for marketing.

Cynthia spoke frequently with Nicole, who told her the new Huntleys website was a magnet to customers, that their social media presence and careful digital advertising was bringing custom from further afield than ever. Cynthia mused on the idea. Social media was not so different to footfall. Their jewelry popping up on people's mobiles was the equivalent of all the merchants of the past displaying their wares in the big glass windows of Cynthia's corner shop, her own House of Clubs.

How she loved having both Émile and James at home with her in Provence! The life and chatter in the old building was exactly what she'd imagined when she'd first fallen in love with the place, in total contrast to her isolation a mere month ago.

She and Émile left croissants for James in the morning as he slept off more jet lag.

When they ran into him on the street hours later, as they carried home their groceries for the day, he was subdued—something was troubling her son.

They ate lunch together under the chandelier, then James asked for a private conversation with her. He'd been polite about it—James was always polite—but it was awkward. She'd felt chastised, as if she were the child, and James the parent, as if her joy at her new life with Émile, their delight in every moment, were somehow irresponsible.

Émile was magnificent. He didn't take offence—he merely went to the kitchen to clean up their lunch and prepare a casserole for dinner, leaving her alone with James in the beautiful front room.

Cynthia was taken aback. The last thing she'd expected was for James to ask her so directly about money. She didn't envy him his task of keeping the business afloat, but did he have to bring his worries here, where she and Émile were so happy together?

James grilled her about how often she'd loaned Will money, about how much she'd spent at the markets, and about how she was meeting the costs of Will's fashionable Vegas addictions clinic.

Then he quizzed her about her plans for all the treasures stuffed in the spare rooms. Did she really intend to keep them all, or would she sell them one day?

She explained her vague ideas about renting out rooms to tourists in the summer for extra income if necessary, or renting out the shop.

And what were her plans with Émile, he wanted to know. Was he paying rent?

She pointed out her French friend more than paid for his board and lodging through the repairs he carried out, and that the very bed James slept in was practically created by Émile.

"No need to get offended, Mum. Émile's cool. I care about you. I don't want any Frenchman taking advantage of you."

"He's Belgian."

"Whatever."

They stared at each other.

"Now, since we're having frank conversations, James, how are you?"

"You mean 'where are my grandchildren'?" he laughed.

"Exactly."

"I've met someone."

"Tell me."

Cynthia sat back and admired her eldest son, his handsome face more animated than ever, all the worry lines replaced by a sudden, intense joy as he described the woman who had stolen his heart.

As Cynthia began to understand the reasons for his newfound determination to turn Huntleys' fortunes around, her secret smile expanded to a real one.

"I've never been more serious, Mum. That's why I wanted to see you in person. She's a jeweler, and immensely talented. She doesn't even realize. She's only new to the game. She works with silver, creating affordable pieces, but she has so much more potential. There's so much Jim can share with her, teach her. She has all the ideas I've never had. She has a designing mind, just like Jim's. He likes her. You'll like her. Her name is Stella."

"So why didn't you bring her?"

"I will. I will now. I'll be able to. Now that you can help me get things back on track, and as long as things go well enough with Will. It's only then I'll have something to offer her. I want to marry her. I've never wanted anything more."

Cynthia jumped up and threw her arms up around his neck before running to the door, calling out to Émile.

"Darling! Champagne! Champagne!"

And so their big confrontation became a moment to toast the future.

Next day, Saturday, she encouraged James to visit the markets with her, and he gravitated towards all the antique jewelry for sale.

"You know there's no jewelry store here, Mother," he said.

A future opened up before them.

She and Émile would help James take Huntleys to the next level. They would open a branch right here, right in the extraordinary front room, making Huntleys international.

She could see it all. Émile would create the display cabinets. She would sell off some of the excess antiques, the silver serving spoons and crystal pieces that so many visitors loved.

With her lifetime of dealing in jewelry, there was no one better placed than Cynthia to find suitable antique jewelry at the markets, both high end and costume jewels. France was awash with art nouveau and art deco pieces and everything older and more recent. She'd clean them, make simple repairs and display them for tourists and locals, and send others back to Sydney to complement newer items created by Jim and this Stella person of whom James spoke so highly.

Émile and Cynthia traveled to Nice again to farewell James when he headed for Las Vegas. She was glad James cared about Will. Would his visit help her wayward son make the most of the clinic? She hoped so. They boys always got on so well in their childhoods. If anyone could help Will make the most of the clinic's opportunities, it was James.

After leaving the airport, she and Émile went down to the shore, where the little waves lapped at the stony beach. The rocks chinked on each other as they tumbled—such an oddity after the simple fresh swish of waves on Australia's golden sands.

Everything about life was looking up. From the crucible of conflict with James came the gem of an idea.

"When the children criticize me, I'm ashamed, as if I were a selfish little girl again, and not their mother, the experienced adult."

"I understand."

It was hard to walk on the stones, so they made their way back up to the promenade and walked, hand in hand, as they talked.

"I really had no idea the finances were so bad."

"James is a good man, Cynthia. I can see he does not like to say these things to you. But let us talk of our new plans. I am excited."

She stopped and faced him, catching his other hand in hers, this beautiful man. He was the gift in her life, whatever else might happen.

"*Our* new plans? *You're* excited?"

He nodded, the light in those green gold eyes as bright as ever in the winter sunshine.

"I miss my shop, Cynthia. I loved the retail life. Every hour, a fresh challenge, another thing to fix, a problem to solve for a customer; so many people in my life, old and new, and no two days the same. And to be able to be with you day and night, no longer on the road. This is my dream, Cynthia. I cannot wait to begin."

She reached her hands up to his neck and he smiled and bent his head and found her lips. They kissed for so long that three cyclists rang their bells as they rode past.

...

Back in the front room, now known as their boutique, House of Clubs, Émile began work creating the display cabinets, refashioning from parts of other shops, demolished or modernised. Cynthia barely heard her phone ring over the noise of Émile's sander. It was Kath.

"Wait a sec, Kath. I can't hear a thing in here. What's news?"

"It's done," said Kath. "We're in, and all the boxes are unpacked and I'm sitting down for the first time in four months and I. Don't. Have to. Do another thing! All those lists! I've thrown them out. I'm on top of the world."

Kath and Bob's new apartment on the edge of Sydney Harbour gave them views of ferries and party boats and yachts and tugs and the light on the water night and day.

"It's so beautiful, Cynthia. It was worth the effort. Now, how about you? What's the latest with that sexy Belgian?"

"Oh Kath. We do have news! We're opening a store together in my front room, the one with the beautiful chandelier. He's busy building the cabinets for it right now."

"No! Tell me?"

"It was James's idea, but we're all behind it. Huntleys is going global. We're opening a French branch."

"Oh but that's great. When? Or is it? Weren't you tired of running the business?"

"This will be quite different to the Bondi Junction store. It will be tiny in comparison. We'll run it as we like; and any trade we do will be a bonus. We're here anyway. We'll have a bell out the front, and a sign, 'back in three weeks' if we wish to take a break and go exploring. We're going to offer estate jewelry, as well as some of Jim's engagement rings and a range of our best-selling contemporary pieces, and also a few things in the more affordable range. Oh, and Kath. Did I tell you James has met someone? I couldn't be more excited."

"Well, that was always going to happen, Cynthia. James is a catch. Tell me more."

"Her name's Stella and she's very talented. She's a jeweler, too. James says she's a brilliant designer. She put up a stall in front of Huntleys, with all sorts of clever things—upcycled coffee pod earrings, for example. Can you imagine? Anyway, for our store over here, our House of Clubs, the population in Provence really swells in summer, especially with tourists from the UK, the US, Scandinavia and even Australia. So we'll have something for everyone. Everyone wants a memento of their travels. What do you think? I'll be able to get rid of some of this clutter."

"Fabulous idea. You know—I've worried about you, Cynthia. After all those years in retail, you must miss it; some aspects at least. You were always so good with the customers, and you balanced the books, and managed the payroll. Then you leaped right in and built that Southern Highlands house, but Nicole was right. Once it was done, you were bored in Bowral—you weren't nearly ready to retire. You needed the stimulation of moving to France, and now you've succeeded at that, you need a new challenge. Otherwise you'll keep on buying French furniture until there's no more room in that place."

"You know me too well, Kath. You're right. I'm really very excited. Émile and James and I planned it all before he left, and Émile's already making great progress. Émile is retrofitting some beautiful old cabinets. I did go a bit wild purchasing antique bits and pieces when I arrived, so we'll have plenty of smaller items to sell as well; some silver spoons and candlesticks, and some crystal—souvenirs and gifts which might appeal to people a bit more widely than jewelry on its own.

"We even have space for a few larger items, such as beautiful chairs and a small table for example, or a beautiful dresser—the sorts of things Émile restores so cleverly. These things are quite affordable from the markets, but most tourists don't have time to go find them, and Émile is so clever, he can restore them quickly, and we can still keep our mark-ups fair. We'll gain a reputation. Tourists can't eat and drink all day. Almost everyone in this village has to walk past our store. Oh, and I'm offering free English lessons. Our store will become a hub, a community resource. Please visit us, Kath. Come for the opening, you and Bob. You can travel now, can't you, now all the hard work is done? I can't wait for you to meet Émile. You know, Kath, maybe I was becoming a bit of a hoarder when my life was so empty."

"You think so?"

"Jimmy's death was tough on all of us."

"And you took on so much."

"Yes. But life is better now …"

"With that Émile."

"It is."

What Cynthia didn't tell Kath was that she'd caught Émile brooding from time to time, staring into space. What was troubling him?

Chapter 33

James phoned from Vegas to say Will appeared to be making excellent progress—though he was a little worried there might be something going on between Will and his therapist, a Dr Lisa Bakker.

Cynthia shook her head. Trust Will to push the boundaries. Surely such relationships were against the rules. They certainly were in Australia. She only hoped he was making progress, as James believed.

A few weeks later James phoned her again, telling her of Will's firm plans to stay in the US, and more news. Will, too, would open a branch of Huntleys, in Boulder City, where Lisa lived—so Huntleys would have stores on three continents and be truly international.

"But is that sensible, James? Will isn't known for being responsible. And you and I both know what a huge responsibility that is, to handle stock, and supply and sales, and accounts. I'm exhausted just thinking of it all, but excited, too. With our experience, we can do it when we're asleep on our feet. Which is fortunate, as that's often what's required. But Will has never been responsible for more than a tiny part of Huntleys."

"Well, I know this will surprise you, but Will's plans are watertight. Scottie and I've given them the third degree, and we're in touch with Will every few days. So far, so good. He completed that three-week program and he goes back to see Dr Peters regularly, for follow ups. You were right about the clinic. By all measures, it seems excellent, and Will was a different person when I saw him over there. It's like he's finally grown up—I'm convinced of it, even though I'd be the first to admit I thought it would never happen."

"I hope you're right, James. I'm not doubting your word, but we all know Will. Oh well. A store will certainly keep him busy enough to stay out of trouble. Do you think maybe that was part of his problem; that he was always a bit bored?"

"Maybe."

"And there I was, always smoothing the way for him, because of his grief, because he was my youngest, my baby."

"I don't think you can take responsibility for all of our failings, mother. We're grown up now."

"You're wonderful, James."

"Well, you're right about that." And they laughed.

A couple of weeks later, as Émile was positioning two sturdy benches into place outside her door—he'd found the wrought iron ends at a market and replaced the timber—so everyone could come and sit in the sun outside her shop, Cynthia had another surprise phone call, this time from Sydney. She checked her watch and did the calculation. It was Saturday evening over there.

The whole family had gathered at Nicole's apartment—even Will who was back in Australia to rent out his apartment. She'd had a few more calls from Nicole about dates with Scottie. Could this call be significant?

For the first time, Cynthia wished she was there with them, admiring the lilac and peach afterglow of the sunset reflecting off Sydney Harbour on a late summer's evening.

At the emotion in her voice, Émile rushed to her side and she put the phone on speaker just in time.

"We're engaged, Mum!" said Nicole.

"Oh, Nicole and Scottie, my darlings! *Félicitations*! You'll have to come to France and meet Émile. And stay here for your honeymoon!"

In Sydney, everyone was talking at once, saying "cheers" and clinking their glasses.

"Now, Will," said Cynthia. She couldn't help it. She'd always be his mother; always love him to bits. After coming so far, would he throw away the progress he had made? "Are you being good?"

"Sparkling mineral water, Mother."

"Never!"

She hadn't been fishing, but Will's words gushed out.

"Look, I really need to thank you, Mother," he said. "I don't care who else hears me say this. That clinic saved my life. I can't thank you enough. I hate to think where I'd be if you hadn't paid up front and told me about the free food."

He rushed on, telling her not to worry, but he'd been in the paper again—something about being spotted at Jupiter's in Vegas with two young women.

"It was a total beat up, as usual. I'm on the straight and narrow now. It's true I've got my eye on someone from the clinic, but it sure isn't that Mindy or Shelly. You're aware of the plans for my US branch? Yes. We're working out the details. That's why I'm here. How's your own store? You know I'll race you. Let's find out which of us can open the first international branch. I bet I'll win."

"You always were a winner, Will," Cynthia said. "We all want you to keep on the right track. We need you to do the right thing. I think this is a good bet for us to have, don't you?"

"I'm excited, yeah, but not as excited as I am about Nicole and Scottie," Will said. "So when's the big date, guys?"

Émile popped champagne and brought full glasses into the front room as Cynthia listened. Her eyes sparkled with gratitude and emotion, and she leaned against him as the phone was passed around in Sydney.

...

Behind their Australian accents, Émile pieced together who was who; old Jim with his gravelly voice; James, level-headed as usual; Nicole quite different to Cynthia; and Scottie, self-conscious. There was someone else there, too. Another woman—like him, on the edge of the family, warmed by their vitality and closeness.

Cynthia laughed and cried with them and plied them with questions. No, there was no date, yet. Yes, they'd consider honeymooning over in France.

When Cynthia hung up, she sat still, smiling into the silence.

He placed his hands on her shoulders and drew her to him, wrapping his arms around her.

"You need to go to them?"

His question surprised her. She pushed away from him.

"No. Not at all. They'll come to us. You'll see. Did you notice the quiet one? I wonder if that's Stella. I'll bet James didn't introduce us because he didn't want to spoil the moment for Nic and Scottie."

How he loved Cynthia; so perceptive.

"You and I have serious work to do, Émile. Will has set us a challenge and we have to take it up. This will be a life saver for him. Imagine. This is Will's first long-term plan; his first plan ever as far as I can remember. This shop race is serious. If he can keep his mind on our competition, and truly follow through and create our store, it will keep him away from all those short-term distractions, the parties and bars and other temptations."

Dear Cynthia. Did she believe Will could change so completely?

"We have to help him change, Émile. These first few months will be crucial. Will you do this with me? You understand retail. If we carry out our side, and truly create our store, and keep Will up to date with our progress, it can only help him. James was right. Will is different. Did you notice? That clinic has changed him. It's exactly what we all wanted. This is brilliant. So much good news in one day! You'll help me, won't you, Émile? Let's take some pictures right now of our space and some of the things we plan to sell, and send them to Will."

And so they took a selfie with the benches and shop in the background, its new display cabinets clearly visible, along with some of Émile's power tools. Then Cynthia laid out a selection of silver and crystal treasure she'd collected from nearby markets but would be happy enough to sell from their new boutique.

Will shot back a thumbs up emoji. That was different for a start—this from the man who never answered his phone. Maybe Cynthia was right and Will Huntley really had turned a corner.

Not for the first time, Émile admired the formidable mind of Cynthia Huntley. He saw again how she'd held a business together for her children in the wake of her husband's death.

This beautiful woman was not so different to Will. She too could drift. But in her eyes and the set of her head were the same stoicism, determination and loyalty he'd detected in James.

"The race is on, Émile."

"I am right beside you, my Australian. Let me show you how closely I support you."

He led her upstairs to the bedroom. He pulled the slide from her hair, and he made love to her, until they fell asleep, curled together.

Next day, Will emailed her a copy of his business plan. It was impressive. That evening, he phoned, bursting with details. She put the phone on mute while she told Émile it was the first time since Will's childhood that Cynthia could remember he wasn't hung over. She put the phone on speaker again as he shared more details.

His shop wouldn't stock jewelry alone. It would mostly stock adventure wear.

"House of Hearts," he said. "Get it? Healthy hearts. But it's also for Lisa. You'd love Boulder City. It's so different. It's no city. It's in the desert, set up in the early 1930s. Model city. No gambling. No chance I'll stray, eh. Lisa's got me over all that anyway. They built the Hoover Dam from this town. So much concrete. Did James tell you? We went on the tour."

"Exciting." Would he tell them more about this Lisa? Apparently not.

"So. How's Émile the French lover?"

"He's Belgian, darling."

"Whatever. So. The race is on. I'll bet I can open my store faster than you can. No money involved for the winner. This bet is just for fun. What do you say?"

"Well, Émile and I already have plenty of stock. I'm going to let some of my antiques and old wares go. I did have a bit of a spree when I arrived, but there's plenty more at the markets, as you've seen, and I'm going out with a new eye now, to find old jewelry. Can't wait."

"Stock. Yes. I'm going to have to stitch up some deals with suppliers in Europe, so I might drop in again some time."

"You must. Come and see our Huntleys House of Clubs, our French branch, our own boutique."

Chapter 34

Through the rest of winter, Émile was able to base more of his work in Cynthia's village. As a couple of big contracts near Nice came to an end, he spent more and more time in her front room, creating the bespoke glass cabinets, fitting showcase lights and adding a secret safe for the most valuable items.

For the first time, Cynthia opened the doors engraved with clubs not merely as her property, but also as their gift store, their House of Clubs, and neighbours dropped in to admire their wares and ask about their plans.

Cynthia spoke in English or French, and as word spread she'd be glad to help anyone with their English studies, including children, the villagers' reserve began to thaw. Nanette and Inès were her most frequent visitors, when not busy giving tourist information. Inès loved discussing Australia, especially the birds and animals.

Émile ventured into the attic one day, hunting for a small spare piece of wood to finish the underside of a shelf, and came upon an old sea chest full of letters and other documents, many of them in English.

Cynthia was enchanted. All work sorting and polishing finds to sell in their store halted as she tried to work out the origin of the materials.

She rushed into the room with a document, waving an arm to catch his attention, and he put down his power saw and removed his ear protection, catching her in his arms.

She spun around, leaning against him as she pointed at the piece of yellowed paper and scrolled through her phone to a Wikipedia article.

"It's a love story, Émile," she said. "I'm guessing that the Frenchman who lived here more than two hundred years ago, way back in the late 1790s, was a soldier who went to Ireland to support the Irish Rebellion. They called it *l'expédition d'Irlande*. There were 12,000 of them who went to Bantry Bay in County Cork. The Irish rebels joined the French against the British, but they lost. It was the Battle of Ballinamuck. It says here all of the Irish soldiers were executed!"

He held her close.

"But it turns out, I really think, that the soldier who came here after the battle had fallen in love with his Irish friend's sister, because there's this series of letters. So Émile, it was the retired soldier—he was the one who carved the shamrock symbol on our doors. There's a letter about it, where he tells her he is waiting for her, that he chose the clover leaf and clubs symbol to stand for faith, hope and love.

"And look, here's one back from her, and she's actually drawn the shape at the top of her letter. It's so romantic. And Émile—the fact that all his letters are here—that means she kept them and so she must have come to him, right here, through these doors. Can you imagine? It's so exciting. We'll have to ask everyone if they knew anyone Irish who lived here."

She was on fire with her news. The local paper ran a story about it, sharing news of Cynthia and Émile's House of Clubs shop, with its small antiques including jewelry. Émile carved more club symbols on the back of their sunny benches.

When Will paid them a flying visit while on his tour to find suppliers of adventure wear, Émile reserved his judgement about the young man. He didn't want to see Cynthia's good nature abused, but he had to concede that for once, there was no alcohol on Will's breath and he was fired with purpose.

Will's examination of Émile's cabinetry was astute, and this time he took his time before he spoke. Was there a little more respect?

"A craftsman *and* helping my mother," Will said, shaking his hand as he was about to leave.

"Your mother, she does not need help," Émile said.

"Touché. Still. It's great she's so happy."

Was it a compliment? The young man's smile was as charming as ever, but the mere fact he'd even thought of someone else's wellbeing was an improvement. If Will kept on the straight and narrow he could do well in his new store.

"Come to my opening," Will said, catching Émile's eye, then hugging Cynthia.

"When? Have you set a date?"

"Soon. Nic's helping plan it. We'll let you know."

...

There was no way Cynthia wanted to miss the opening of Will's store. Why was there no mention of this Dr Lisa Bakker? Was she still in the picture? But why else would her son go to all this trouble to create a store in Nevada?

Nicole had mentioned something about Will finding some opals in the desert, and polishing one up for Lisa while he was in Australia, but that had been months and months ago.

She longed to ask him about the young doctor who'd been part of the treatment team, but bit her tongue. Relationships between patients and therapists were taboo.

She took Will to her front doors as he was leaving. She ran her fingers around the carvings on the doors, to tell him the story of the soldier and the Irish woman.

"Can you imagine, Will? It was years before they were together. I checked all the dates on their letters. And each letter would have taken weeks to arrive, going by land and sea. It's unimaginable these days. Look at these clover shapes. Did you know that as well as the holy trinity, they symbolize faith, hope and love?"

"'Faith, hope and love.' Nice one, Mother." In the past, he would have mocked her sentimentality. Not this time.

His handshake with Émile was firm. Was there a new mutual respect?

Will's back was straight and his step purposeful.

What was the symbol for a parent's love, she wondered? The shamrock would do.

...

Émile and Cynthia discussed the progress of their own shop and their opening plans as they flew into the US via New York.

"Émile, let's not have a grand opening, nor regular opening hours for our store. I want to be able to come and go. Let's go to Paris together if we feel like it. Or to see Maxime, or that festival. What do you call it? Ommegang."

Émile's expression changed. Again his face fell.

"What is it?"

"Maxime wants me to see him at Ommegang."

"Of course you must go."

Émile winced.

"What's wrong, Émile?

"The rainbow float, I do not mind. But Quinka colors, the gold and purple. This makes me angry."

"Quinka stole your son and your shop and your livelihood. You have every right to be angry."

He squeezed her hand.

"I try to forgive."

"Yes, but it's a bit hard to forgive a multinational corporation. A person maybe, but not a company."

"You understand this."

"I love you, Émile. Oh look!" Cynthia pointed as the wing dipped and they circled in above the famous statue, to land. "Liberté!" The statue was impossible to miss.

Their days in the legendary city were full of sightseeing and encounters with popular culture they'd both absorbed all their lives, from movies, music and television shows.

The US accents were larger than life, the shopfronts astounding, and the fact the city was open all night exhilarating and exhausting after their quiet French village.

At Vegas airport, they hired a car and made their way to Boulder City, the day of the opening.

Nicole and Scottie were busy fastening a huge blue ribbon around the outside of Will's shop, but when they saw Cynthia, Nicole dashed down from the ladder so quickly Cynthia was worried she might fall.

They hugged, while Émile and Scottie shook hands and introduced themselves. Cynthia hugged Scottie, too, once Nicole released her. She'd never seen her daughter so happy; glowing.

296

"One of Jim's?" she asked as she admired Nicole's engagement ring, a large pear cut, flanked by smaller ones along the shaft. Unusual. Was this one of the diamonds she and Jim had brought back from Belgium all those years ago? Where were they—those shields and the rhomboids, the triangulars and half moons? The kites and lozenge and trapezoids. There were even a couple of pentagonals, if she remembered rightly, and at least a couple of hexagonals and octagonals. But where had they all gone? She'd have to ask Jim some time.

"Of course," said Scottie. "Jim sends his very best wishes, of course. He wanted to be here, and he specifically asked me to tell you he's thinking of you and the whole family, Cynthia, but he said you'd understand how much he hates to fly, after Korea."

"Yes. That's Jim," said Cynthia. She must make the trip to Australia to catch up with him again, and soon.

Will emerged from inside the shop, phone to his ear, apologetic, and gestured to some people inside to come out with him.

James emerged, holding the hand of a young woman with curly dark hair. She was small, with bright eyes, shy and fierce.

"Mother, I'd like to introduce Stella Rhys, my fiancée."

"Oh, James, you didn't tell us! I'm over the moon! Stella dear, come here and let me meet you properly, the woman who has captured my son's heart. How brilliant!"

"Stella's a jeweller in her own right, Mother. We were going to tell you, but there's just been so much else going on, what with Nic and Scottie's wedding next month and Will's shop opening, and all our improvements to the business back in Sydney. Stell is an integral part of that. She works closely with Nicole these days, and also with Jim, designing. It's a long story. We wanted to tell you face to face."

"Well, I'm absolutely delighted for you both. What a wonderful surprise!" said Cynthia, though there was a question in her heart. If this woman was so integral to James's life and business, why hadn't he told her more about Stella, and sooner? Surely this was no way to find out such important news, when they were all flat out helping Will open his store.

"Alright, enough chit chat," said Will. "Mother! Émile. So pleased you could join us. Come and let me show you how to work this American till. James, Nicole, the stage is arriving at four o'clock. Can you set up the mic, please?"

The store was extraordinary. Huge screens displayed snowboarders and rock climbers and daredevils in wingsuits surrounded by wilderness. It made Cynthia's heart pound.

When all was set, and the sun went down, and the smell of free pizza from Jeronimo's, next door, wafted in the dry evening air, James took to the stage.

"Good evening, ladies and gentlemen. I'm James Huntley the Third, of Huntleys House of Diamonds."

Cynthia admired the way her eldest son could command a crowd. Maybe the Australian accent helped, but there was no doubt he was eye-catching, his travelling t-shirt and jeans replaced by a pale grey suit. For a moment she wished Jimmy was here beside her to witness the expansion of their business to the US and their impressive children, now all so grown up and taking their places in the world. Émile was steady at her side. Could he guess at the note of sadness? She leaned against him and he squeezed her shoulder.

"When my brother Will said he was going to open a branch of Huntleys right here in Boulder City, it was unexpected to say the least, but you people have quite a place here, don't you!"

There was applause and a few cheers.

"Now, Will here, my younger brother, is an unusual man," said James. "He's always pushed the boundaries. Not content to stock jewels for the romantic hearts among us, like our Australian branch, Huntleys House of Diamonds, and our French branch, Huntleys House of Clubs, Will was determined that this American arm, Huntleys House of Hearts, will mainly carry things for what he calls 'healthy hearts'—adventure gear for the great outdoors you have around here."

James held out his arms. "Tell your friends about us," he said. "This store is sure to be a real treasure for your beautiful town. I encourage all of you to come in tonight and browse. Come in and find out what we have on offer for yourselves and the special people in your lives, and if we don't have what you need, let us know. We'll do our best to source it for you. But now I'd better move over for Will."

Amid more applause, strikingly handsome in casual outdoor wear, Will jumped onto the small stage beside James and smiled. A hush came over the crowd. Everyone felt Will's presence.

"Admirable," Émile whispered. She squeezed Émile's hand.

Will welcomed everyone, offered them discounts, and was even polite to the media, triggering a frenzy of photographers' flashes. When he introduced an older woman to the stage, Cynthia held her breath. Could this be that special therapist, Lisa, who'd helped transform her son?

"I now call to the stage a very talented and generous person, whose devotion to Boulder City and the health of the local businesses is unequalled, and who every day gives away her time and expertise for free to people like me, and that woman is none other than Sondra Martin, Secretary of the Boulder City Chamber of Commerce."

So. Not Lisa.

"Ladies and gentlemen," said Sondra. "This young man deserves our congratulations. I've never witnessed a person work so hard to make their dream a reality. Not only has Will Huntley here transformed our old travel agency into the most extraordinary shop of treasures you've ever imagined—good things for a healthy heart and healthy life—he's been working with our events committee to help plan a new event.

"So stick around a little bit longer, and you reporters, you listen up," Sondra said. "Tonight, as well as opening Huntleys House of Hearts, we're announcing the International Boulder City Skyrun and Charity Ball."

Sondra knew how to work a crowd. They whooped and cheered.

"And the prize? You all come in and admire it, won't you? It's a magnificent Nevada Black Fire Opal, set by the founder of Huntleys, Jim Huntley, a master goldsmith from Sydney, Australia!"

Cameras popped amid cheers and applause, reporters firing questions.

"How many people are you expecting to compete?"

"What's the exact date of the competition?"

"How much are you investing?"

"Why are you doing this?"

"How's the Contessa?"

Will took to the stage again. "Thank you, Sondra," he said. "It's now time for us to cut the ribbon and invite the crowd right inside. I'll be glad to take media questions in person right here, beside the door, if you reporters would like personal interviews."

A few more cameras flashed in his face as he posed for the media with a huge smile, framing his shop with his arms.

"But right now, I'd like to welcome my sister, Nicole, to the stage to cut the ribbon," Will said. "Nicole has made this ceremony possible. She's a key part of our expanding Huntleys global empire."

"That's our cue," whispered Cynthia, and she and Émile slipped back inside, behind the till, where a radiant Nicole in bright yellow snipped the blue ribbon with a huge pair of scissors which flashed in the spotlight.

Customers rushed in, exclaiming over the screens and the displays, and there was soon a huge queue. Cynthia rang up sales and Émile wrapped the goods. She was busier than she ever remembered being at Huntleys, even during Christmas sales. Time flew.

In an instant she registered that Will was beside her, trying to catch her attention.

"Mother, this is Lisa, the woman who changed my life. Lisa, Cynthia."

Cynthia's heart leaped as she nodded and smiled at the tall blonde woman in a striking red dress beside her son. She was surprisingly athletic, with kind eyes. So this was Lisa, the miracle worker. What a shame she was too busy to meet her properly. She focused on Will and Lisa, scanning for clues. If there was a link between the two of them beyond respect and a professional relationship, it was impossible to discern. They barely touched, yet something was there, something electric. Controlled—that's what it was—on both sides. Intriguing. The old Will had never had an ounce of self-control.

Cynthia smiled her apologies, gesturing at the queue and busy counter, with the next customer waiting.

"I hope we'll meet again, Lisa," Cynthia said, locking eyes with the miracle worker. Did she ever! Will and Lisa had already turned away, and she strained to listen.

"And over there, that's Nicole, my sister, and behind her is Scottie, her fiancé. And you remember James?"

The next morning, they met for breakfast in Will's apartment above the shop, where Will flipped pancakes and brought bacon and eggs out of the oven.

"Sensational," said Scottie.

"Not bad," said James.

"Thanks," said Will.

Was that a first?

Stella poured coffee. Nicole yawned. Where was Lisa?

"Mum," said Nicole.

"Yes, darling?"

"Scottie and I, we wanted to ask you about your house."

"In France?"

"No. We thought we'd get married in Australia. Could we hold the wedding there, do you think? Next spring?"

"I'd love that, Nic. Of course!"

Stella and Cynthia washed up together.

"James tells me you're a designer, Stella."

"I'm not qualified, if that's what you mean, but I've enrolled to do some courses."

"Oh, I'm not talking about qualifications. He says you're prolific; that your work is favored by film stars; that you've won an award, and sold your designs in Hong Kong. That's impressive."

"I suppose it is, when you put it like that."

"I have a design idea for merchandise, Stella. Perhaps you're interested?"

The washing up flew by as they discussed the club or clover shaped keyring, with the Huntleys House of Jewels, HHJ, symbol on it.

"Oh, I like that," said Stella. "That's a fantastic give-away idea. And I could design one for Will's store, featuring a heart; and one for the Sydney store with a diamond."

"I like her very much," Cynthia told Émile afterwards. "She's very poised. She doesn't gush. I gush a bit, don't you agree?"

Émile smiled and kissed her.

Chapter 35

S oon after, she and Émile were on an airplane again, flying south and further south, via Dubai, then swinging into Sydney, circling in from the north over the famous harbor, with its arched bridge and signature opera house.

"Twenty-two hours, Cynthia," said Émile, standing and stretching then sitting again.

"You're so tall, Émile," she said. She'd slept well, nestled in beside him. "But it will be worth it. You'll love it."

They'd left Nanette and her daughter in charge of their shop, with instructions to only open for an hour or two on the quietest days, and a note in the window asking customers to phone the tourist bureau to be let in. Minette adored Inés, who always turned up with some morsels of extra food, and piled her bowl high with crunchies before leaving. Cynthia's phone dinged at all hours with her young friend's pictures of the sleek cat.

The next few days were a whirl of preparations, with Scottie and Nicole to marry at Cynthia's Southern Highlands property.

James, Stella, Nicole and Scottie remained wary of Émile at first, baulking at *"faisant la bise,"* but Émile couldn't seem to help it, and soon, everyone was doing it, even Jim, laughing.

It became the gesture of the wedding, as the guests arrived in her French country house. To say Cynthia was over the moon was an understatement. All the dust covers were swept off her beautiful antique French furniture, and the French doors flung open to the courtyard which ran along the whole northern side of the gracious house.

Caterers in black with crisp black and white striped aprons handed around the canapés and champagne in her courtyard.

Kath was her usual frank self.

"So this is your handsome Frenchman!" she said.

"Émile, this is my oldest friend, Kath, and her husband, Bob, and for the record, Émile is Belgian."

Kath clapped her hand over her mouth and stared at Cynthia, who blushed. They laughed.

"I'll let you in on the joke, Bob," Kath said. "Cynthia had the most dreadful prejudice against people from Belgium.

"Stop it, Kath. I was very immature about that."

"Well I'm glad that's over," said Kath. "Very pleased to meet you, Émile. You've clearly been an excellent ambassador."

They all laughed as Émile and Bob shook hands.

Cynthia almost cried to see Nicole's school friends grown so tall, now with careers, partners in tow, and several with babies in a pouch or stroller. She crossed her fingers for Nicole and Scottie. Or would James and Stella beat them to it?

"Mrs Huntley!" The greetings were mutual. She was delighted to introduce Émile beside her and to explain she now lived in France and they were welcome to visit.

"Oh but this beautiful house!"

"It's not going anywhere," said Cynthia. "We'll be back and forth."

Will was the biggest surprise. Fresh back from the US for a quick visit, he'd definitely changed, and for the better. There was something restrained about him for the first time ever, his insouciance replaced with a sense of mischief just held in check. To Cynthia's eyes, it made him even more attractive. Perhaps now he'd find the right life partner, and would give up using a string of women for nothing more than a good time, never willing or able to commit to them or see them as people, rather than accessories. If James was correct, Will had his eye firmly on that lovely Dr Lisa Bakker, not that there'd been anything to suggest they'd been a couple when they'd all met up at the launch of House of Hearts.

As she checked her hair in the mirror over the fireplace, Will strode towards her, the healthiest she'd seen him for years, eyes dancing, one hand in his pocket. What was he up to now?

"I hoped I'd catch you, Mother."

"Thank you so much for making the trip, Will."

"Good to be here. Mother, I actually have a little something for you."

"No!"

"I want to thank you. Your booking that clinic for me … You saved my life."

"That's a bit extreme." She'd never seen her son so serious.

He shook his head.

"I'm not exaggerating, Mother. The suicide rate in Vegas is almost twice the rate it is anywhere else in the US. I was on a one way path to nowhere and that's for sure; and it was you who saved me. Well, technically, the clinicians saved me, but you got me into that clinic. I'll never forget what you did for me. It must have cost you a fortune."

"You're my fortune, Will; you and James and Nic."

"Oh, I almost forgot." Will reached into his pocket. He pulled out a small flat velvet box in deep blue, and handed it across. "Open it. You've got time."

Cynthia smiled. Will had always been impatient. Some things never changed.

She pulled up the lid, and there, inside, nestled in black satin, was a gold bracelet.

"It's for you. Try it on. I'll help you with the safety catch. I'm sorry I took the other one. I needed it to pay my gambling debts, but there are none of those now, and you'll be pleased to hear this wasn't bought with gambling money, either, and nothing will be, ever again. This is the first thing I bought with my first clear profit from the House of Hearts."

The bangle fitted perfectly. As Will's young fingers fastened the catch, she grabbed his hands and squeezed them.

"You didn't have to do this, Will. But thank you. I love it."

"I absolutely did. And I'm paying you back the money for the clinic, too, in instalments. It will take a while, but it's the least you deserve. I'm seeing Scottie senior in the city before I go back to the US to set up the repayments. It's the right thing, so don't even try to talk me out of it."

"Oh, Will. What I hope you will understand one day, is that a parent will do almost anything for their child. I'm so, so proud of the new you. You're certainly making the most of your fresh start."

They exchanged a glance. Maybe now her son would speak to her of Lisa, but just then, out in the courtyard, James rang a gong.

Everyone moved to the orchard for the ceremony as the sun began to set, the balmy evening a bonus.

At Nicole's insistence, Cynthia and Jim walked her down the small aisle, to a Scottie beaming with the loyalty and sincerity Cynthia had always hoped Nicole would recognise in him.

Cynthia squeezed Nicole's arm as she let her go, and moved to the front row where Émile had saved seats on either side of him. As Jim took his seat on the other side it was impossible not to notice how stooped Jim had become—Cynthia recalled how tall he'd been at her marriage to Jimmy—but he was more distinguished than ever now in his pale grey suit, his white hair like a silver crown and blue eyes more striking than sapphires.

Émile reached for her hand as the couple said their vows, and she tucked her arm inside his. It was so good to have him there beside her, this man who could never bring back Jimmy, but could be here with her for these moments, for her children, and for her. After a decade of brusque loneliness, who could have suspected that love would call on her again in the form of this tall Belgian?

After the congratulations and photographs, celebrations moved to the marquee, hung with chandeliers and filled with white draped chairs tied with huge bows. The tables were set with crystal and silver candelabra and white flowers were everywhere.

After speeches, there was dancing in her courtyard strung with fairy lights, and Émile, so dashing in his dinner suit, and so attentive, held her close.

On her way to freshen up between numbers, Cynthia passed a cluster of Nicole's old school friends.

"OMG, Nic. Your brothers! I had such a crush on both of them, and now they're even more eligible! OMG."

"Too late," said Nicole. "James is engaged, so you've missed your chance there."

"Nooooo. Okay. Will, it is."

Cynthia observed Will closely but as far as she could tell, he kept to sparkling mineral water.

In demand on the dance floor, Will paid nobody special attention, except perhaps Cheekie Boom, the one-woman band, rocking it on her electric guitar and drum machine, and everyone knew he'd have no luck there.

He was on a flying visit, he'd explained—"off to meet some sky run organizers in the Snowys while I'm here. It's full speed ahead for the Black Opal Sky Run back in Nevada. We're on countdown."

Will's adventure shop was trading well. There'd been no more requests for loans from him. Nor had James complained about Will spending more money than he was making, so that was a good sign.

Come to think of it, she hadn't heard much from James at all.

Since she'd noticed the engagement ring on Stella's finger at Will's shop opening, she'd kept expecting they'd announce a wedding date, too, but the one time she'd asked, James told her he and Stella were "staying low key—to give Nicole and Scottie the limelight." How thoughtful he was, her eldest son. It was difficult not to swell with pride every time she thought of him.

She loved catching up with Kath and Bob, who were loitering near the desserts table.

"That Émile," said Kath. "I can see why you fell for him. Bring back *'faisant la bise'* I say. Get him to teach Bob, would you?"

"Are you loving retirement?"

"No. I hate it. Of course I'm loving it! Bob's doing half the housework finally, and we're flat out researching our world trip. So you'll see us again soon, my friend. I'm taking Bob back to France to meet all my distant French relatives, and then we'll descend on you. We're exploring dates. Any recommendations for hotels in Paris?"

The new couple cut the three-tiered cake. Just before Nicole and Scottie were due to leave for their secluded honeymoon hideaway, the women and a few of the men, gathered. Nicole turned her back and tossed the bouquet, and a school friend caught it.

Émile pulled her close and brushed her cheek with the back of a finger, tender.

"*C'est quoi?*" he said, his eyes full of concern.

Were her thoughts so obvious?

"I wanted Stella to catch it," she said.

"Ah, these Australians—they are so superstitious," he said with a smile so infectious, she kissed him, right there, in front of everyone, and he drew her close until she pushed him away.

"We have to wave. My daughter's all grown up!" and she rushed to Nicole and hugged her tight, then stepped back with everyone else who was waving and cheering, and the newlyweds jumped into Scottie's Tesla and disappeared down the drive.

Now Émile touched a fingertip to her face again, this time to wipe away her tears, and she leaned into him and cried.

"Happy tears," she said.

"*Bien sûr,*" he said. Of course.

Later, when the guests had departed and they retreated to the master suite, Émile smiled at her as he undid his bow tie and went to her to unzip her dress. He kissed her neck so slowly the blood rushed to her cheeks.

"Cyntia," he said, in that way of his, with a "t".

"Mmmmm?"

"The bouquet."

"Mmhmm?"

"Perhaps you wished to capture it yourself."

She turned to him and pulled him close.

"You should be so lucky, you Belgian."

And then they kissed.

If nobody slept much, nobody minded.

"That's one way to deal with jet lag," said Cynthia, snuggling into bed with Émile for the few hours before he donned a beret and one of the striped aprons to cook sausages, bacon and eggs for all the family and friends invited back to the courtyard for the barbeque breakfast.

"I'm so happy, Cynthia," said Dianne. "I remember back when Scottie and Nicole were in preschool together. I think our boy made up his mind about his future wife back then!"

Cynthia nodded. Somewhere she had a photograph of the two of them holding hands near the swings, but Nicole had told her to get rid of it when she'd been in high school. Thank goodness her daughter had finally seen the qualities of Scottie that made him such an excellent ally for James in the world of business, and would make him an excellent life partner for her.

"They've certainly all grown up," said Ron. "You know, you'll want to have a chat about the business structure now you're going global and the next generation is becoming so involved."

Dianne frowned at his serious tone of voice.

"Not today, Ron. Today is for celebrating," she said. "Ron sees so many family companies in his work, you understand, Cynthia. Succession planning is important and it can become quite … fraught if it's left too long."

"Of course," said Cynthia.

"Maybe while you're all here in Australia," said Ron.

But the happy couple were going away for their honeymoon, Will departed for the US the next day, and Cynthia and Émile had purchased their return tickets to Nice. Their flight left a few days later.

When all the guests had departed, Émile helped Cynthia replace the drop sheets over all the furniture, but she hesitated at Eleanor's old writing box on its ornate side table near the front door. She found the key and opened it, laying back the lid to expose the writing surface inside.

"*Un coffre au trésor?*" said Émile.

"*Mais oui*. Yes. It's a treasured box of treasures alright, though maybe not conventional ones."

"Show me."

Cynthia laughed, holding up first a chipped old inkwell, and then some ancient grey blue metal writing nibs.

"I suppose these were Eleanor's," she said. "The box was fairly empty when she gave it to me, so I added a few of my own treasures when I moved here. She lifted one of the internal lids and pulled out a small pale blue book, well thumbed.

"My English to French pocket dictionary," she said.

"But I had one the same," he said. "French to English."

"Obsolete technology now, of course, what with all those apps and online translators, but it's precious to me," said Cynthia.

She riffled through another compartment and brought out a soft handkerchief, twisted to make a tiny swag, which she unrolled, revealing a small pile of tiny white objects.

"Do you have the tooth fairy in France?"

"What is this?"

"The tooth fairy leaves a coin for each baby tooth." Cynthia rolled the sharp pearls in the palm of her hand with one finger.

"But this is the *la petite souris*, the little mouse," said Émile.

"No! A fairy mouse? Don't tell the children."

"You love this box, Cyntia. We will take it back with us?"

"No need," she said, as she wrapped the teeth once more and closed the tiny chest. She ran her hands over the polished surface and covered it with the pale cloth.

Émile went to lift the box. "You are sure? Oh. This is solid, this box. Quite heavy, yes? I was thinking it could go on my lap in the airplane, but …"

"We have more than enough treasures in France, thank you, Émile. And best of all, we have each other."

313

After she locked her front door, they stood together in the peace of the garden, absorbing the dappled sunshine and breathing the fresh country air. A whip bird sliced the silence.

"I like your house," said Émile.

"I hope we'll come back often," Cynthia said. "I need to leave France regularly under my visa, anyway. We can always close the shop for the winter months, when there'll be hardly any custom."

"Spend our winter in Australia's summer? I like this. I like 'south'."

"Oh, there's so much more of Australia I'd love to show you, Émile."

"But of course."

In the airplane on their way back to France, Cynthia asked Émile about Maxime.

"Enough of my own children, Émile. You fitted in so well with everyone. Thank you. Has Maxime been in touch?"

"He messages me sometimes. He sends pictures of Liam in bars and restaurants. He asks me about Ommegang."

"That's important, Émile. This is good, isn't it?"

"He wants Quinka to sponsor a float. I am not so sure."

"Why not?"

"Ommegang. My grandfather took me. We marched together in our traditional uniform, the one I have left for Maxime back in his old bedroom, the one he ignores."

"We've spoken about this, Émile. Wasn't Maxime afraid he'd offended you by taking that job?"

"Yes. And he did not want to tell us he was gay."

"But you've accepted that. And you like Liam."

"Yes."

"So what's the problem?"

"He wants the Quinka float to be about LGBTQI employees."

"But what's wrong with that? That's good, isn't it? You're open minded about people's sexuality, aren't you? About Maxime's choices?"

Emile winced.

"Oh that. That is not a problem. It is the Quinka colors—the yellow and the purple. I detest them. I don't want Quinka to spoil Ommegang. It is wrong. For so many of us, they destroyed our businesses."

"Yes." She held his gaze and squeezed his hand. "I see." Émile sighed and rested his forehead on the window pane, staring out at the endless blue.

"Émile?"

"Yes?"

"Is Ommegang always the same?"

"No. When I was a boy, it was, but now … It is commercial. Many companies have floats, or they sponsor drinks or food or cardboard hats."

"So Maxime isn't the first person to suggest something new."

"No. But I do not want to be part of it."

"Has he asked you? I know what a loyal man you are; how much you value traditions, and how clever you are at repairing your vintage motorbike—all those things—and I respect you for it. Everyone does. You've seen how well our small antiques sell. Many people appreciate the best of the past …"

"But … you say I am too old fashioned."

"I'm the last person to turn away from things that are old fashioned, Émile! You've been to my Australian house, full of everything old. But we both know we can't stop time, whether we want to, or not..."

"And?"

"And if Maxime has asked you to Ommegang …"

"I must go?"

"You won't regret it. It will be a reunion, won't it? Won't Roddy be there?"

Émile shrugged and swung his head back to contemplate the universe. Cynthia worried that a gulf had opened up between them again. But she loved her own family. Surely Émile loved his only son. He deserved that chance to keep their relationship healthy. If she could encourage him to keep in touch with Maxime, surely that was the right thing to do.

Émile was more silent than usual, clearly still troubled.

Back in Provence, Émile's mood remained subdued. Whenever they discussed his pending reunion with Maxime, his voice was clipped. It was all duty. He sighed a lot.

Maybe it was good for them to have some time apart. She kept her own mood chirpy to make up for his silences, but her voice sounded forced, even to her.

The picnic under the cherry tree was her idea—something they could both look forward to, away from the chores of the shop.

"We'll close up early on the day you're due back," she said. "I'll pack a picnic. It will be romantic. In spring, the cherry tree will be in bloom."

He kissed her and held her close, then headed north again on his old motorcycle. She missed him already, but at least she had her English students to keep her busy, and word was spreading about the shop. They hadn't opened with any great fanfare. It was what Nicole called "a soft opening"—completely different to Will's, but their profit was tracking well enough.

If she missed Émile, there wasn't much she could do about it. She sent him text messages from time to time, but was anxious not to intrude on his time with Maxime and his old colleagues.

Her tulips were in bloom when Cynthia headed out with the picnic, thrilled with the anticipation of seeing Émile again and finding out all about Ommegang, Maxime-style.

So when he didn't show up on time, and she hadn't heard from him, she shivered in the spring chill.

Chapter 36

Cynthia shook out the picnic rug and laid it under the cherry tree, the bubble gum fragrance of the white blossoms blending with wafts of lavender. Joy in Provence.

She was glad to sit after the walk up into the hills. Petals fell like snow around her.

She patted the back of her French twist and peeped in the picnic basket to check that Émile's favorite pie, still warm, was upright and the chocolate cake not too squashed.

A couple of doves strutted and cooed, while sun and shadow played on the shapes of the ancient roofs in the village below, like so many pieces of pastry.

She pulled the lapels of her pale pink blazer closer in the too-cool spring air. Tiny fluoro green leaves among the blossoms promised warmer weather, but she'd been too optimistic.

As the sun began to drop, she longed for Émile, with his leather jacket, his smile, that little scar on his cheek, those eyes with their sense of fun, and a sizzling kiss or three.

Émile should be here by now, his arm warm around her shoulders. They'd agreed to a romantic picnic lunch under this tree—so where was he?

She checked her watch and phone for the tenth time. Reception was poor on this side of the mountain. Was "no news" "good news"?

A cold wind from across the mountains sent a shiver down her spine. Surely this wasn't the end of her French adventure.

She drew her legs beneath her and pulled half of the rug across her lap against the strengthening wind, as she sifted the fallen petals through her fingers, remembering.

A thousand scenarios rushed through her head as she waited. Had Émile gone back to his first wife after all?

Had his old motorbike lost a wheel on a steep hill and he was in Emergency, with memory loss?

Had someone stolen his phone?

She nibbled on a dried apricot and tried to wrest her thoughts back to something more positive.

Had he got the date wrong, and she'd have to wait here all night? She shivered again. She'd have to give up soon. She hadn't even brought a torch.

It was time to abandon this silly plan.

She tried his phone number, but it went through to voicemail again. "I love you, Émile. I hope everything's okay."

She scrolled through her emojis and found a clover symbol and sent it. And then another.

Had he gone back to Angelica—Angelica with endless money to spend; Angelica who adored him and didn't nag him to reconnect with his son and confront the enemy that had changed his life.

Or maybe he'd simply embraced his life of freedom again.

She stood up and did star jumps to warm herself up. Forget that. Quinka had brought him a better life, a life with Cynthia, who adored him. Why hadn't she pointed that out to him?

Maybe she didn't like Belgians after all.

A motorbike roared and she turned her head to listen more carefully. Was that Émile's old engine? No. It rattled even more than his ancient vehicle, if that were possible.

She picked up the picnic rug, shook the cherry blossoms off it and began to roll it up when the engine stopped.

A tall man came out from behind some lilac bushes and strode up the embankment. She really must get her eyes tested again.

He pulled off his helmet.

"So sorry I'm late, Cynthia. My trip, it took twice as long with this thing. Roddy's friend, he found it in a barn in Flanders, and we all thought it would be good for you. But attaching it…" He shook his head.

"I should have phoned you to tell you I was running late, but at every moment I revved. I hoped I could save time."

What was he talking about?

Émile took the blanket from her. "Let me lay this out again. I am famished. I dropped in on Angelica."

She knew it. So that was it. He'd gone back to her after all.

"To Angelica…"

He stopped and smiled at her.

"You're not jealous, Cynthia?"

"Don't laugh at me, Émile. Yes. I might be a little bit jealous of Angelica. Very jealous. Anyone would be, the way she looks at you."

"... to ask for the use of her chapel. She's all in favor, by the way. She wants to cater for weddings and said she'd let us use the whole chateau for nothing if we wanted, as a practice for her staff and suppliers."

She stared, holding her breath.

"You're marrying Angelica?"

He laughed, took off his leather jacket and draped it around her shoulders. The warmth was heavenly and her teeth stopped chattering, but he ignored her question.

He burrowed inside the picnic basket and pulled out the pie and spatula. "Ah, my favorite pie! Thank you."

"Émile?"

"Actually, it is you I wish to marry," he said, and gave her an enormous grin. "There's enough room at the chateau for us all to stay—your whole Huntley family, and Kath and Bob, and Nanette and Inès, and Jacques, and Roddy. And Maxime and Liam. You were right. Ommegang was not so bad. Not so good, but not so bad. I will tell you, as long as you will marry me."

She poked him with the bread stick.

"Is that a 'yes'?"

"Just kiss me, you crazy Belgian."

It was only afterwards she saw the contraption, screwed to the side of his ancient motorbike.

"It is a sidecar, a Lionne, so you can travel in comfort, however old we grow," he said, and he swung open the little door and ushered her inside, placing the empty picnic basket on her lap.

And they cruised back through the soft hills fragrant with lavender, down to their House of Clubs.

If you loved *House of Hearts*, you might enjoy

House of Diamonds

Handsome James Huntley the Third faces a challenge or two at his Bondi Junction jewelry business.

Sparkles fly when newbie jeweller Stella Rhys sets up her home-made jewellery stall outside his shop.

She steals the limelight at his expensive PR stunt, and then she steals his heart.

Instant enemies, and fighting their attraction to each other, Stella and James become entangled in a social media war.

In this "enemies to lovers" romance, **will this dazzling couple ever work out what to do with an engagement ring?**

House of Diamonds is the first volume of Amber Jakeman's fast-paced, heartwarming *House of Jewels* series—with an international flavour—featuring the romantic fortunes of three generations of jewellers; the extended Huntley family. The books may be read in any order.

Praise for *House of Diamonds*

"Stella is an interesting character. Easy to read, feel good book. We need more of these kinds of books. I enjoyed it. I am looking forward to reading the rest of this series." Kris Revson

"Loving House of Diamonds… It's the perfect 'bedtime read'. I really enjoyed it. More publications, please. Please put my name down for Book 2." Annette

"Congratulations on a well crafted and delightful page-turner! The world of jewellery is a splendid backdrop to your romance, as are Sydney Harbour, Bowral and the south of France, with more glimpses of Boulder City perhaps in the eagerly awaited next book. Keep writing!" Sparkle-lover

House of Hearts

House of Hearts is Volume 2 in the *House of Jewels* series.

What does it take to be lucky in love? Opposites attract in *House of Hearts*, set on the edge of Las Vegas.

Gambling addiction therapist Dr Lisa Bakker never breaks rules, but her bad boy client Will Huntley, good-looking youngest heir to an Australian jewelry business, breaks them all.

The one rule neither can ignore is the two-year dating ban between clients and therapists. Will calls Lisa his "Queen of Hearts" but her hard-won career hangs in the balance. *What will it take to win her hand?*

Praise for *House of Hearts*

"… a wonderful love story with a number of twists in the plot… I really enjoyed it."

"Was amazed at your extensive knowledge on counselling procedures and rules, a myriad of psychological conditions, and gambling addiction (and the triggers). Great research!" Jen

"I could not put it down."

"Many congratulations on another bestseller." Annette

"I really liked it and can't wait to pass it on to my book-reading friends." Robyn

House of Spades

House of Spades is Volume 3 in the House of Jewels series.

Can love call again later in life? He calls her a trespasser. She calls him a hermit and thief.

Free spirit and serial single Flame Rhys has sworn off love, but try convincing her reclusive neighbor Ross Archer.

Fiery redhead Flame accidentally rekindles the widower's passion for life, for his land and a wife.

But is there more to Flame than meets the eye, as Ross's daughters suspect?

Praise for *House of Spades*

"Your book inspired me to rewild parts of my property."

" ... some delightful insight into the subtropical climate and people of northern New South Wales."

"Flame is awesome."

Full House

What can you do when you've friend-zoned the one you love?

Nicole Huntley, marketing manager for her family's international jewelry business, froze out family friend Scottie back when they were teenagers.

Now he's the Huntleys' financial advisor. Newly divorced, the affable Scottie needs somewhere to stay. Nicole offers him space, never expecting to fall for him — hard.

But when fate deals the Huntleys a high-stakes fresh hand, "conflict of interest" threatens to shatter her family, destroy their retail empire — and to break her heart.

Get ready for the showdown in *Full House*, Amber Jakeman's latest international heartwarmer in the Huntley House of Jewels saga.

Amber's contemporary love tales — on the sweeter side — may be read in any order.

Amber Jakeman's *House of Jewels* series features the romantic fortunes of the extended Huntley family.

The books may be read in any order.

House of Diamonds

House of Hearts

House of Clubs

House of Spades

Full House

Don't miss out!

Visit www.amberjakeman.com to find out how to order other novels by Amber Jakeman. Sign up to receive occasional email updates.

About the Author

Partial to sunsets, picnics and poetry, feel-good fiction writer Amber Jakeman was a journalist, ghost writer and editor before succumbing to her addiction to uplifting endings.

She writes from her tiny apartment on the edge of Sydney Harbour, creating historical and contemporary fiction with an international flavor, including romance, on the sweeter side.

When not writing, Amber enjoys time with family and friends, sailing with her husband, travel, walking and savoring other writers' creations.

Amber Jakeman acknowledges Australia's first storytellers and offers respect to Indigenous people past and present and to their descendants.

Visit www.amberjakeman.com to find out how to order other novels by Amber Jakeman, and sign up for occasional email updates.

About the Publisher

Lorikeet Press publishes feel-good fiction for readers of all ages. If you enjoy books with uplifting endings, you're in the right place.

Visit www.lorikeetpress.com for more information.